KILL
A
STRANGER

Also by Simon Kernick

The Business of Dying
The Murder Exchange
The Crime Trade
A Good Day to Die
Relentless
Severed
Deadline
Target
The Last 10 Seconds
The Payback
Siege
Ultimatum
Wrong Time, Wrong Place
Stay Alive
The Final Minute
The Witness
The Bone Field
The Hanged Man
Dead Man's Gift and Other Stories
We Can See You
Die Alone
Kill A Stranger

KILL
A
STRANGER

SIMON
KERNICK

HEADLINE

First published in 2020 by
HEADLINE PUBLISHING GROUP

1

Cataloguing in Publication Data is available from the British Library

Hardback ISBN 978 1 4722 7095 5
Trade paperback ISBN 978 1 4722 7096 2

Typeset in Sabon by CC Book Production

Printed and bound in Great Britain by Clays Ltd, Elcograf S.p.A.

HEADLINE PUBLISHING GROUP
An Hachette UK Company
Carmelite House
50 Victoria Embankment
London EC4Y 0DZ

www.headline.co.uk
www.hachette.co.uk

For Sarah, who provided encouragement
and support all the way through.

DCI Cameron Doyle

Justice. I've spent a thirty-year career being paid to uphold it. I've had successes, sure. I've put no fewer than twenty-six killers behind bars, as well as numerous other lowlifes who've committed serious crimes. But almost to a man and woman, the people I sent down were either poor, desperate or, in some cases, just downright stupid.

The truly successful criminals, the ones with the money and the power, they've always been a far harder proposition. They've got the resources to fend you off time and time again. Eventually your bosses tire of the fight and decide to leave them in search of easier targets. That's how it works, especially when success in police work is all based on performance targets.

But that's not how I work. Call me old-fashioned, but I never give up. I'm patient. I'm methodical. And in the end, I get there. However long it takes.

And I'm here now. Ready to close the curtain on a case that's been troubling me for a long, long time. I've got three murder suspects in this police station, and a trail of dead bodies. I need to hear from each suspect what happened in the twenty-four hours leading up to their arrest. I want to let them tell it their way, with as little interruption as possible. Give them the rope to hang themselves.

Because right now, I think they're all lying.

1

Matt

A word to the wise. Appreciate every waking second of your life. Breathe in the fresh air. Smell the roses. Don't put off things that'll make you happy. Do the stuff on your bucket list. Now. Don't waste your time with worry. Pretty much everything you've ever worried about never happened.

So live.

Jesus, live. Because let me tell you this. Even if you think your life's a long line of disappointments, it can always get worse. Much, much worse.

And it can all happen in an instant. Like it did that night.

It was just short of 1 a.m. when I got out of the car with a yawn and walked to the front door of the cottage. The rain had stopped but a chill November wind still blew hard across the fields. A light was on in the living room, though I knew Kate wouldn't still be up. She was an early bird. It was rare that she ever lasted past 11, especially now she was pregnant. She might be only a couple of months gone, but she'd suffered a lot from morning sickness, which was one of the reasons we'd returned home to England for a few months, so we could get access to the best healthcare.

I was in a good mood as I went inside. I remember that. Thinking that I'd had a good evening in London, that life was going well. That I had a lot to look forward to.

I locked the door behind me and took off my shoes, cutting the light and using the dying embers from the open fire to guide me as I crept through the living room, trying not to make a noise. Kate was a light sleeper, and she wouldn't take kindly to being woken. I hadn't given her a time I'd be back from London – we don't have the kind of relationship where we have to be in each other's pockets – but I knew this was on the late side, so I took the stairs one at a time with exaggerated slowness, trying in vain to stop them creaking and whining beneath my feet. That was the problem with character cottages. They never shut up.

Our bedroom door was open a foot and I tiptoed past it into the bathroom. I washed my face and cleaned my teeth, and even stopped for a few moments to smile at my reflection in the mirror. 'We've come a long way, you and me,' I whispered. Which was true. We had. Thirty-six years. Some big ups, some even bigger downs. And then finally, when all looked lost, the biggest up of them all. Falling in love, against the odds, and starting a whole new life in the sunshine.

I took off my clothes in the bathroom, switched off the light and slipped into our bedroom, gently closing the door behind me and listening, just to be on the safe side, for the telltale sound of Kate's breathing as she slept.

Except I couldn't hear it.

The window frame was rattling a little from the wind and I wondered if that was obscuring the noise, because she was definitely in bed. I could see her in the darkness. She was almost completely covered by the duvet, though I could make out the bulge of her figure under it, her head poking out of the top.

But she wasn't moving. At all. Not even when one of the floorboards creaked loudly under my bare foot.

This was a result. She was sleeping heavily for once.

Gently I pulled up my side of the duvet and lay down in the bed, stifling a yawn, feeling that warm pleasure at the prospect of sleep.

And felt it immediately. A cold, clammy wetness on my arm.

Frowning, I slid my hand across the sheet. It was soaking, yet Kate still wasn't moving.

Something was wrong.

I lifted my hand from under the duvet, saw the darkness of the stain on my palm, and cried out. 'Oh Jesus.'

Instinctively I grabbed Kate's shoulder, which was when I realised she was wearing a coat.

'Kate? Kate?' I shook her. Nothing.

Panicking, I reached over and switched on the light, blinking against the sudden brightness, and yanked back the covers.

She was lying on her front, fully clothed, her head turned

sideways towards me, pale blue eyes staring blankly into space.

I'd never seen a corpse before, but straight away I knew the woman in front of me was dead.

But the thing was, it wasn't Kate.

2

Kate

If you've never been in a situation like this before, you just can't understand it. I'll be blunt. It was absolutely terrifying.

The nightmare started just like that. Bang. I literally woke with a start, and realised that I was being flung around in complete darkness in a suffocating confined space. I tried to open my eyes but couldn't. Then tried to open my mouth. I couldn't do that either. I was utterly disorientated, with an intense throbbing pain between my eyes.

For another confused few seconds I couldn't compute what was going on. My first thought was that I was in some incredibly vivid dream, where I could actually experience pain and discomfort. Then, as my head banged against something metal and hollow, and the artificial sound of an engine forced its way into my consciousness, it finally dawned on me that I was being transported somewhere in the boot of a car.

My first thought was my baby. I'm two months pregnant. He or she – and I have a gut feeling it's a she, don't ask me why – will be my first child, and already I felt that intense, indescribable bond with her that I've heard about from so many mothers. Without thinking, I tried to reach for my belly to protect her from all the violent movements, but I couldn't do that either. I was lying bunched up in a tight foetal position, with my hands tied painfully behind my back and my feet bound together. I was also blindfolded and gagged.

And that was when the panic set in. I wanted to throw up, and that made me even more scared, because I knew that if I did, then the gag would cause me to choke on my own vomit. My breathing was getting faster and faster, and I felt close to hyperventilating for the first time in years.

I had to calm down. But you try it when one minute you're flat out asleep, the next you're trussed up going God knows where. It's a lot easier said than done. I could feel everything running away from me. I had to slow my breathing. For the baby's sake.

Calm, calm, breathe slowly, I kept telling myself, like one of those crappy mindfulness apps that rich Pilates-loving women of a certain age all seem to have. Take stock. Think positive.

I tried to. It felt almost impossible. And yet . . . A chink of hope popped into my head like a light switching on. Because I was still alive, and if whoever had snatched me from my bed wanted me dead, I'd be dead. Simple as that.

The thought went a very small way to consoling me, and I finally felt my breathing come back under control.

I could tell that I was still in my silk pyjamas, but a thick blanket had been placed over the top of me, presumably to keep me warm. Again this meant I was better to them living and breathing.

And obviously, the most important thing was to keep it that way.

All my life I've had to fight. I grew up in a single-parent family where we had next to no money. According to my mum – who basically told me nothing else about him – my dad wasn't interested in having anything to do with me. And my mum's boyfriends (and there were quite a few of them) tended to just come and go, passing through as if she was just a tired port of call on the voyage to better things. But while they were there, they tended to treat both of us with varying degrees of contempt. In other words, there wasn't a lot of love to go around and I grew up harder than people think.

As a consequence, I don't scare easily.

I tried to remember how I'd got here. My last memory was heading up to bed. I'd spent the evening at home in our new rental cottage while Matt was catching up with old friends in London. He hadn't asked me to go with him, and I would have said no anyway. On a wet, miserable November night, the last thing I needed was to traipse up to town. Instead, I'd relaxed by the fire, watched some crap TV and read my book – a hard-boiled thriller I wasn't really enjoying. Then I'd headed for bed at about 10.30, 11, something like that, leaving the light on downstairs for Matt.

I'd locked the doors. I remember that.

I'd read some more, turned out the lights and gone to sleep. Then what?

I racked my brains. It was a huge effort. My head was

killing me, a heavy white pain, accompanied by a terrible raging thirst and an unpleasant chemical smell in the still air of the boot.

That smell. It was suddenly familiar.

I remembered waking up from a light sleep, almost before I'd really gone under, and sensing the presence of someone else in the room, thinking it was Matt . . .

And the next second a silhouetted figure looming out of the darkness, thrusting a wet cloth with the same chemical odour I was smelling now – but much stronger – over my nose and mouth. I had another vague memory of struggling violently against whoever was holding me down, but I couldn't honestly say for certain whether it was real or imagined.

And that was it.

God knows how much time had passed. Ten minutes. Two hours. As I lay there bracing myself for bumps in the road, the car made a sharp turn and stopped. A car door opened, then I heard a gate opening with a whine.

Now we were travelling up a gravel track in a gentle curve. I calculated the distance, knowing that any information I could get might assist me later. Fifty metres. One hundred. Going fairly slowly.

The car stopped and the engine was cut. Two doors opened. Which meant two kidnappers.

I took a deep breath, swallowed. Waiting. Scared of what was going to happen next.

The boot opened and I felt two pairs of hands on me, one yanking off the blanket, the other untying my feet. I was hauled from the car into a strong wind that my silk pyjamas, bought in tropical Colombo, did nothing to protect me from.

I shivered violently, making muffled sounds beneath the gag, hoping they'd have some pity and remove it.

The blanket was thrust back round my shoulders and my feet untied, but no attempt was made to remove the gag or the blindfold. They led me, each one holding an arm, for a distance I counted as thirty-six steps before they stopped again. Neither of them spoke. I tried to smell them. That way I'd be able to detect whether or not they were male or female, but the lingering chemical smell in my nostrils was playing havoc with my senses. I managed to bump against the one on my left, immediately bouncing off, estimating that he was a stocky male, two or three inches taller than me, so about five ten. Both had firm grips, making me think the one on my right was a man too.

The one on the left temporarily let go of me as I heard him unlock a door. I never seriously considered running. Where the hell was I going to go with a blindfold on and my hands tied behind my back? There was no way I was going to risk hurting my baby.

I remained utterly passive, my heart thumping hard in my chest as I was led inside. I immediately caught a whiff of damp and smoke, strong enough that it overpowered the chemical smell in my nostrils. It was as cold in there as it was outside. That told me something important. Not only had they got into our locked cottage, but they'd found a building nearby to hold me in. Judging by the silence on the walk from the car, it was suitably out of the way. This kidnap had been well planned by people who knew what they were doing. More importantly, if they were holding me here, it meant they weren't intending to kill me yet. They wanted something from me first.

Bide your time, I repeated to myself as I was led slowly through the building, down a corridor, through a door and then up half a dozen steps onto what felt from the sound it was making beneath my feet like some sort of wooden stage.

They brought me to a halt and turned me round so I was facing the other way. The man on the left moved away for a few seconds before returning and slipping something over my head.

I was still telling myself to stay calm. That there would be a way out of this. Right until the moment the rope tightened around my throat.

Which was when I realised it was a noose.

3

Matt

The woman lying dead in the bed that I shared with my fiancée was young. Early thirties, with dark brown hair tied into a ponytail, and still wearing a pair of black-framed glasses. Her clothes were ordinary. A dark blue puffa jacket, jeans, black trainers. She was lying on her front with her head angled sideways and her arms down by her sides. It was clear that she'd been placed in that position and then covered with the sheets.

It looked like her throat had been roughly cut. From the depth and width of the wound, it could only have been caused by a large knife. Semi-dried blood had leaked onto her collar and jacket, and a large pool had formed on the sheets round the upper half of her body. There were splatter marks all over the duvet cover and the headboard, as if she'd been standing facing the bed when the attack had happened.

I couldn't bear to look at her for more than a second at a time . . . yet my eyes were drawn to her like magnets. I was shocked; I was confused; but I also felt a guilty sense of relief that it wasn't my fiancée lying there.

But this left its own mystery. Where was Kate?

I looked round the room. There was no sign of any kind of struggle. Everything was as it should have been. The book she'd been reading – a thriller with an attractive but hard-looking woman on the front cover – was open face-down on the bedside table, next to a half-drunk glass of water that would definitely have been upended in a fight.

But I was certain she wouldn't have gone out alone at this time of night either. We had two rental cars, and hers – a white Audi A3 – had been parked outside when I'd got home. Even so, I switched out the light and walked to the window, pulling back the curtain and looking out across the field that ran along the side of the house. There was no one there. The field was waterlogged from all the rain of the last few days, making it close to impassable. I opened the window and poked my head out so I could see into the back garden, just in case she'd decided – which would be completely out of character – to take a wander in the middle of the night. She hadn't.

I was pulling my head back in when I spotted something through the trees lining the end of the field. It was an unfamiliar parked car. I couldn't see the make or the colour, but it was the first time I'd seen a car in that spot in the six days we'd been in this cottage.

I closed the window and switched the light back on, deliberately turning away from the woman's body. I didn't want to look at her as I paced the room, trying to figure out what on earth was going on.

14

Someone must have taken Kate. The same person who'd murdered the woman in our bed. That was the only logical explanation I could think of.

But why? We were an ordinary couple. There was nothing that exciting about us. We ran a small boutique hotel together in an old plantation house up in the hills of western Sri Lanka, part owning it with a Sri Lankan businessman. We made enough money to live comfortably, but not a huge amount. We'd lived there together for just over a year and had been back in the UK for less than a week. During that time we'd had very little interaction with anyone, barring my trip to town that night, not even our neighbours in the village. We had no enemies that I was aware of. There was no reason for any of this.

And yet clearly for someone there was.

I forced myself to look down at the dead woman properly for the first time. I noticed that she had a phone clutched in her right hand. I didn't want to touch it. I didn't want to touch her either. The sight of her lying there – a corpse that only a few hours ago had been a living, breathing person with hopes and dreams and memories, and her whole life in front of her – made me feel nauseous. And yet I needed to know what was going on.

The phone had to have been deliberately placed in her hand by someone. Which meant it would provide a clue.

I reached down towards it, trying hard not to think about what I was doing.

And then immediately jumped back as, without warning, it started ringing: the ringtone a loud, old-fashioned car horn sound that would have sounded faintly ludicrous if it wasn't for the fact that the phone was vibrating in the woman's soft dead hand.

It rang once, twice. Three times. If I picked it up, I could find out who she was. But it also meant that I'd have to tell the person at the other end what had happened to her. It occurred to me that, with her body in our bed, I was a potential suspect in her murder.

The phone kept ringing. Curiosity was killing me. Who was she? Why was she here?

The ringing stopped as suddenly as it had begun. After a few seconds' pause, I found some gloves in one of the drawers and put them on, then reached down and gently tugged the phone from her grip. It came free easily. Rigor mortis had yet to set in, which I guessed meant that she hadn't been dead very long. But then I knew that from the way the blood hadn't yet dried completely. For all I knew, it might only have been a matter of minutes.

Which meant the killer could still be here.

I listened but could hear nothing bar the wind. I told myself that if the killer was still here he'd have ambushed me when I'd come in – and he hadn't.

Even so, I looked behind me towards the door, just in case someone was lurking beyond it, before examining the phone.

The missed call was from an unidentified number. The phone itself was a Huawei smartphone, and when I pressed the home button, it immediately opened to reveal a screen containing the usual apps: weather, photos. I checked the pictures. There were none. I went to the list of contacts. Again, nothing. Then I saw an unread text message. There was no number, just the name of the sender. Matt Walters.

Me.

I swallowed audibly and opened the message, reading it slowly, with a growing sense of dread.

This phone is secure. Only I have the number. Use the Tor browser app already installed to go to the following site. 1298aband4141qq3.onion. You will get the answers you're looking for there.

I didn't know much about the dark web, but what I did know was that it was where bad things happened. Throwing the covers back over the dead woman so I didn't have to keep looking at her, I quickly located the browser on the phone – the need to know what was going on stronger than my fear of what I might see – and followed the instructions from the message.

At first it simply showed a blank black screen. Then something appeared to start loading. A few seconds later, an image appeared that I knew immediately would stay with me for the rest of my life.

Kate was standing on what appeared to be a stage. The room was illuminated by two bright lights in the background. She was dressed only in her pastel silk pyjamas and shaking visibly. I remember thinking how beautiful she'd looked when I'd left for London that afternoon – lean, more athletic than petite, with her soft feminine features, the sprinkle of freckles across her nose and cheeks, and her hair the colour of autumn leaves.

Now she was blindfolded with a black scarf, which covered the space from her forehead to the bottom of her nose. Two loops of rope round her midriff pinned her arms to her sides. But it was the noose round her neck that grabbed my attention. It was made of thick hangman's rope that was pulled tight as it disappeared towards an unseen ceiling, and as I looked down at Kate's feet, clad in a pair of black socks, I saw that she was only just managing to keep them on the wooden floor.

The message was clear. A couple more pulls on the other end of that rope and she'd be dead.

It took me a couple of seconds to realise that this wasn't an image but some kind of webcam footage. In the bottom left corner of the screen was a digital clock. It read 01.28 – which meant it was live.

On the screen, as if sensing something, Kate inclined her head to her left. 'Who's there?' she called out uncertainly, the fear in her voice obvious, even though the tinny webcam audio was distorting the sound.

A few seconds later – while I was still processing the fact that my pregnant fiancée was in a strange room with a hangman's noose round her neck – a figure moved into camera shot. I could tell straight away that it was a man. He was dressed in a long black coat that was far too big for him. The hood was pulled up over his head and he was wearing an old-fashioned gas mask that completely obscured his face. He stood next to Kate, facing the camera, and I could see that he was about three inches taller than her, making him five ten.

The man waved a gloved hand at the camera, staring at me from behind the gas mask.

Kate seemed to sense his presence and craned her neck in his direction. 'Whoever you are, just talk to me,' she said, clearly trying to keep her voice calm. 'We can sort this out.'

The figure's only reaction was to stop waving at the camera. He didn't turn her way.

After a moment, he walked slowly towards the back of the stage, partially obscured from view by Kate's body.

'Please,' she continued, as the figure crouched down out of shot. 'I know you're there. I'm pregnant. And I'm willing to let this—'

She never finished the sentence.

There was a sound like a pulley being turned, and suddenly her whole body was yanked upwards three inches, so that only her toes were touching the floor.

She made a sound that was part gasp, part cry for help, and I could see that it was taking all her effort to retain her balance. If the man in black turned the pulley one more time, that would be it. She'd be throttled to death.

'What the hell?' I shouted at the screen. 'Don't do this, for Christ's sake! Please, please!'

But of course, neither of them could hear me. This wasn't an interactive video.

I watched as Kate balanced there, her face rigid with fear. Waiting.

The seconds passed. Three. Five. Ten.

Then I heard the pulley being turned again and I howled

in frustration and horror, drowning out the noise on the film as I watched my pregnant fiancée die.

Except she didn't. Instead, her body relaxed as the rope lost a little of its tautness, and her feet were once again almost flat on the floor.

The man in black came back into view and walked past Kate without looking at her before exiting to the right of the shot, the same way he'd come in.

A few seconds passed, and then, without warning, the picture went black as if the power had been turned off.

I tried to log back in, but nothing happened. The feed was lost. I waited a minute, counting the seconds, the tension rising in me in waves, then tried again. No luck.

In a wave of directionless anger, I threw the phone at the floor. I couldn't believe what I'd just seen. My fiancée – the first woman I think I've ever truly loved, pregnant with the first child for either of us – had been abducted by someone who meant her serious harm. But what did he want? And why the hell was he taunting me like this?

On the floor, the phone began to ring again. I stared as the vibrations moved it in an aimless circle on the Persian rug, knowing this was no coincidence.

I bent down and picked it up. Another unidentified number. 'Hello,' I said unnecessarily.

'It's time to talk.' The voice was one of those robotic, disguised ones you hear in films.

My mouth went dry. 'What do you want?' I managed to croak.

'You saw the position your fiancée's in,' the caller

continued. 'We can kill her at any time. It'll be an unpleasant way to die. Strangulation rather than a broken neck. Only two people in the world can save her. I'm one of them. And you, Matt, are the other. But for her to survive, you have to follow three rules.' He paused, as if revelling in his power. 'Rule One: do not tell anyone what's happening. Police, friends, *anyone*. The moment you do, Kate dies. Rule Two: keep this phone with you at all times. Rule Three: follow your instructions to the letter. I'm not going to lie to you. It's going to be hard. You're going to need a strong stomach and an even stronger heart. But you have the best motivation. Succeed, and you and Kate will be reunited, with her unhurt. Fail, and you'll never see her again.'

'Please don't do anything to hurt her,' I said, conscious of the acquiescence in my voice, and knowing that my pleas would almost certainly fall on deaf ears. 'She's pregnant.'

'All the more reason to succeed, then,' said the voice with a casualness that both scared and angered me.

I paused. 'What do you want me to do?'

'First thing. That corpse in your bed. Get rid of it. Make it disappear.'

'What do you mean? How? Where?'

But I was already talking to a dead phone.

4

Matt

Back in the day, I was an actor by profession. I did it for the best part of ten years, which sounds a lot more impressive than it actually was. For most of that period I was a waiter, a shop assistant, a minicab driver and, at one point, a not especially successful children's entertainer. The acting roles were few and far between, and mostly bit parts, so there's not much danger you'd ever have recognised me in the street.

But there was one role that always stood out for me, and which I'd had high hopes for. The show was a drama on Sky called *Night Beat* that, though critically acclaimed, only lasted one six-part season. My role was DC 'Jonno' Johnson, one of the team of murder squad detectives operating out of a fictional London borough. To be honest, I was probably the least important member of the team, with a handful of lines in each episode, but I performed them well, and was optimistic that it might lead to something more substantial. I threw myself into the part too. I immersed myself in true-crime books and documentaries, and found a mentor in a decorated Scotland Yard detective who became an invaluable source of information. As a result, I gained a thorough understanding of how the police work in their investigations. And the single most important thing I learned is that it's not like Sherlock Holmes. Or indeed like *Night Beat*. It's slow, methodical and mundane, and most people are caught because they make mistakes, or because they had a prior relationship with the victim.

I had no prior relationship with the dead woman in our bed. This, in theory, gave me some advantage, although how that advantage was going to help was unclear as I looked down on her unmoving form beneath the sheets, the phone still in my hand, my mind working in overdrive.

I figured I had two choices. One: call the police immediately and let them use all their resources to find Kate before this man did what he was threatening to do and killed her. Or two: do what he'd ordered me to do and immediately become involved in a very serious crime. And of course still not have any guarantee that he would let Kate go unharmed.

My first instinct was to call the police, because this was way too big for me to deal with alone. There was something reassuring about the idea of pouring my heart out to a tough, no-nonsense, problem-solving cop like DCI Luca Pacelli, the star of *Night Beat*, who'd be able to ride roughshod over the rules, using even the slimmest of leads to find where Kate was being held, and effect a rescue at the very last minute that would see her released unharmed (although only by the skin of her teeth) and leave her kidnapper dead, just as he deserved. The problem was, detectives like Pacelli don't exist in real life. They have to follow the rules. The slimmest leads took time to turn into concrete evidence, and in real life the police were usually up against criminals who were, to put it bluntly, idiots.

The man who'd abducted Kate was no idiot. Her kidnap had required significant planning. He'd not only got inside the house and taken her without a struggle – which wouldn't have been easy; my fiancée's no shrinking violet – but he'd also managed to kill someone else and dump her body in our bed. All without leaving a single thing out of place.

It struck me then that there had to be two of them involved. What I'd just described wasn't possible with only one person. This was even more unnerving, and it was made worse by the fact that they'd almost certainly been watching us. And if they could break in tonight without leaving a trace, then they'd almost certainly been in here before. Which meant they'd bugged the place. It made perfect sense. After all, the phone in the dead woman's hand had begun ringing only a couple of minutes after I'd entered the room.

I looked round wildly as if I was suddenly going to spot a hidden camera, then told myself to cool it. It didn't matter whether there was one or not. I was clearly dealing with professionals who, for whatever reason, had planned their operation meticulously. I thought about contacting former DCI Geeta Anand, the woman who'd done so much to fill me in on the way the police operated for my *Night Beat* role. But she was a civilian now, having left the force more than five years back, and I knew what she'd say. Get the police involved. If I didn't, there was no guarantee that she wouldn't do it for me. I couldn't risk that.

So that was it. I made my choice. To do what the man on the phone had told me. I had to get rid of the body.

A stupid move, you might think. Especially as that was unlikely to be the end of it. But I'd ask you to put yourself in my position for a moment. I'd just seen the woman I cared for more than anyone else in the world – the woman who was carrying my tiny two-month-old baby – standing precariously on tiptoes with a noose around her neck. At the mercy of some lunatic in a gas mask who'd killed once already and was threatening to do the same to her. I had to try to get her back, even if it meant carrying out a truly grim task.

And it didn't get much grimmer than what I was about to do.

Or at least so I thought at the time.

I pulled back the duvet on the bed and looked down at the dead woman. They often say that the dead wear peaceful expressions. This woman didn't. Her expression was utterly blank, her blue eyes staring into the middle distance. I wondered what her story was.

There was only one way to find out. Taking a deep breath and ignoring the fact that someone could be watching, I grabbed her with both hands and turned her over so she was lying on her back. Her coat was zipped up to the top and there was a large bloodstain on her chest.

I partially unzipped the jacket, which was when I saw

that several deep stab wounds had penetrated the sweatshirt she was wearing, clearly aimed at her heart. And yet they hadn't penetrated the jacket. I wasn't sure what this meant and didn't have time to think too much about it. Instead, I meticulously searched through her pockets, finding nothing in any of them. Whoever had killed her had taken away anything that might be used for identification. They weren't going to make this easy for me.

Now it was time for the hard part. Reaching down, I hooked my arms under hers and hauled her off the bed. Her feet hit the floor with a thud and I had to tense all the muscles in my upper body to keep the rest of her upright.

I'm forever ashamed about what happened next. Instead of hauling her out by the shoulders, I did it by her ankles, because that way she was less of a weight. At first it felt horrible, coming into contact with her steadily cooling skin. Even through the gloves and her socks, I could still feel it. But I did a good job of pushing my distaste to one side and getting on with the job, although I did gag while I was dragging her body down the staircase as her head thumped hard against each of the stairs.

In the end, the whole thing took several minutes and a rest break before I'd unceremoniously dragged her to the front door.

I turned off the outside light and stepped into the wind, watching as the clouds scudded across the night sky, occasionally showing glimpses of a butter-coloured half-moon. Our cottage was situated opposite the village allotments and was remarkably private, which was the reason we'd chosen it. There were a dozen or so other cottages on the other side, but all a good hundred yards away. Although ours was semi-detached, the house next door was separated from it by a thick stone wall, and it faced out onto the road in a different direction, so we never saw the owners.

I checked that the coast was clear, then opened up the rental car's boot, which, since I was driving a new Discovery Sport, was fairly spacious. I went back and got hold of the body, by the shoulders this time, and dragged it across the gravel. Finally, with a huge effort and one last furtive look over my shoulder, I manhandled it inside and covered it with a picnic blanket I'd got from the cottage, before shutting the boot with a temporary sigh of relief.

Temporary, because getting rid of a body was no easy task. I couldn't just take her up to the woods and bury her. It would take forever to dig a deep enough hole, and I didn't even have a shovel. I couldn't burn her either, not without drawing a huge amount of attention to myself. And even considering these possibilities made me nauseous.

Ultimately I had to accept that the body was going to turn up somewhere and the point was to get it as far away from here as possible. My best option was the nearby river. It was already coming close to bursting its banks, thanks to the almost record-breaking levels of recent rainfall, and was flowing fast enough to transport her a long way downstream.

I felt awful dumping this poor woman like this, I want you to know that. But she was dead. There was no way of bringing her back. At least if I did this and got Kate back, then some good would have come from the situation.

Having made my decision, I reversed slowly out of the driveway before turning right onto the single-track road that led round the allotments, then right again in the direction of the river, passing alongside the field that sat across from the cottage. Slowing down, I spotted the car I'd seen earlier from the window of our bedroom. It was an ordinary-looking dark-coloured saloon, not especially new, partially hidden by undergrowth where it had been driven onto the bank at the side of the road. I didn't recognise the make, but then I've never been interested in cars. However, it was parked in a spot where it couldn't be seen from any of the houses around here, and where, more importantly, it had a direct line of sight to our cottage.

Stopping to take a look while I had a body in the boot wasn't an option, so I kept on, driving slowly and carefully, bypassing the village centre. I was terrified that at any moment I might get stopped by the police for some minor discrepancy, even though I'd yet to see a single officer during the six days we'd been in the country.

I needn't have worried. We were in a surprisingly quiet area of south-east England. I only passed one car on the ten-minute journey to the place I'd hastily identified as the best spot to carry out my plan – the other side of the river, where I'd been out walking two days earlier.

I cut the headlights as I came down the track that led to the river, passing a large detached house where there were still a couple of lights on inside. A security light was immediately triggered, bathing the car in an unwelcome bright yellow glow, and I instinctively turned my head away in case there was a camera. That was another problem I faced. Nowhere was completely isolated and there were cameras recording your every move.

The track reached a dead end near the riverbank and I parked close to the side of a hedge and switched off the engine.

Which was when I heard a dog barking. Loudly. It was coming from somewhere in or around the detached house behind me.

'Oh Jesus,' I whispered, leaning forward on the steering wheel with my head in my hands, wondering again what the hell I was doing. I'm not a bad man. I'm not even a brave one. I'm normal. Maybe even a coward. And yet here I was, slumped in a car with the body of a murdered woman in the boot, drawing attention to myself at every turn.

I sat back in the seat as panic began to tear through me. I forced it down, thinking of Kate with the rope around her neck. I knew that for once in my life, I had to be strong.

The security light went off and the dog stopped barking. But the longer I sat in here the riskier it became. I had to move. Now.

I got out, looked towards the house, and – seeing no movement – hurried to the boot. I didn't dare look behind me as I opened it, removed the blanket and hauled the woman out by her shoulders. With a burst of strength I never knew I had, I managed to close the boot one-handed, then drag her towards the river, using the car as cover, moving as quickly as possible.

Rather than go straight down to the exposed bank, I

turned onto the footpath, which was screened from the house by trees, and continued down another ten yards or so to where there was a gap in the foliage and, exhausted, dropped her unceremoniously close to the water's edge.

I stood panting in the darkness while I got my breath back, feeling strangely exhilarated, as if I'd just done a really good scene in a single take. Because that was the thing. The more time passed, the more I got used to what I was doing, and the less human the woman seemed. She'd become a problem that needed solving.

The water lapped right up to the edge of the path, twisting in angry little whirlpools as it tumbled downriver, only just contained by the banks. Another day's rain and this footpath and the area around it would be flooded. In that respect, my timing was fortunate.

With one final deep breath, and realising there was no way back from this, I went down on my hands and knees, ignoring the slippery mud I was getting all over myself, and pushed her like a log into the water, grunting hard with the effort.

I'd assumed the water would take her like one of those Hindu funeral pyres you see on documentaries about the River Ganges, but it didn't happen like that. Instead, she stayed almost still, turning slightly this way and that, caught in one of the mini whirlpools, forcing me to shuffle forward so that my knees were in the water and give her another hard shove. She went out about a foot before floating straight back. Cursing under my breath, I moved deeper until the water reached my thighs and I could feel its strength. It struck me how utterly ridiculous and yet weirdly fitting it would be if I was dragged to my death while trying to get rid of her body.

Luckily, that didn't happen. I gave her another push, and this time, thank God, the river took her and she began to drift steadily away.

I got to my feet, took a couple of steps backwards so I was out of the water and breathed a sigh of relief.

Which was when the torch beam fell on me and a man's voice said: 'Excuse me. What is it you're doing out here exactly?'

5

Matt

I almost jumped in shock, especially as the body was still very much in view as it began its rapid journey downriver.

I had to think fast. 'Jesus, you scared me,' I said, shielding my face from the torch beam while simultaneously trying to obscure the man's view of the body. 'Do you mind not shining that in my eyes?'

It always pays to be polite, and it worked this time, as he lowered the torch so that it was now shining on my very wet lower half.

I could just make him out. Middle-aged, a little rotund, roughly my height and dressed in what appeared to be the classic country look of wax jacket and gumboots. His expression was like the tone of his voice: confident, snooty yet not unfriendly. Mind you, I'd have been confident if I had a dog like his: a big German shepherd on a lead, who was staying very calm and still but also carefully sizing me up, as if he was choosing which bit of me to go for.

'So what *is* it you're doing?' he repeated, staring at my wet, filthy clothes.

But that was a good thing. I wanted him looking at me and not out into the river. I'd already concocted a story and sighed theatrically, careful not to appear panicky or suspicious. 'If you must know, I had a huge argument with my wife. A bad one. I took a drive to calm down. I was walking here the other day, so I thought I'd come back and just sit by the river. Unfortunately, as you can see, I slipped over and almost fell in.' I looked down at my clothes and then back at him, making a 'what can you do?' gesture. 'So all in all, it's been a pretty bad night.' Which, of course, was something of an understatement.

'Sorry to hear that,' he said, seemingly satisfied. 'I heard you driving past our house. The only people who usually come down here at this time of night are kids smoking drugs and leaving litter all over the place. We've had a lot of trouble with them lately. That's why I came out to have a look.'

'Well, you can't be too careful,' I said rather pointlessly, deciding that the body was going to be out of sight by now and that it was time for me to make a rapid getaway. The less this guy knew about me the better. 'Anyway, I'd better get back and change out of these clothes. Hopefully the wife will have gone to sleep.'

And then, as I started towards him, trying to act as casual as possible, the unthinkable happened. 'Don't I recognise you from somewhere?' he said, lifting the torch up so he could see my face better. 'I've definitely seen you. Have you been on the telly? Yeah, you definitely have. What have you been on?'

All through my acting career, and in the enforced hiatus since, I've been waiting to be recognised by someone – anyone. Just one tiny nod to whatever talent I might have had. To make it seem like it hadn't all been a colossal waste of time and effort. And now the one time in my whole existence I desperately wanted to remain anonymous, someone – at last – fucking had.

And you know what? This guy wasn't going to let it go. Even in the gloom, I could see that. Denying it would just make him suspicious.

I stopped next to him and smiled ruefully. 'I was on that cop show on Sky, *Night Beat*. DC Jonno Johnson.'

'Never heard of it,' he said emphatically.

I genuinely felt like slapping him then, but that clearly wasn't going to be much help. 'Well I don't know where then,' I said with a shrug, taking the opportunity to glance casually across at the river, just in case the body was out there in plain view, stuck in reeds or something, which would have been just my luck right now. Thankfully, though, it was gone, and hopefully hurtling rapidly through the English countryside a long way from me and my new-found friend. 'Anyway, goodnight,' I said and started past him. But I could feel his eyes still on me, and before I knew it, he was walking in step alongside me, the dog between us.

'No, it was something else,' he said. 'It's on the tip of my tongue . . .' He stopped. 'Oh yes, that's it. I remember now.'

I stopped too, intrigued.

'That advert. You're the chap injured in the car crash, the one where you end up in the wheelchair, crying. Your wife has to comfort you. "When there's nowhere left to go, call Hannett and Stowe, the compensation specialists."'

Jesus. I remembered that horrendous scene where, in a neat bit of role reversal, I broke down in tears in my wife's arms on screen until she had the bright idea of calling the ambulance chasers at Hannett and Stowe, who miraculously made everything right again with a big wodge of cash extracted from someone else's insurance company.

I always thought of that advert as the lowest point in my professional life, and this bastard remembered it word for word. No wonder those leeches at Hannett and Stowe were making so much money.

'Yeah, that's me,' I said, relieved to be back at the car.

But he wasn't giving up chatting yet, asking me if my wife and I were new to the village and, God forbid, even inviting us round for coffee.

In the end, I had to promise that we'd stop by for a cup of tea at the weekend if we had the time, before finally I turned the car round and, as he stood there waving at me with a big smile as if he'd just met Marlon Brando, I drove away thinking that now there was no way back, because there was a witness who could put me at the scene of the heinous crime I'd just committed, making it very hard for me to deny my role in it.

And I know what you're thinking. That this is all very convenient. But it's the truth. I swear it.

6

DCI Cameron Doyle

Matt Walters wears an expression of injured innocence as he recounts his story. It's as though he can't believe he's been flung into this terrible situation. He looks at me pleadingly with those last words:

'And I know what you're thinking. That this is all very convenient. But it's the truth. I swear it.'

Let me tell you, Matt. You have no idea what I'm thinking.

I've been across the table from hundreds of suspects over the years, listening to them attempt to wriggle out of the crimes they've committed, or try to blame others for them. Most of those suspects are easy to read. It's obvious when they're lying. But to give Matt his due, he hasn't paused once so far in his retelling of the events that led him here. Nor so far has he contradicted himself.

But then he's an actor by profession – and he's had a few hours to get his story straight. And truth is, I don't like him. I admit there might be an element of jealousy in this. Even amidst all the cuts and bruises, you can tell he's a good-looking guy – a boy-next-door charmer type – who looks ten years younger than the age on his birth certificate. DS Wild commented on it as we watched him through the two-way mirror before the interview. 'Not bad,' she'd said with a lazy half-smile. 'Not bad at all.'

That wasn't something I wanted to hear. I've had a thing for Tania Wild ever since we started working together three months ago. The problem is, I'm fifty-one, and look every inch of it, right down to the thinning hair and extra stone in soft flesh I carry round my waist. She's fifteen years my junior and out of my league in every way.

So here I am, looking at a man who is my polar opposite. Who is trying to convince me that I should believe him. So I do what every good detective does when they've got the suspect talking. Nothing. I don't give him any help. Neither, credit to her, does Tania. She just sits back in her seat with her arms folded across her chest, an expression of vague scepticism on her face.

I motion for him to go on.

And as he starts talking again, I wonder if he has any idea what his fiancée's been saying to us. Or who she really is.

Because she's a very, very interesting one.

7

Kate

I've had some horrible moments in my life, but my God, nothing compares to the sheer ice-cold fear you experience when you believe you are about to die. And when one of my kidnappers cranked a pulley somewhere behind me, and the noose round my neck suddenly tightened, lifting me onto my tiptoes, I was utterly convinced it was the end.

What got me most was that it was so unexpected. They'd removed my gag, so I'd relaxed just a little. I'd tried to engage them in conversation and made a point of telling them I was pregnant, but to no avail.

And then right out of the blue, I was being half strangled, my toes barely touching the floor, knowing that one more crank of the pulley would be it. The end of my life. The injustice of it felt almost too much to bear.

Seconds passed. They felt like minutes. Hours. Every nerve in my body tingled. And it's true what they say. It was the most alive I've ever felt.

I heard the pulley crank again. This was it.

And then the rope loosened enough for my feet to sink flat to the floor and the pressure round my neck to ease.

A moment later, someone walked past, their footsteps loud on the hollow stage. I heard them going down the steps and the door shutting. Silence.

I sighed with relief. It doesn't matter how bad a situation is – if you've been seconds from death, anything else is tolerable. These people wanted me to know they could kill me any time, but this wasn't the sole reason why they'd tightened the rope. Everything felt choreographed. The bright lights shining through the blindfold; the ropes binding my arms; the noose; what felt like a stage beneath my feet. As if it was for someone else. A threat of what would happen if they didn't cooperate.

I knew who that person was. Only too well.

And it wasn't my fiancé, Matt.

8

Kate

I don't know how much time passed before I heard the door open again, but it was no more than five minutes.

One set of footsteps came towards me, moving purposefully, and instinctively I tensed again.

And then I felt the ropes round my arms being untied and the noose being taken off. This time I could smell the person much better, the chemical odour having largely disappeared. I got hints of expensive deodorant, leather, soap and masculinity.

'Open your mouth,' said a robotic male voice, disguised by some app or machine.

I felt another rush of relief as a bottle of cold fresh water was pushed to my lips. I drank the contents greedily, water splashing down my front and making me shiver in the cold.

'Thank you,' I whispered as he took the bottle away, knowing I had to establish some kind of relationship with my captor.

He then said something unexpected: 'I'm sorry I had to

put you through that. But it was necessary. No harm will come to you if you do what you're told.'

I didn't believe him, but it was best to go along with it for now. 'I will,' I told him. 'But could you give me that blanket again? I'm freezing.'

He put it over my shoulders, holding it in place with his arm as he led me off the stage and through a door. We were going the way we'd come in, and I could tell from behind the blindfold that he was using a torch and that the interior of the building was dark. As the space opened out again, I guessed we were back in the entrance foyer. My feet were no longer bound, there was no sign of the other kidnapper, and freedom was only a few yards away . . . but I'd already decided not to try anything stupid.

I figured we were going to the car, but instead he guided me to a staircase on the other side of the foyer and led me up two separate flights onto the second floor, then down another long corridor, which smelled more strongly of smoke than downstairs. I silently counted the steps I was taking as we turned into one room, then immediately right into another much smaller one.

'All right,' said my abductor. 'Sit down here.'

He let go of my arm and I carefully placed myself down on what I immediately realised was a toilet seat. I was in an ensuite bathroom, which made me think this place had been a hotel at some point.

He told me to stay still, then put the torch down on the floor. I heard the sound of chains rattling.

'What are you doing?' I asked nervously.

'I'm keeping you secure,' he said, wrapping the chain twice round my left ankle before attaching it to something else.

That was the only moment I genuinely considered making a bolt for it. I knew that once I was chained in place, I wasn't going anywhere. But I remained still and acquiescent while he fixed a padlock to my leg.

'Can you release my wrists, please?' I pleaded. 'The cable's really tight. I won't do anything, I promise.'

'I'm sorry. I need to keep you completely secure. It won't be for long.'

'How long?' I asked, careful to remain polite and calm.

'I can't tell you that. It depends on too many factors.'

I didn't ask him what those factors were. Instead I asked him the obvious question. 'Why am I here?'

My abductor stood up with the torch. 'I think you know the answer to that,' he said, and then left the room, double-locking the door behind him.

And that, of course, was the big problem.

I did know the answer.

9

DCI Cameron Doyle

Kate. She's an interesting one. Sure, she looks like a kidnap victim. Her long hair's a twisted, tangled mess; she has big, black bags under her eyes; there are deep red marks on her wrists from where the cable tie bit into her flesh, and further marks on her left leg from the chain that had been wrapped round it.

So yes, she looks the part. But does she sound it? That's the question I've been asking myself as the interview goes on, and the fact is, I'm not sure. I once led a raid on the house of a violent drug dealer suspected of kidnapping his ex-girlfriend and holding her hostage over a debt. We found her in a back room blindfolded, gagged and chained to a radiator, where she'd been for the previous two days. I'll never forget how traumatised she'd been. She was taken straight to hospital and was unable to speak to us for the best part of another two days. When she finally did, it took hours to coax the story from her.

I know it's crude, but on a trauma scale of 1 to 10, I'd have that girl at about 9.5. And I'd have Kate on about 4.5

at an absolute push. Which still means she could be telling the truth. But the fact that she's so lucid and talkative just doesn't sit right with me.

Something else. I don't like the way she immediately lawyered up before saying a word to us. Her brief is a hard-as-nails silver-haired woman from a top-notch London firm. The kind who costs you six or seven hundred an hour plus VAT. Of course, she's perfectly within her rights to get legal representation, but if I were an innocent kidnap victim eager to tell my story, and without a guilty conscience, I might not have made such extensive preparations.

Kate has secrets she doesn't want us to know about. I have an idea what some of them are too.

And they don't cast her in a very good light at all.

10

Matt

The loud blast of an unfamiliar ringtone woke me from a worryingly deep sleep, and for a couple of blissful seconds I had the pleasure of not knowing where I was.

Then I recognised the car horn sound and everything came back to me in an unwelcome flash: the abduction; Kate with a rope round her neck; the body of the anonymous woman slipping into the darkness of the river. I was back in the nightmare.

I must have fallen asleep on the sofa in the living room and I patted at my pockets with increasing urgency for the phone the kidnapper had left behind. It was still dark outside, and I knew I hadn't been asleep for long. Not allowing me to rest was another way of keeping me pliable and disorientated. But I had no choice but to go with it.

I found the phone and shoved it to my ear.

The robotic voice of the kidnapper broke the silence. 'How did you get rid of the body?'

'The river,' I answered tightly.

'Did you weigh her down?'

Jesus Christ. What kind of conversation was this? 'No. But she floated off downriver.'

'She'll be discovered soon enough. It would have been a lot easier if you'd buried her. But at least nothing connects her to you. Hopefully by the time she's identified, you and Kate will be reunited and on your way back to Sri Lanka.'

It scared the hell out of me that he knew so much about us. 'Look, I've done what you've told me. Now please can you release her? I'm willing to let all this go. I won't talk to anybody.'

'Of course you won't, Matt. You're no longer in a position to. Because you're implicated now, aren't you? You've dumped a body in the river and your DNA's all over it. All it would take is one anonymous call to the police and you'd be a step away from a murder charge.'

He was right. He had me now. But that was still a lot better than the alternative, which was never seeing my fiancée again.

'But I don't want you to have to face a murder charge,' he continued. 'That doesn't benefit me at all.'

'Then what *do* you want?'

'For you to do exactly what you're told. The first thing you need to do is go to the garden shed. Inside you'll find a black backpack, tucked in behind the log stack on the left. Bring it to the house and open it. I'll call you back in five minutes.'

The line went dead and I got to my feet. The world had dried out a little and there was the faint pinkish glow of sunrise to the east. I looked at my watch: 7.20. I'd slept for longer than I'd realised but I still felt like shit. It had without doubt been the strangest and most gruesome few hours of my life, and I had a grim feeling it was only going to get worse.

The rental cottage had a long, narrow garden which ran down to a small orchard, with a disused chicken coop on one side and the garden shed on the other. I could see the car from last night on the other side of the adjoining field. Still in the same place. Still empty. In the daylight, it was even more obvious how much of the cottage – not just the side, but the garden and, more importantly, the driveway in front – would have been visible to anyone inside the car. It was a perfect concealed spot to watch us without being noticed, and I was certain that whoever had been in that car had been spying on us. I wondered if it was the dead woman.

Shivering against the cold, I hurried down to the shed. It was bolted, but not padlocked, so anyone could have got access to it.

I found the backpack easily enough. It was exactly where he'd said it would be. It felt comparatively light in my hand as I strode back to the cottage, both eager and scared to open it.

I put it down next to the sofa and made a cup of strong black coffee to fortify myself. I was walking back into the living room when the phone rang again.

'Have you looked inside?' he asked, his tone suspicious.

I stared at the backpack. 'Not yet. But it's in front of me.'

'Open the main compartment.'

I put down the coffee and, with a deep breath, unzipped the bag and reached inside, my hand immediately finding a hard plastic handle. I knew straight away what it was.

The knife was a long black thing, tucked into a leather sheath, the kind I imagined Special Forces operatives carrying. It looked brand new. I put it down beside me and rummaged further inside, quickly locating an A4-sized white plastic folder. It was semi-transparent and I could see a photo inside, as well as a bunch of keys. Propping the phone between my shoulder and ear, I took out the photo and inspected it.

It was a high-resolution shot of the top half of a man in his mid to late fifties. Taken, it seemed, without his knowledge. He was walking outside, his head stooped forward, almost sinking into his coat as if he was hunched up against the cold. He had slightly unkempt grey hair that was long at the back but retreating steadily on top amidst a fairly angry comb-over; a thick beard of the same colour, and heavy-rimmed black glasses. For some reason, I was convinced he was an academic of some kind, maybe a university lecturer who'd lived the high life just a little too much. There was a second photo in the folder, which was a much more close-up version of the first, and I could see that the man's cheeks were liberally sprinkled with broken veins, and his nose was the bulbous kind that comes from too much drinking. Other than that, he looked pretty ordinary.

'Are you looking at the photo?' said the man on the phone, making me wonder if he had a spy camera in here too.

'Who is he?' I asked.

'He's the man you're going to kill if you ever want to see your fiancée again.'

11

Matt

I was too shocked to speak. No one expects to be on the receiving end of a line like that.

The caller filled the silence. 'I said you were going to need a strong stomach and an even stronger heart. This is your time to step up to the plate, Matt.'

'Look,' I said desperately, 'you're making a mistake. I'm not a killer. I'm a guest-house owner, for Christ's sake.'

'Beneath the surface, everyone's a killer,' he said with harsh finality. 'Desperation makes animals of all of us. And animals can kill in cold blood if it's necessary for their survival. Or the survival of their offspring. And it's necessary for the survival of yours.'

'Please. Don't make me do this. Anything but—'

'Do you remember the rules, Matt? You do what you're told. End of story. That way you get to be reunited with your fiancée and unborn baby. You don't get to pick and choose what you're prepared to do. You are going to kill this man. We've even provided you with the weapon to do it with.'

I couldn't believe I was hearing this. It was insane. I'd never hurt anyone in my life. The last time I'd so much as thrown a punch was during my first year at secondary school, and even then I'd missed. 'I'm not stabbing a man I've never met and I know nothing about,' I said instinctively, real anger suddenly rising to the surface. 'I'm not doing it.'

'Then your fiancée dies,' he said, in a dangerously calm tone. 'As does your unborn child.'

His words stopped me dead. I was dealing with a man who'd already left the dead body of a young woman in our bed. I was going to get no mercy here. And yet, like all people capable of empathy, I still held out hope that everyone had some goodness in them.

'Please, I'll do anything else. Whatever you want. We can get you money, anything . . .'

'Are you finished? You're wasting valuable time.'

I stopped, defeated. 'Yes,' I said, realising I was actually contemplating doing this. 'I'm finished.'

'Good. Now grab a pen and paper.'

I went into the kitchen and found a notepad and pen next to the cooker.

He then gave me a street house number and postcode and told me to write them down.

'Memorise those details, then destroy the piece of paper. This is the address of the man you have to kill. You're going to do it this morning. Do not arrive before ten a.m. or after ten thirty. Let yourself in using the keys in the plastic wallet and wait for him to return home. When he does, he will be alone. Ambush him and kill him. He's not an especially big man, or fit, so it won't be too hard.'

I still found it almost impossible to believe what I was hearing. He wanted me to do it in a matter of hours. I wanted to interrupt, to beg him to reconsider. But I didn't. I kept quiet. Because I knew what his answer would be. That if I wanted my family back, I had to do it. That anyone could be a killer if necessary.

And the most terrifying thing? He was almost certainly right.

I kept listening.

'I don't care how you do it,' he continued, 'but I suggest using the knife. Aim for the heart. If he dies quickly, there'll be a lot less blood. Make sure with utter certainty that he's dead. When you've finished, leave. As soon as I have confirmation you've done it, we will arrange returning your fiancée. Do you understand?'

I understood all right. I also understood that I was being set up. Because this man was obviously not afraid to take risks. And yet he was sending me instead. Which meant he wanted me to take the rap for it.

He repeated the question, the robotic voice hardening.

'I want to talk to Kate. I need to know she's all right.'

'No.'

'Fuck you. Let me talk to her, or I don't do it.' I was desperate to wrestle back some control of the situation while I still had leverage.

'Then she dies,' said my tormentor. 'I'll gut her. I'll cut out the foetus.'

51

'You piece of shit.'

'That was a very foolish thing to say. I'll let it go for now. If it's any consolation, the man you're killing is no angel. The world won't miss him, I promise you.'

'Who is he?'

'There's no need for you to know anything about him. Just complete the task you've been given.'

'What if he's not there?' I said desperately.

'He will be.'

The line went dead and I sat back on the sofa, staring at the ceiling and feeling like I was being dragged down a rabbit hole from which I would never emerge. I had no power in this situation. And yet I knew I had to go through with it because, in the end, there was no alternative. I was already involved. I'd dumped the body of an innocent young woman in a river. My DNA was all over her. If I went to the police, who would believe me? And what would happen to Kate and our unborn child?

Not for the first time in my life, I felt completely alone. A sacrificial lamb with no way back and a way forward that was almost certainly going to end in disaster. But why? I knew I hadn't done anything to deserve it.

But what about Kate?

Because as I sat there taking stock of the situation, it occurred to me that I really didn't know her that well at all.

12

Kate

The hardest knock I ever had in my life was when I was sixteen and my mum sat me down and told me she had cancer.

Well, that wasn't quite how it happened. She actually sat me down and told me that Bill, her on-off boyfriend of the past few months – a slimy double-glazing salesman with dyed blond hair and bad teeth – had left for good after she'd finished with him. 'Good riddance to bad rubbish,' she'd concluded, a phrase she'd used more than once to describe a relationship break-up (although it was usually the lacklustre boyfriends doing the finishing). *Then* she'd told me she had cancer. I'd just got home from school. It was only two months until my GCSEs.

She'd told me not to worry. That the doctors had caught it early so the prognosis was very good. That she'd get better.

Except she didn't. She began chemotherapy for stage 3 breast cancer the following week, and I watched with mounting terror as she went slowly downhill. We'd never got on that well. We had our moments. Like when we were watching a film on TV together, sharing a big pack of salted popcorn. But ultimately I resented the fact that she'd always put her boyfriends before me and that *her* happiness had always seemed more important than mine. I hated her weakness, the fact that she'd remained forever trapped in her dull, thankless existence in our poky little flat in a forgotten part of a forgotten town.

Yet in the end, she was all I'd ever had. I had no brothers or sisters. Mum had miscarried when I was four, having fallen pregnant by her fiancé at the time, Dave, a would-be entrepreneur who'd been the nicest of the bunch but who'd ended up in prison for fraud. Her dad had died before I was born. She didn't get on with her mum, who lived up in Scotland with her new husband and who I'd only met once. Her only sibling, my Auntie Julie, lived in New Zealand, where she had her own family.

What truly hurt me was that I'd been so powerless in the face of Mum's deterioration. I'd always stood up for myself: against bullies, against my teachers, against Mum's boyfriends. And too many times, against Mum. I'd prided myself on my ability to stand tall even when others were keen to strike me down at the knees. And yet that strength was of no use in the face of cancer. That summer was the worst of my life as I watched Mum's hair fall out, her body become thinner and paler, her hospital stays get longer each time.

And then in early October, the consultant in charge of her care came by the ward when I was visiting her. I'd started a job on the tills at the local Sainsbury's and had come straight from work. I'd been there for my usual half-hour, talking vaguely with forced cheeriness, trying not to notice how sick Mum looked, how she seemed to be visibly shrinking before my eyes, and was just about to go when the doctor approached us with a rictus smile on his face.

He asked if he could have a word in private and, without waiting for an answer, drew the curtain round the bed so we couldn't be seen by any of the other patients. He pulled up one of the plastic chairs so he was sitting across the bed from me.

'I need to talk to your mother about her progress,' he told me, 'so you may want to wait outside for a few moments.'

My mum turned her head towards me, managing a weak smile. 'You don't have to stay, love,' she said.

It irritated me that they both treated me like a child. I was only weeks away from my seventeenth birthday and already vastly more independent than many people twice my age. 'It's okay, Mum,' I said, taking her hand. 'I can stay. I'd like to hear this.'

The consultant turned to Mum and gave her the bad news – straight and with limited emotion. In spite of their best efforts, the cancer had spread to her bones and liver and her condition was now terminal. With continued treatment, she had as long as six months. Without it, her time could be measured in weeks.

I'd always thought I'd be the one able to handle the news best, but it was Mum who kept her emotions in check. She thanked the doctor while I buried my face in her bedcovers and sobbed silently, and she gently stroked my hair in a way she hadn't done since I was a young child.

Finally I regained control of my emotions and sat up, wiping my eyes with the back of my hand.

Mum was looking at me gently. 'You're going to be okay, love. You don't have to worry. I've made arrangements.'

I frowned. 'What kind of arrangements?'

'From now on, you're going to have a thousand pounds a month put into your bank account.'

I looked at her like she'd lost her mind. 'You don't have any money.'

'You're right, I don't,' she said after a pause, looking ashamed at the fact, which made me feel guilty for bringing it up. 'But your father does. I called and told him about the circumstances and he's agreed to make sure you have that money. He's promised me faithfully he'll pay it.'

It struck me as bizarre that a man I'd never met, and who'd never shown any interest in me, would suddenly start giving me money now, and I said as much.

Mum gave me the kind of look that suggested I wouldn't understand, which would have pissed me off royally if she wasn't so ill. 'He's always paid that money to me. It's what's kept us going all these years.'

I felt like saying she hadn't spent it very wisely considering the lifestyle we'd led while I'd been growing up. It hadn't exactly been hand to mouth, but it had been hard. But instead I asked the question that I'd never had a satisfactory answer to for all these years: 'Who is he?'

She sighed. 'It's best you don't know.'

'How can that be? He's my father. I have a right!' I'd raised my voice instinctively, the anger that I've always carried rearing its head.

Mum looked mortified, and I realised a long time afterwards that it was shame for the way she'd treated me. At the time I misconstrued it as defensiveness.

'I'm sorry,' I said through gritted teeth, 'but I need to know. When I lose you, I'll be alone. It's not right that I don't have a chance to meet him.'

I was playing the guilt card, and for a few seconds, Mum didn't speak. When she did, her words were like hammer blows. 'He's told me there's no way he wants to meet you.'

I swallowed hard, telling myself that I didn't need the approval of someone I'd never met, but I can still remember now how awful those words made me feel, and for the first time I wondered if Mum was lying to me, and if it was her stopping me from having a relationship with my father.

'I'm sorry, love,' she continued. 'I didn't want you to hear that, but he made it a condition of giving you the money. He said he'd stop paying if you ever approached him.'

'Why?' I asked incredulously.

'Because . . .' She paused. 'Because he's a bastard and he doesn't care about you.' She took my hand in hers and gave it the gentlest of squeezes. 'I've always been there for you. That's why I'm finding this so hard, because I'm leaving you behind. But don't go looking for him. If he ever stops paying you, call Auntie Julie in New Zealand and she'll deal with it.'

But I never did let it go. I couldn't. I had to know his

name, and what this whole thing was about. I asked her every time I visited, even as she continued her inevitable journey downhill. I badgered her. I told her that I'd travel to New Zealand and demand answers from Auntie Julie if I had to. I ignored all her warnings about how no good would come of it, and eventually, finally, she told me his name.

And so began my own journey, which more than twenty years on would finally lead to the place where I was now, chained up and blindfolded in the bathroom of an abandoned hotel that smelled of stale smoke and damp.

Because one way or another, this was all about my dad.

13

Matt

I was thirty-five and single, and living in a one-room rental flat just off the Holloway Road, when I realised that I was never going to be a full-time actor. Some people realise it far quicker than I did and manage to forge successful alternative careers. Others go a lifetime taking bit parts and scraping by because, like any of us, they don't want to have to admit to themselves that they walked the wrong path.

I didn't want to admit it either. It was far easier to live in hope that that elusive major role – the one that would finally catapult me to stardom – was just round the corner, and that if I could just be patient a little longer, it would finally happen.

I think the rot had started to set in after *Night Beat* ended its run. No new speaking parts turned up at all. Nothing. It was just voice-overs, and that terrible ad. Phil, my agent, told me to think positive. 'Positive things happen to positive people,' he always liked to say. But then he also used to say meaningless shit like 'You've got to put it out to the universe' and 'Only by looking through the rain do you get to see the rainbow', so I wasn't hugely encouraged.

Then one night while walking back to my flat from the bus stop nearby, having just done an eight-hour shift in a bar in the City catering almost entirely for overpaid, arrogant and staggeringly rude twenty-something twats, I was mugged. For those of you fortunate enough never to have had someone pull a knife on you when you're alone at night, it's hard to explain the feeling of utter terror it engenders.

My assailants were three kids of about sixteen, and they all had knives. I remember walking past them as they stood on the corner of the street next to mine, already feeling the tension build, trying to look as tough as possible, like my character DC Jonno in *Night Beat*, who would have just given them the eye and then continued on his way. But I guess it proved that I wasn't as good an actor as I'd hoped, because just like that, I was grabbed roughly from behind by my coat collar and pulled round so I was facing one of them. I saw the glint of the blade only inches from my belly, and before I'd even fully registered it, the other two were flanking me on either side.

Three knives. All poised and ready to use. I felt my legs go weak. I was so damned scared I wanted to vomit.

They made me empty my pockets. The lead one still had hold of my collar. He jabbed his knife into my jacket so I could feel the tip of the blade pushing against me. He was grinning beneath his hoodie, revelling in my fear. I gave them everything. My phone, my watch, my wallet. Even my Fitbit.

Afterwards, they ran off and left me there, their laughter and rapid footfalls echoing across the empty street, and I burst into tears. Powerless and humiliated, standing there crying: that was when I had my epiphany. It was time to change direction completely.

I'd always dreamed of travelling the world but, for whatever reason, had never done it. So a few months later, with five thousand pounds to my name and the bulk of my belongings in a backpack, I flew to Mumbai and spent a fortnight travelling down the west coast of India to Kerala. Life was good. I felt free. More importantly, I felt safe. People were friendly. There were no muggers lurking on street corners. Occasionally, I experienced that pang of worry so many middle-class Westerners get – that I wasn't thinking about my future, that I should be looking for a proper job rather than spending what little money I had. But those pangs never lasted long. I was meeting fellow travellers of all ages and creeds, with their own stories of abandoning the rat race. Talking to them just showed there was so much more to life than plodding along endlessly until I finally conked out.

My next stop was Sri Lanka, and that was where it all changed. Barely two days after I'd landed in Colombo, I walked into the lobby of Royston House, a small boutique hotel on an old colonial tea plantation high in the forested hills of the island's interior, where I was greeted by the hotel's co-owner, a young Englishwoman, who knocked me off my feet the moment I met her.

I've never been the kind of man who believes in love at first sight, but this was completely different. There was just something about Kate that drew me in. She was beautiful for a start, with long auburn hair and bright blue eyes, and a lean, sun-kissed body. Then there was her wide welcoming smile, the air of warmth that came off her. Her accent was a brave attempt at Home Counties but veered more towards Essex, and wasn't what I'd expected. Still, as we shook hands and she handed me a welcome smoothie of turmeric, ginger and mango, I realised that even her voice was endearing. There was something sweet about it.

Another thing. Kate was relentlessly chatty, and there was something almost manic about her need to talk, as if she'd only just come off a vow of silence. But do you know what? I like to listen, and that made everything between us just seem to work. In the week I stayed at Royston House, I found out that she was single and I think I must have made my feelings plain, even though I was trying hard not to. On my last night, we stayed up drinking beer and talking on the veranda long after all the other staff and guests had gone to bed, and when it was finally time to say goodnight, we looked at each other for a long moment like they do in those old Hollywood movies, and then kissed.

And that was that. Although nothing further happened that night and I left the next day, taking a taxi to a beach resort on the east coast, it was clear that we had the makings of something special. For the next week, we talked on WhatsApp or Skype at least once a day, and the bond between us continued to grow, and then at the end of my stay on the east coast, we agreed that I should come back to Royston House.

At first I stayed in my own room, which I paid for by

doing various jobs round the hotel, but within a couple of weeks, I'd moved permanently into Kate's small villa in the grounds.

That was just over a year ago. Since then, our life together had blossomed. We'd got engaged, she'd become pregnant, and we now effectively managed the hotel as a team.

I loved Kate. She made me incredibly happy. But how much did I really know about her? Because for all her chattiness, she was evasive whenever we talked about her past. I like to discuss things in depth, but every time I tried to get her to open up, I was gently, subtly but firmly rebuffed. I sometimes wondered if that was the reason Kate didn't drink much. Because she was worried it might loosen her tongue.

She's got a hidden scar that runs along the top of her forehead that looks like it must have come from a serious accident. When I asked her about it, she said she'd fallen from a first-floor window at the age of twenty-one when she was drunk, and had ended up in hospital with amnesia, unable to remember large parts of her life. I knew she'd grown up in England – an only child in a single-parent family – and that her mum had died. They were the only details she was prepared to share. Apparently she'd come into some money from an inheritance, which was how she'd managed to buy into the hotel eight years earlier, and she'd been making a decent income from it ever since. At least until the terrorist attacks a few months earlier, which had seen bookings collapse. That was one of the reasons why we'd decided to come back to the UK, with a view to having the baby here before returning to Sri Lanka when things picked up again.

It was Kate's idea to come back to the UK. At the time, it had seemed sensible. The healthcare was far better for a pregnant woman. It would also give us a break from the hotel, which was close to empty most of the time and could easily be left in the charge of our highly efficient duty manager, Raj. For me, it would be a chance to see my mother and brother – not that I was especially close to either of them – and to catch up with friends in London.

I wanted to introduce Kate to everyone – to show her off, if I'm honest – but it seemed she wasn't keen to reciprocate. She didn't seem to have friends or family here. Or at least no one she wanted to introduce me to, which was probably why she'd suggested we rent two cars rather than one. We might have only been back in the country six days but already Kate had arranged to meet up with a girl she hadn't seen since school. I'd wanted to go along with her, if for no other reason than to hear about my fiancée from someone who'd known her before me. But Kate hadn't wanted me to. She'd tried to act casual about it, but the upshot was there was no way she was going to let me be there, and I wasn't really given any good reason why.

So she'd taken her rental car for the lunch and come back a few hours later, and when I'd asked her how it went, she'd talked only vaguely about it – 'it was nice to catch up'; 'she's looking good for her age', that sort of thing. I remember thinking at the time that something about it didn't sound right, but I let it go, because there seemed to be no reason why Kate would lie to me about meeting up with a friend.

But now, after last night, her secrecy seemed far more sinister. Someone clearly hated her enough to commit murder, abduct her and threaten her with death – and then blackmail me.

I stared down at the photo of the man I was supposed to kill. What information could he possibly have that connected him to Kate? Why did he have to die for it?

But even if I could find out the answers to those questions, it wasn't going to help. I either had to do the deed or locate Kate in the meantime – which was impossible, given that it was already 7.30 a.m. Right now I only had one obvious lead. The dead woman, who I suspected had been watching us. She had to be involved somehow. I decided to search her car in the small window of time left before I had to leave for London.

It was beginning to get light as I walked out of the cottage's front door and took a right down the track that bordered the village allotments. At this time of year, the plots were largely empty. There were lights on in a few of the houses opposite, but I couldn't see anyone outside. I turned onto the single-track road I'd driven down the previous night, which ran parallel to the field beside our cottage, and followed it to the dead woman's car. Parked between two trees, it was almost completely hidden from anyone who came this way.

Raindrops were still dripping from the bare branches of the trees, and I pulled up the hood of my coat to keep them from landing on my head, looked round to check no one was watching me and tried the driver's-side door. I was wearing gloves to keep myself from leaving prints on the handle, because I was in enough trouble as it was without contaminating yet another crime scene.

Thankfully, it was open. I peered inside, squinting against the dim light, turning on my phone torch to see better. The interior was clean and tidy. I climbed in, sitting carefully in the driver's seat and closing the door. I remembered what my police mentor Geeta had always told me: the key to solving a murder is knowing the victim's story. In most cases, the best way is to start at the end – the murder scene itself – and work backwards.

My first impression had been that the woman had died in our bedroom, stabbed as she stood by the bed. My search of the car turned up no sign of a struggle or bloodstains – and there would have been a lot of blood – which seemed to confirm my theory. But I couldn't understand why she was in our bedroom in the first place. There was no evidence of forced entry into the cottage. Someone had let her in – and there'd only been one person inside.

Kate.

And yet that didn't make sense either. It was possible that the woman had gone inside with the kidnappers, but it would have been extremely difficult, and risky, to kill her and overpower Kate at the same time. And if she had *been* one of the kidnappers, then what was this car doing here? And why hadn't it been locked?

In the end, I was turning up plenty of questions but no actual answers. But I was sure of one thing. This woman had been watching us. There was a half-full litre bottle of mineral water in one of the cup holders and a thermos flask the same size in the other. I unscrewed the lid and took a sniff. Coffee. She'd been here for the long haul. I looked towards the cottage. From the driver's seat I could see our bedroom window perfectly.

Why were you watching us? What did you want to know?

I leaned over and opened the glove compartment and saw it immediately, sitting on top of the car's owner's manual. A single loose paper receipt. I took it out and inspected it in the torchlight. It was from the BP petrol station in Gerrards Cross, and the date was three days earlier. The time 2.46 p.m.

That was the day Kate had met her friend. And one of the only things she had told me about it was that they were meeting in Gerrards Cross.

Had this woman been following her?

Or, more worryingly, did the two of them know each other?

14

Kate

Matt. I was desperate to know if he was okay. So much so that I'd actually dreamed about him. In the dream, we were back at the hotel, in our private villa high above the rainforest, sitting in the plunge pool looking out over an amazing view I've never grown tired of. Naked, sipping champagne . . .

And then *bang*. I woke up shivering and cold. I'd fallen asleep, but in the absence of light, it was impossible to tell how long for. The blanket had fallen off and my whole body felt stiff and painful – especially my arms where they were pinned behind my back. I was also starving hungry. I hadn't eaten a thing since a tuna salad I'd put together the previous night, and I hadn't even managed to finish that.

I sat up against the toilet seat, shaking myself awake, and used my teeth to get the blanket back on.

For a few minutes I sat there pondering my options, until finally I realised I had absolutely none. The silence in the building was unnerving, and a terrifying thought struck me: what if they'd simply left me here to starve to death? No one was going to find me. Not until it was far too late.

And then before the idea could continue its germination, I heard the sound of a door closing somewhere down the corridor, followed by faint footfalls getting closer, and the bathroom door being unlocked.

I moved my feet out of the way as the door opened and someone stepped inside. I caught the same smell of expensive aftershave and knew it was the man who'd brought me in here earlier. It smelled stronger this time, as if he'd recently reapplied it, which meant he'd either been out or he kept a supply here. It made me wonder how a man who took the trouble to buy and wear expensive, subtle scent had ended up being a kidnapper. I've always been interested in people and their various quirks, and I knew my best bet was to continue trying to engage with him, because he was the key to whether or not I got out of here alive.

'Hello?' I called out, my voice reflecting the fear I felt. 'Who is it?'

'It's me,' he answered, the voice still disguised. 'I've brought you water and some food.'

'Thank you.'

I heard him put something down on the floor then crouch down close to me. He told me to open my mouth and proceeded to put another bottle of water to my lips, holding it while I drank.

After that he spoon-fed me some Weetabix in cold milk. I was surprised by how gentle he was. It seemed that he bore me no ill will. That he was doing this for someone else. But in a strange way, that made it worse. Because if he was a professional criminal who didn't have a moral issue with kidnapping a pregnant woman and holding her hostage in squalid conditions, then it was unlikely he'd have too many qualms about killing her either.

Even so, I was encouraged by his small act of kindness and I asked him if he'd mind untying my hands. 'The cable's very tight, and they feel numb. I won't try to escape or do anything stupid, I promise. I wouldn't do anything to endanger my baby.'

'I'm sorry,' he said. 'I can't. But you won't be here long.'

I thought of Matt again. I wondered how he was reacting to my disappearance. He'd been like a puppy around me ever since I'd told him I was pregnant, and I knew he'd be terrified for my safety. Unless, of course, something had already happened to him. 'Where's my fiancé?' I asked the kidnapper. 'Is he okay?'

'He's alive and well.'

'Is he here?'

'No. But he's safe. And you'll be reunited with him soon enough.'

I had some serious doubts about that. But then I was doubting a lot right now, and I needed some answers. 'You claimed last night that I knew what this was all about. I've got some ideas, but I need to know for sure. So, why am I here?'

He leaned forward and I could feel his breath on my face. It smelled of mint and coffee.

I suddenly felt very uneasy and regretted asking the

question as a gloved hand pushed my hair back above the line of the blindfold, and a finger ran gently down the long pale scar that crossed my scalp just below the hairline – a scar that only a handful of people in this world were even aware of.

'You're here so we can talk about this,' he said quietly. 'You remember how you got it, don't you?'

I tensed before I could stop myself, and breathed out slowly, trying to sound calm. 'I had a fall.'

'It was more than a fall, wasn't it?'

'I don't know. I have no memory of it. It put me into a coma and gave me amnesia.'

'That's interesting,' said the man, almost playfully. 'And how far before your fall does your amnesia stretch?'

I knew what he was getting at. 'I don't know. A while. I have a lot of memory blanks from before. It was bad. I was in hospital a long time.'

'I know. Two months. And under police guard too. Things have gone a lot better for you since then, though, haven't they? Money. A new life in the sun.'

'You seem to know a lot about me,' I whispered. But of course he did. He – or whoever he worked for – had planned all this.

'I do,' he said. 'But there's more I need to know. And you're going to provide me with the answers.'

'I'll do what I can,' I said, knowing exactly what he was driving at.

'You'll do more than that,' he said, his words taking on a more ominous tone. 'You'll tell me the absolute truth, and you won't use amnesia as an excuse. Because if I think you're lying to me, I'll have to hurt you. Badly.' He paused. 'Do you understand?'

Suddenly he didn't seem so nice any more. And I knew he wasn't lying. He would hurt me. It was possible – maybe even likely – that when he finished asking his questions, he'd kill me anyway. I had to think. To plan my next move. There are very few puzzles that don't have a solution, and I had to make sure that this wasn't one of them.

'Yes,' I told him quietly. 'I understand.'

15

Matt

Ultimately, it didn't matter what other clues I might find, because time ran out. Barely half an hour after my search of the car, I was driving towards the address in London that the kidnapper had sent me.

The man I'd been ordered to kill lived in a 1950s terraced house close to a railway viaduct, on a long residential street of near-identical homes not far from Wembley Stadium. I was almost an hour early, and it was one of those dark, gloomy November days that threatened torrential rain at any moment. There were only a handful of pedestrians on the street and, being London, no one took any notice as I drove slowly past the house, navigating speed bumps and making sure I had the right address. Number 46. There was light coming from inside the ground floor. I assumed the white Ford Fiesta parked on the carport directly outside belonged to my proposed victim.

I made a mental note of the number plate and continued driving at a steady speed. I passed under the viaduct, not wanting to stay too close to the house, and found a parking spot on an adjoining street half a mile away. As soon as I stopped, I typed the registration number into my iPhone. I knew I had to get as many clues as possible to the identity of my target, even though I still had no idea how I could do it without drawing attention to myself.

After that, I settled back in the seat to wait. I was wearing a cap, pulled down as low over my face as I could manage without looking suspicious, and staring down at my phone like any normal person would.

And all the time my heart was racing as I realised what I was about to do. The knife – the murder weapon – was under my seat. At some point this morning I was going to be called upon to use it. I tried to imagine what it was going to feel like to kill a man I'd never met before. Just the thought of it made me nauseous. I was sweating and my hands were shaking. It was very similar to the feeling of utter terror I'd got just before I went on stage for the first time in my first proper acting role – a big part in an Agatha Christie play running at the Theatre Royal in Windsor. The stress had made me want to vomit, and I'll always remember one of my co-stars, a much older actor who'd had a half-decent career in TV, putting a supportive hand on my shoulder and saying: 'You've just got to look at it this way: what's the worst that can happen? It's a play, not the end of the world.'

His words had reassured me at the time, and I'd gone out on stage and all my nerves had disappeared, because he was right. In the end it *was* just a play not the end of the world. But this . . . this was totally different. This was killing a man. Ending his life. Risking imprisonment. This could easily be the end of my world.

And yet if I didn't go through with it, I risked losing my fiancée and our unborn child, and then my life as I knew it – the life that I'd lovingly built up this past year – would be over too. It was like I was trapped in a vice, with no way forward and no way back, its jaws slowly crushing me.

I had a straight choice. Let two lives of people close to me be lost, or end the life of someone I didn't know. In the end, it could only ever go one way, and this was why I was sitting here counting down the seconds, knowing I had to drive the fear out of my mind and do what I'd been ordered to do.

But Jesus, the half-hour I sat there in that car was the most unpleasant of my life. Yet it was also one of the shortest. I kept looking at my watch, willing the time to slow down, to grind to a halt, to give me more time to think of a way out of this, even though I knew in reality there wasn't one. More than once I punched 999 into my phone, thinking that I had to call the police, give them the responsibility of finding Kate and saving her from this faceless killer, but each time, I stopped myself. The jaws of the vice were too tight. There was no time, and the chances were they'd never believe my story about the body in our bed. A body that I'd made disappear. I also reconsidered calling Geeta. Telling her everything, asking for her advice. Because one thing about her was that she always seemed to know what to do.

But this time she couldn't help.

I have no choice. That was what I kept telling myself. *I have* no *choice.*

I looked at my watch: 9.55. It was time.

Taking a deep breath, I put the car in gear and pulled away from the kerb just as it began to rain, big heavy drops that splattered against the windscreen, suddenly becoming the kind of torrential deluge that sends people scuttling inside, providing me with much-needed camouflage.

Conscious that I was going to have to make a quick get-away, but one that didn't look too suspicious, I found another parking spot on the road running parallel to the viaduct, less than fifty yards from my target's front door. Leaning down in the seat so I couldn't be seen by anyone still foolish enough to be outside, I put on my gloves, then removed the knife, still in its sheath, from under the seat and slipped it into the inside pocket of my jacket. Then, with a final check of the watch – 9.59 – I felt in my jeans pocket for the keys to the target's house and got out of the car, hurrying down the street, head down, as the rain pelted down on me.

As soon as I rounded the corner, I saw him. My target. Thirty yards away. He was dashing to the driver's side of his car. I recognised him instantly, even though he was pulling the collar of his coat over his head in a vain attempt to keep the rain at bay. He was taller than I'd been expecting, and thinner too. But there was no doubt it was him, and the thought that I was looking at a living, breathing human being on an ordinary street who had no idea that he was about to die almost made my legs go from under me, and I visibly stumbled.

Thankfully, he didn't even look my way as he jumped inside the white Fiesta, quickly reversing out of the carport before driving away in the opposite direction. I knew without looking at my watch that it was almost exactly 10 a.m. Kate's kidnapper had known exactly what time he'd be leaving, which only served to confirm how dangerous were the people I was dealing with.

I was almost hyperventilating as I approached the house. The light was still on downstairs and I had a terrifying thought that there might be someone else in there. A woman or a child. Then what the hell would I do? I had no answer to that question, and I just had to hope the kidnapper's intelligence was as reliable as it appeared to be.

Without dropping my pace, I glanced round to check the street was still empty, then hurried up to the front door, pulling out the keys. The target had double-locked it, which was a relief, because it meant that the house was unoccupied.

I opened the door and stepped inside, half expecting an alarm to go off, but I was met by silence and engulfed in a wave of centrally heated warm air. Double-locking the door behind me, I wiped my feet on the mat to avoid leaving any incriminating footprints and looked round. I was in a narrow, tired-looking hallway with a staircase directly in front of me. The place smelled vaguely of cannabis mixed with incense sticks. A cardboard box almost overflowing with books sat in one corner, with a suit and a couple of other jackets piled on top of it. Other than that, and a mirror shaped like a smiling sun hanging from one of the walls, it was empty.

I glanced at my reflection in the mirror's dirty glass. The man who stared back at me looked wide-eyed and haunted, as if suffering some terrible shock, nervous exhaustion pumping out of every pore. It was all so different to the face I'd seen last night in the mirror of the pub washroom. Then I'd been happy. Returning to London in triumph, having finally made something of myself.

I turned away, not wanting to see myself any more, and looked around for clues that might give me some kind of leverage later. The nearest door opened to a lounge with a matching sofa and armchair, facing a cheap-looking TV on a corner unit. There were a couple of bookshelves along one wall, but they were empty. It felt like a house rather than a home. It also looked like its occupant was planning to leave.

There was a stack of washing-up in the kitchen sink, and an open box of cornflakes on the worktop. The sight of it stopped me in my tracks, because it reminded me that this was a man who'd woken up this morning and carried out his usual routines, including eating his breakfast cereal, all the time expecting to still be alive at the end of the day.

And my job was to make sure that didn't happen.

Creeping back into the hallway, I went over to the box in the corner and gently lifted the jackets with my gloved hand. The topmost book beneath them was a well-thumbed tome called *Influence: Science and Practice*, which appeared to be some kind of psychology self-help manual. Under that was another equally well-worn psychology textbook. The rest were a selection of fiction paperbacks.

Replacing the jackets, I headed upstairs and into the main bedroom. The bed was unmade and a large suitcase crammed with clothes sat on top of it, which confirmed that this man was definitely planning on leaving. There was a single chest of drawers next to the bed, but they were all empty. I opened the large free-standing wardrobe only to find nothing but a few items of clothing and a pair of shoes.

Frustrated, I spent the next ten minutes carefully looking for any clue to this man's identity – and what possible connection he could have to Kate. But he'd almost cleaned the place out. Clearly he didn't want to be found, and I was reminded of what the kidnapper had said about him: that he was no angel and the world wouldn't miss him. It was scant consolation for what I was about to do, but at least I wasn't killing a complete innocent.

Except was I actually going to stick a huge knife into a fellow human being and watch him die? Even thinking about it made me nauseous. And it wasn't as if my intended target wouldn't resist. He'd fight for his life, and he wasn't a small man. So there was no guarantee I'd even be able to kill him, no matter how determined I was.

But if I didn't . . .

I tried to shift myself forward in time a few hours to see how this would pan out, but the fact was, I had absolutely no idea. Except for one thing. Whatever happened, my life was never going to be the same again. I'd already dumped the body of a murder victim, so I was forever destined to be looking over my shoulder, wondering if it would come back to haunt me.

The car horn ringtone sounded in my pocket and I cursed myself for forgetting to put the phone on vibrate. It was 10.25. Once again it was an unidentified number, but I had absolutely no doubt who was on the other end.

'Where are you?' demanded the robotic voice. I thought I detected frustration in his tone.

'At the target's house,' I whispered.

'He's on his way back now. He'll be there shortly. Be prepared.'

I felt my stomach clench and had to fight to control my breathing. This was it. 'I am,' I said, even though I wasn't.

'Good,' said the voice. 'Because you have new instructions. Before you kill the target, you are to get some information from him. When he arrives, ambush and incapacitate him. Use the knife as a threat, but keep him alive and conscious. He'll be scared. Get him to lie down on his front, then put your knee in his back so that he's completely subdued. Tell him you'll kill him unless he answers the following question: where is the master copy? Tell him if he doesn't produce it right now, you'll cut his throat. You're supposed to be an actor. Make him believe you. Tell him if he gives you the copy then you'll let him live.'

I felt a sudden burst of hope. I had no idea what this master copy was, and knew the kidnapper wouldn't tell me, but at least now there was a chance of getting out of here without committing murder.

'If a copy exists, he will have it on him,' continued the voice. 'It will be in the form of a flash drive or a micro cassette. It may even be hanging from a chain round his neck. If he refuses to cooperate or says there isn't one, stab him in the gut. Then ask him again.'

'Jesus Christ,' I whispered. 'Please don't make me torture him.'

'It'll be the target's choice to cooperate and your job to convince him that he should do so. All I'm interested in is the master copy.'

'And if he gives it to me, I can let him go?'

'*When* he gives it to you, finish him off.'

My heart sank. Not only was this nightmare not ending, it was getting worse. I took a deep breath and told him that I understood, because it was the only way to buy myself some time to think.

'As soon as I have confirmation that he's dead, we will arrange swapping the master copy for your fiancée. But let me make one thing crystal clear. Do not look at the contents. For your own sake as much as anyone else's.'

I had no idea what he meant, but I didn't like the sound of it. I told him I wouldn't.

'Now don't let yourself or your fiancée down,' he said. 'And remember, I'll be watching.' With that, he ended the call.

I'll be watching. What the hell did he mean? Did he have a camera in here that I hadn't spotted? It was possible. Why not? He had the keys to the place. It stood to reason he'd install a camera. But then why had he asked where I was? If he could see me, he'd know.

All these questions were flooding through my head, threatening to overwhelm me. Even if there was a camera

81

here, there was nothing I could do about it now. Instead, I walked over to the window and looked out onto the street. The rain had stopped and the sun was attempting to peep out from behind the clouds.

And as I stood there, the white Fiesta came driving down the road towards me. I moved back from the window, my whole body trembling as I fought to keep control of an escalating, sickening panic.

My victim was here.

16

Matt

I crouched, dead still, in the darkness of the wardrobe. The air was hot and stifling, and a bead of sweat dripped down my forehead, leaving more of my DNA in what might well become a major crime scene. I'd pulled on the scarf I'd brought with me so that it covered my face beneath the eyes, and in my gloved hand I held the unsheathed knife.

The panic had stilled now, replaced with clarity-inducing adrenaline. I knew I had to be strong – to act like I never had before, to bend this man to my will. I had a plan. It was basic, but it might just work. Kate's kidnapper badly wanted the drive or tape or whatever it was. If I could get it, there might be room for manoeuvre. Maybe we could somehow fake this man's death. It was a solvable situation. I was sure of it.

Downstairs, I heard the front door opening and then closing with a loud bang, as if he was in a hurry. No matter. He had to come up here if he wanted his suitcase.

I waited. My knees felt stiff, so I stood up, my head scraping against the rail.

And then he was moving quickly up the stairs. He went into the toilet and I heard him take a long, loud leak and clear his throat. It was utterly surreal being in someone's house like this, listening to their most intimate moments. The man didn't wash his hands but came striding into the bedroom, only feet away from me, and I heard him closing the suitcase with a loud exhalation.

It was now or never.

I came out of the wardrobe fast, the adrenaline coursing through me.

The door only just missed him as it flew open. He had his back to me, leaning over the bed, and was turning around just as I gave him a hard shove.

It wasn't hard enough. He fell forward towards the bed but managed to right himself, darting off to one side before I could grab him properly.

I was now between him and the door. He turned to face me and spotted the knife, taking several steps backwards towards the window before realising he'd trapped himself. His hands were held out in front of him in a defensive posture. Sheer terror was etched across his face.

I now saw him properly for the first time. He was even thinner up close, with that pinched, haunted look you sometimes see on obsessive middle-aged runners. He also looked older. Mid fifties at least, maybe pushing sixty, skin lined and sallow, his small dark eyes round and sunken. He looked ill.

I immediately felt both guilty and frightened. My acting skills melted away as I stood rooted to the spot, waving the knife at him. 'Where's the master copy? Give me the master copy now!' I demanded, realising my voice was so badly muffled that it was almost unintelligible.

I pulled the scarf away from my mouth with my free hand and took a step towards him, trying to stop my knife hand from shaking. 'Get on the floor!' I shouted, trying to put some force into my voice.

But though he was scared, he didn't look compliant. His eyes were darting all over the place and I could see I was in danger of losing control of the situation.

I took another step forward, pointing the knife towards his chest, and he stepped back again, closer to the window. 'Look, I don't know what you're talking about. But if you leave now, I won't call the police.' His accent was educated, the voice authoritative, though it was still tinged with fear.

Something switched in me then – maybe it was the knowledge that if I failed even to get him to comply with me, there was no way I was going to get Kate back – and suddenly I was Matt the actor again. DC Jonno Johnson. A man who wasn't going to stop until he got the answers he needed. 'I said I want the master copy! Give me it or I will fucking kill you.' My voice carried weight now. 'And get down on the floor.' I took another step forward, more confident this time.

He retreated round the bed, backing up towards the wall now, still keeping his hands out in front of him, with me matching him step for step.

Then he stopped. Five feet separated us, maybe less. He was looking me right in the eye now, and I could see he was calculating whether or not to comply.

I tensed, ready to lunge forward so that he'd know I was

serious. 'Just give me the fucking master copy, that's all I want,' I hissed, conscious that sweat was pouring down my forehead and into my eyes. It was stifling in here. I felt sick. And something told me he was going to make a break for it. I had to do something.

I blinked hard, trying to clear my vision.

And that was when he made his move. Taking a rapid step back, he reached behind him and grabbed the lamp from the bedside table. For a sick-looking man he moved extremely fast, but that's what you do when your life depends on it. Before I could react, he'd flung the lamp straight at me, and as I brought up an arm to deflect it, he jumped onto the bed and raced across it, heading for the door.

By a stroke of luck, he tripped on the suitcase and fell head-first off the other side, smacking into the wall and landing on the floor in a heap. But he was far too close to the door and freedom, and he was already scrambling to his feet.

I couldn't let him go. That would have been the end of everything. So I ran after him, grabbing him by the back of the collar as he tried to stand up and yanking him back-wards, careful not to catch him with the knife. 'You're not going anywhere,' I grunted.

Struggling out of my grip, he lashed out, trying to smash an elbow into my face. I dodged the blow, but he kept coming, his face only inches away from mine as if he was going to land a headbutt, his fingers tugging at my scarf, pulling it free so that suddenly my features were exposed.

'You bastard!' he shouted, his expression furious now, and then with a roar, he did attempt the headbutt.

I managed to turn my head and the blow was a glancing one, but I stumbled and, realising I was in danger of losing my footing, I started fighting back, and shoved him backwards.

And then his eyes widened and he let out this weird gasp that seemed to last for several seconds, which was when I realised with a sense of real shock that I'd accidentally stabbed him.

Pushing him away, I looked down and saw the knife buried deep in his upper thigh.

'Oh Jesus.' I pulled it out without thinking, looking down at the bloodied blade, then at him, watching frozen to the spot as he staggered backwards, banging against the wall, the blood pumping out now in great gouts. I no longer cared about the fact that I'd been unmasked. Right now, that was the least of my problems.

I couldn't move. It felt like I was trapped in the middle of a nightmare with a starring role. As I watched, he clutched at the wound with both hands, the blood seeping through the gaps in his fingers in an unstoppable flow.

Then he slid down the wall, staring at me with wide confused eyes, his face rapidly turning a ghostly white, and I knew that he was dying.

I wanted to help him, but felt perilously close to throwing up. The sight of blood has always made me queasy, and to see so much of it right in front of me was almost too much. But a little voice in my head – the voice of self-preservation – came out of nowhere and told me I couldn't afford to throw up. It would leave my DNA all over the place.

I had to think like a detective. Jesus, I had to think like a *man*. The guy in front of me had information I had to get hold of or Kate and my unborn child would die. It was as simple as that. You have to believe me when I tell you I was trying to do the right thing; that I had no choice but to do what I did next.

As he sat sprawled awkwardly against the wall, making strange little whimpering noises, I crouched in front of him. I was still holding the knife, but now it was down by my side and out of sight, because I knew that it was far too late for any threats to work now. 'For God's sake,' I implored him. 'Tell me where the master copy is. My fiancée's life depends on it. She's pregnant.'

His eyes flickered. I was losing him. Blood continued to spill down his leg. 'Help me,' he whispered, the words little more than a croak.

'I will,' I said, pushing my gloved hand over his, trying in vain to help stem the blood pouring out of his wound. 'Just give me the copy. That's all I need.'

'Can't help,' he said faintly, and then his eyes closed and he let out a long, gentle sigh.

'Please, please wake up,' I begged him, bringing my face close to his.

Nothing.

I slapped his cheek. Hard.

Still nothing. His head drooped to one side. If he wasn't already dead, he soon would be. There was no way I was getting any answers from him now.

Even so, I slapped him again, harder this time, the panic

tearing through me. I grabbed his collar, shook him, unable to take in what I'd just done. I'd killed a man. Worse, I was assaulting him even as he lay dying in front of me.

But I had to get that information.

Without stopping to think what I was doing, I unzipped the top of his coat, looking for the drive that the kidnapper had said he might be wearing on a chain round his neck. It wasn't there, so I reached into the outer pockets of the jacket, rummaged around, felt keys and a phone. I pulled out the phone, shoved it in my own jacket, somehow managing to compute in all the mayhem that it might come in useful later. I searched his trouser pockets next, my hand feeling the warm wetness of the blood as it soaked through his clothing, realising that I was acting like some sort of ghoul but operating pretty much on autopilot. Still I found nothing. I reached into the pocket on the other side, not sure what I was even looking for now.

And that was when I heard it.

A loud, ear-shredding scream.

17

Matt

My head snapped up so fast I almost pulled a muscle in my neck.

There she was. Just in view round the corner of the bedroom door frame, standing at the top of the stairs, her mouth gaping open. A short-haired woman in her forties, dressed in a shiny black raincoat and leggings and holding a bunch of keys, staring straight at me as I crouched over the body of the man I'd just stabbed while still clutching the knife I'd used on him.

I stared back at her, during which time three things instantly dawned on me. One: I was no longer wearing the scarf, meaning there was now a witness who could ID me as the man's killer. Two: I looked exactly like a murderer as I searched the body, not someone who'd killed this man accidentally. And three, and right then most importantly: this woman – whoever she was – might be in possession of the master copy I needed.

'It's not what it looks like, I promise you,' I said, putting on my most trustworthy expression and slowly getting to my feet, making sure I placed the bloodied knife on the floor in an effort not to panic her.

Not surprisingly, the gesture didn't work. The woman screamed again, just as loudly, and turned and started running down the stairs.

I couldn't lose her. She had a key to this place so she obviously knew the target well, meaning right now she was my only hope, so I took off after her, desperation giving me a turn of speed I'd never known I had.

She was fast too, almost on the last step when I caught up, slamming her in the back and sending her crashing into the front door before yanking her back round and using both hands to hold her up by the collar of her raincoat.

'Don't even think about screaming!' I hissed, trying to ignore the terrified look on her face. 'I'm not going to hurt you. But I need the master copy.'

She stared back like a rabbit in headlights. 'You killed Piers.'

'I didn't mean to. It was an accident. You've got to help me. They're going to kill my fiancée.'

'You liar!' She suddenly began to struggle hard in my grip and I didn't know what to do. I couldn't hit her, surely.

But I couldn't let her go either. I took a step back, still holding onto her lapels, and slammed her into the door again, my face contorted in anger as I thrust it close to hers. 'I'll kill you if you don't give me the copy, I swear it.'

'I don't know anything about a master copy, I promise. And please stop. You're choking me.'

I realised that I was pushing the balls of my fists against

her throat as I clutched at her lapels, and I loosened my grip slightly.

'But you know what this is all about, don't you? You know Piers was involved in something. Something bad.'

She hesitated. And that confirmed it. She knew more than she was letting on. I could see it in her eyes.

And I noticed something else. She was wearing a cheap-looking but thick metal chain round her neck. It looked oddly out of place. I stared at it and knew instinctively that it held the master copy.

I grabbed hold of it and pulled, thinking the chain would snap. It didn't, but it did fly upwards from under her clothing, revealing a single black flash drive on the end.

'Give me that,' I hissed, grabbing the drive in one hand, ready to give the chain another wrench.

Those were the last words out of my mouth, because the next second I felt an intense, excruciating pain as a knee was launched straight into my groin.

With a high-pitched gasp, I stumbled backwards onto the staircase, letting go of the drive and landing on my behind, clutching uselessly at the place where my balls used to be, because right now it felt like they were somewhere up around my chest. It had been years since I'd taken a shot to the nuts, but you never forget the all-consuming agony of it – like your insides are being smashed with a jackhammer – and I was forced to watch helplessly as the woman yanked open the front door and ran outside, slamming it shut behind her, still in possession of the flash drive. Already I could hear her screaming at the top of her voice that there'd been a murder, and I knew that she'd be calling the police any moment.

Even so, it was a real struggle to get up, and when I did manage to, I had to stand there for a few seconds, holding onto the banister like an old man, until the pain finally began to subside enough to be tolerable.

I had to get out of here. But I had to have that drive too. If I could just catch her . . .

I staggered over to the window and looked out onto the street, trying to stay out of sight. The woman was still out there on the pavement and her screaming had clearly alerted passers-by, because a man and a woman were running over to her now, and she was pointing back at the house. The woman was on the phone while the man – a big guy in his fifties – looked the type who might try to stop me if I went out that way, and probably be successful as well. And the last thing I needed was more people getting a look at my face.

That only left the back way out. Trying to ignore the horrendous throbbing from my groin through my insides, I pulled the scarf back up over my face and took off into the kitchen.

Even before I got there, I heard loud banging on the front door and the muffled shouting of someone outside. I tried the back door but it was locked, with no key in it. Now I could hear the front door being unlocked and then a man's voice shouting that the police were on their way. 'And I've got a baseball bat here!' he added menacingly.

Almost overdosing on pure adrenaline, I tried the window above the sink. But it too was locked.

I could hear footsteps coming down the hall towards me. If it was the man I'd just seen outside, I had no idea where he'd got the bat from, but clearly he was confident enough to confront a killer – and that meant trouble for me.

I looked round wildly and saw the tiny key tucked into the lip of the windowsill. I grabbed it and, with shaking hands, inserted it into the lock, pulling down the handle and throwing the window open.

'Oi!' came a shout from the doorway. 'Stay there!'

I didn't even look round. Instead I sprang, literally one-handed, onto the sink and dived head-first out of the window and onto the patio outside, landing painfully on my elbow before scrambling to my feet and sprinting up the narrow garden. A rickety wooden fence separated it from the one next door, and when I'd put a few yards between me and the house, I scrambled over it and down the other side. A dog immediately started barking loudly and out of the corner of my eye I saw it come running towards me. But I wasn't stopping for anyone or anything and I was over the next fence and into the garden beyond before it could reach me. A train was clattering past on the viaduct, its passengers clearly visible inside, safely ensconced in their own little worlds, completely unaware of the situation I was in. I would have given anything to be in their position now.

The next fence bordered the road where I'd parked my car and it was much higher than the others. But one thing you can only appreciate if you've been in true fight-or-flight mode is that you are capable of things you never believed possible. Without even thinking about it, I sprinted the five yards to the fence and, as far as I can remember, simply ran up it, grabbing the top with both hands and swinging myself over.

As I hit the pavement on the other side, I heard the first siren. It was still some way off but clearly coming in my direction. My car was twenty yards away and I sprinted over to it, keeping my head down, not daring to look back. The keys were already in my hand as I jumped inside and started the engine, pulling out of the space with a screech of tyres and accelerating away from the scene, praying no one had seen me and taken the number of the rental car.

I had no idea where I was going; I just kept driving, trying to put as much distance as possible between myself and the sirens, my fingers tight on the wheel.

Five minutes passed. I hit a main road. Turned left on a whim, joining a long, snaking queue of traffic heading into town. A police car raced towards me on the other side, lights blaring. I was frozen to the seat, thinking that I couldn't continue running like this for much longer, but then it was past me and continuing down the road, weaving through the traffic, its occupants uninterested in me.

The kidnapper's phone vibrated in my pocket. I ignored it. The shock was beginning to take hold of me now. I looked down. My hands were shaking and there were two matching stains on my jeans at the knees, from the blood pool on the carpet. I felt sick. I'd killed a man. Unintentionally or not, he was still just as dead. And it was only my word that it had been an accident. As far as the world was concerned, it had been cold-blooded murder. And now I was a fugitive, and there was a witness who'd seen my face.

My life had changed forever. There was no way back from that. But already I was thinking about the next big problem I had to face, because I hadn't got hold of the flash drive the kidnapper seemed to want so desperately, and that left my bargaining power woefully short.

The traffic began to pick up as the light went green. I took a series of deep breaths and told myself to stay strong, because the alternative was collapsing into blind panic and I couldn't afford that.

The odds might have been stacked heavily against me, but as long as I was free, I had a chance to fix this and get Kate back.

18

Sir Hugh Roper

Cancer.

I'll tell you something about cancer. It doesn't matter how much money you have; how powerful you are; how much you pray to your God. Nor even how perfect your nutritional and lifestyle habits are. Cancer respects none of these things. It can come at you at any time, and it's clever. It conceals itself until it's ready. It was like that with me. Stealthy, beginning symptomless in the prostate before spreading steadily through my liver and kidneys. By the time the coughing began and I noticed the blood in my urine, it had already invaded my lungs, making the end result inevitable.

As a self-made businessman who's worked his way up from the nadir of bankruptcy and a conviction for theft at the tender age of twenty-four to multimillionaire status, seeing off violent rivals, family tragedy and HM Customs along the way, I've always thought of myself as ready for anything, and indeed I'd steeled myself for bad news when I arrived at the clinic to receive the results of my tests.

At the age of sixty-eight, finding blood in your urine and developing a hacking cough means it's likely to be something fairly serious. Even so, I hadn't been expecting to be told by the consultant that my cancer was terminal; that with chemotherapy I had a maximum of a year to live, and without it anything between three and six months.

What does a man do in that situation? Cling on to life, even as it's sucked out of him bit by shitty bit? Or try to go out with some dignity? I decided to forgo the treatment. In fact, I'd even contemplated ending my life with a pain-free cocktail of poisons at a private clinic in Switzerland, but somehow this felt like defeat, and I do not do defeat. Instead, I was going to let the cancer take its course and go out fighting. Like a man.

That had been two months ago now. Since then, the coughing had got steadily worse, as had my weight loss. I'd wanted to keep my diagnosis secret, but as CEO of Peregrine Homes, the UK's premier luxury home development company, with a market capitalisation of over eight hundred million pounds, I had a duty to the shareholders, whether I liked it or not (and I didn't), and so the previous week at a meeting of the board, I'd given them the bad news. I didn't want to stand down. Peregrine Homes was my creation. I'd built it up from scratch, using a huge loan that had almost got me killed when I'd had difficulty paying it back, and I've sweated blood to make it the success story it is today. But there'd been no choice. The board had decided that I would remain chairman while the company's deputy MD, Keith Clappe, would act as CEO until a suitable successor was found.

The announcement had already been made to the media, and since then I've been working from home, and already my workload was beginning to dry up, leaving me pissed off and frustrated. Retirement has never been an option for me. My second wife, Ellen, died suddenly four years ago and I live alone, having not met anyone else I was willing to grow old with. Work, effectively, has been my life.

And now both life and career are almost over.

Ironically, my coughing seemed to have got better in the past week or so and, as long as I didn't laugh, I found I could avoid the prolonged hacking fits. And there was very little danger of me finding much humour from the man sitting opposite me that morning.

Edward Hurst is my stepson. An ambitious and supremely dull young man – as you'd expect from someone who likes to be addressed as Edward rather than one of the shorter and easier alternatives – he was determined to rise to the top in business like his stepfather. I've always had a distant relationship with the boy, which was surprising considering how much time we'd spent together over the years – and how much of a disaster my own son, Tom, has always been.

Edward was eleven when I married Ellen, his mother, a beautiful former model who'd popped him out when she was only nineteen. I've never known the identity of the boy's father but I can say with some certainty that the culprit – whoever he was – had been no oil painting. Edward was skinny in build, and pale, with sandy hair that was already thinning at the crown, and a soft, round face that sat atop his body like one of those old-fashioned sticky lollipops.

He looked like a twelve-year-old in ageing make-up. Having said that, what he lacked in obvious physical attributes, the boy more than compensated for on the intellectual front, being something of a financial genius. He'd come out of the LSE with a first in finance and economics, and Ellen had begged me to give him a chance at Peregrine. I'd been reluctant. I don't do carrying people, and if someone doesn't pull their weight when they're working for me, then they're out. End of. But as it happens things had worked out far better than I could have imagined. The boy had risen up through the ranks entirely on his own merit and he was now the company finance director, with a seat on the board, all at a comparatively youthful thirty-eight.

The problem was that now that I was stepping down, he fancied himself as the CEO going forward, and had been very unsubtly selling himself to me for the last half an hour in what was supposed to be a meeting about the costings of a proposed new luxury development on a lovely strip of greenfield land near Rickmansworth. I admired his chutzpah, badgering me like this when I had barely weeks to live, but it was a waste of time. I could have made it happen. As chairman, and the largest shareholder by some distance with thirty-five per cent of the stock, I had the clout. But as far as I was concerned, Edward had reached his peak within the company, and that was the end of it.

'I know you don't think I've got the killer instinct to take over,' he said in that slightly high-pitched voice of his, finally coming out with what he was here to say – and doing a good job of reading my mind. 'But I can be tough when I need to be. It was me who came up with the plan in 2017 to shave eight million off the bottom line by shutting down Kettering. I let two hundred and forty people go on minimum redundancy payments.'

Which was true. That had been him. But all he'd done was come up with the plan. He hadn't stood in front of each individual to give them the bad news. *That* would have been showing a killer instinct. That's what I would have done, without batting an eyelid. Getting other people to do your dirty work is not the same. It's like when some sycophantic journalist called that arsehole Tony Blair brave for sending British troops into Iraq and I almost coughed up my breakfast. Blair wasn't brave, for Christ's sake! Sitting in your comfy chair sending other men to their deaths is easy. A piece of piss. The brave men are the ones who do the fighting. End of.

I could have told my stepson all of this, but frankly I didn't have the time or the energy. 'Edward,' I said firmly. 'You will get there.' Which was a lie. 'But right now, you're not ready.' Which wasn't.

The boy kept his cool although his cheeks were flushing red like they used to when he was a child. I could tell he was annoyed and doing everything to restrain himself. 'But Keith Clappe as acting CEO? If I can be frank, he's just a corporate yes-man. He's only been with us eight years. He doesn't know the company like I do. I want this chance to prove myself.' He was looking at me with a steady gaze as he spoke, as if he'd been practising it in the mirror. But that's the problem. You shouldn't need to practise. And as

I stared right back at him, not giving anything away, he lowered his eyes in submission, the hyena to my lion. 'I don't want to speak out of turn, of course,' he continued, not quite so confident now, 'but I think you know how much I'm committed to Peregrine.'

'I know you are,' I told him. 'So keep doing what you're doing and your opportunity will arise.' And by then, of course, I'd be long gone and it'd be someone else's problem. It wasn't that I didn't want the boy to succeed. It was just that, when it came down to it, I didn't much care either way.

Luckily, before the conversation could continue any further, there was a knock on the study door and my chief bodyguard, Thomson, poked his large square head round it. 'Sorry to interrupt, Sir Hugh. I've got Mr Burns for you. He's waiting in the sun room.'

Nigel Burns. My former bodyguard and head of security for thirty years until his retirement three years ago. He still did ad hoc work for me, mainly intelligence-gathering. But I was surprised that he was here, especially given that he now lived sixty miles away, and I was certain the reason wasn't going to be good.

I nodded a thank you to Thomson and got to my feet, leaning on my new walking stick, which I hated but which I now couldn't do without. 'We'll talk again on Monday,' I told Edward, and put out a hand.

Edward looked disappointed. That was another of his problems. He wasn't good at hiding his emotions. And he had too many of them to fight his way to the very top in this business the way I had.

We shook and I left the room without a backward glance, asking Thomson to show Edward out.

I own a ten-bedroom Edwardian mansion set in twenty-two acres of grounds in rural Hertfordshire, which I bought for £1.2 million in 1991 after my divorce from my first wife, and which is now worth roughly eight times that, even with the depressed property market. It contains two studies. The one I'd just met Edward in is my main one, for everyday use. The other, the sun room, is a secure soundproofed room with no windows (hence the amusingly ironic name) which I know can't be bugged by anyone, and where I can talk freely.

Only one person knows the code to get inside and that's me, so Burns was in the adjoining waiting room when I arrived.

Of all the people I've ever met, Burns is the most humourless. He makes even Edward seem a wellspring of chuckles. At sixty-six, the bastard is barely two years younger than me but still irritatingly fit-looking, with a strong build and perfect posture, a throwback to his days as an officer in the Parachute Regiment. He's hard, serious, and doesn't get flustered. I'd hired him straight out of the military and we'd seen a lot together, so I trusted him to get things done.

However, the expression on his face – even grimmer than usual – told me something was wrong.

We nodded at each other – two men who didn't need to bother with formalities – and he kept a discreet distance while I punched in the code on the sun-room door and authenticated it with my hand print.

Once inside, I sat down at my desk and took a few seconds to get my breath back while Burns stayed standing opposite me. He had an A4-sized envelope in his hands.

'You've got two problems, Sir Hugh,' he said, without preamble, making it abundantly clear from both his tone and his words that neither of them was his. 'This is the first.'

He handed me the envelope. It was unsealed and contained photographs. I examined them.

'Those were taken last night while he was in London.'

I looked at the photos of my daughter's fiancé and knew that I'd been right to have my suspicions about him. 'Dodgy bastard,' I grunted angrily as I returned them to the envelope. 'Just as I suspected. What's the other problem, Nigel?'

'I've lost contact with the operative watching your daughter. She was meant to call at seven a.m. to give me an update. She didn't and I haven't been able to get hold of her.'

'Have you been down there?'

Burns nodded. 'Yes. The operative's car is there but she's nowhere to be seen. Your daughter's rental car is in the driveway but there's no sign of her either.'

'What about the fiancé?'

'His car's not there. Neither is he.'

I cursed myself for not being more careful. 'You need to find her,' I told Burns. 'And him. Do whatever it takes.'

He shook his head. 'I'm retired, Sir Hugh. I told you that. I'm not getting involved in any strong-arming.'

I eyed him carefully, wondering whether it was worth bringing up all the things I had on him. All the strong-arming he'd done in the past in return for my money. But I immediately decided against it – I've always been good at making snap decisions and following my gut. If he didn't want to help, then threatening him wasn't going to provide the necessary incentive. He'd never been the type to be intimidated, which was what had made him such a valuable enforcer.

'All right,' I said. 'I understand that. But please make sure you're at the end of the phone in case I need your advice.'

I nodded to show that the meeting was over, waiting until he'd left the room before picking up the phone.

It was time to move to plan B.

19

DCI Cameron Doyle

Sir Hugh Roper. What a travesty, making a man like him a knight of the realm.

'How does it feel seeing him in a police interview room like this?' DC Tania Wild asks me.

The two of us are standing at the two-way mirror looking into Interview Suite C. Roper sits alongside his very expensive-looking lawyer, opposite two of my colleagues, DI Marion Webb and DS Sunni Sharma. He's dressed in a thick leather coat that's far too big for him and an open-necked shirt. He looks tired and drawn, but his eyes are still alert. I know that even though we've got him against the ropes, he's nowhere near finished yet. And looking at him now, I'm not sure what I feel. Wariness mixed with a hint of regret that, whatever happens, he won't live to see any trial.

'It's about time,' I say at last. 'The key is making sure he stays here.'

'And yet you didn't want to question him,' says Tania, looking at me out of the corner of her eye with more interest than she usually shows. 'I'm surprised. I thought you'd want to go after the big prize personally.'

'He'll only tell us what he wants us to hear. His lawyer will make sure of that,' I reply, still staring in at him. 'I'd far rather use our time to talk to his daughter and the fiancé. They're the ones who are going to make mistakes.'

'But what if neither of them implicates Roper?'

I've thought about that already, yet I experience a sudden flash of anger at the prospect of him walking free again. 'Even if they don't implicate him, we'll make sure the press get hold of it,' I say, with more emotion in my voice than I'd have liked. 'It'll destroy his reputation. He's always wanted the world to think he's this tough, swashbuckling character with a good heart. The reality is he's nothing more than a sociopathic thug.'

'You really hate him, don't you?' says Tania, and there's a note of surprise in her voice, as if she can't understand why I might be emotionally involved in the case. Because that's the problem. I am, and I know it. I wonder if it's just because I've never been able to catch him. Because he's always been able to best me and I simply can't handle it.

But no. There's more to it than that.

'Let me tell you something about Hugh Roper,' I say to her. 'Back in the early 1970s, when he was first starting out as a developer, he went into partnership with a man named Billy Davey. Billy was quite a lot older, in his forties, and by all accounts he acted as a father figure and mentor to Roper. Or at least that's what Roper wanted him to believe. In reality, Roper used Billy's money to buy up an old warehouse near Smithfield that they planned to turn into luxury flats. The project rapidly turned into a money pit. They borrowed as much as they could from the banks, but when that wasn't enough, Billy decided to pull out. Well, Roper couldn't have that. He knew he'd lose his payday, so he told Billy that he could get finance from family members, which was a lie. Instead, unbeknownst to Billy, he turned to a very unpleasant individual by the name of Vincent Carballion for finance. Carballion was heavily involved in organised crime and definitely not the sort of man you'd want to cross, but Roper clearly thought it was worth the risk.

'Anyway, Carballion lent fifty grand to Roper and Billy's company to help them finish the project. Unfortunately, around the same time, the country tipped into recession, the money ran out again, and when they put the flats on the market, no one was buying, so the whole thing collapsed. The banks repossessed the building, Billy and his wife and kids lost their house, the company went into liquidation, and Roper declared himself bankrupt, so he wasn't liable.

'But the two of them still owed money to Carballion. The best part of thirty thousand, which neither of them could pay. Billy, of course, didn't realise who he was dealing with, until one day he and Roper were grabbed by Carballion's goons and taken to a derelict building in Hackney to meet the man himself and explain why they hadn't paid him back.

'From what I heard, Roper and Billy were made to kneel in front of Carballion with guns pointed at the backs of their heads. Billy was mortified. He couldn't believe this was happening and tried to explain that it was nothing to do with him and all Roper's fault. Now Roper could have manned up and told the truth. He could have taken the rap, but he didn't. He put the blame on Billy. Said that it was all his idea to borrow the money.

'The problem for both of them, though, was that Carballion really didn't care who was to blame. He'd lent the money to their company, so in his eyes they were both equally liable. And now they were in front of him saying they couldn't pay. The story goes that Carballion told them in no uncertain terms that of course they were going to pay, and as a little incentive he was going to punish one of them then and there. So he takes out a ball-peen hammer, the sort you use for banging nails into a wall, and places it on the floor between the two of them. He then takes out a coin and tosses it, covering it with his hand. "We're going to play a little game of heads or tails," he tells them. "Whoever guesses correctly uses the hammer to break every finger on the loser's left hand." He turns to Roper. "You're the one who's going to make the call, but before you do, I'm going to give you a little clue. You've got to decide whether you trust me or not." And with that, Carballion moves his hand away from the coin so only he can see which side it's fallen on. He says to Roper, "If I were you, I'd call heads."'

'Shit,' says Tania, clearly caught up in the story. 'And what did he call?'

'Roper's a cunning bastard,' I say. 'He always has been. He figured that Carballion wanted to punish him more than he did Billy, but he also wanted to give him a chance. He knew the one thing Carballion admired most in a man was balls. And only a man with real balls would disagree with his call.' I pause for a moment. 'So that's what Roper did. He called tails. And he won.'

'And then?'

'Exactly as you'd expect. The story goes that Roper didn't even hesitate. He picked up the hammer and smashed Billy's fingers without a second thought. He then walked out of there and got himself involved with another partner, made some money on his next project, paid back Carballion. Even became friends with him for a while before Carballion got sent down. In fact, Roper went from strength to strength after that.'

'And what happened to Billy?'

'His luck turned the other way. His wife left him, took the kids; he stayed flat broke and in debt; died a few years later of alcohol poisoning.' I shake my head, look at Roper sitting in the interview room with his big-shot lawyer, chatting away, telling his story with an air of supreme confidence. 'You know, Roper didn't even bother going to his funeral. That's why I hate him. The man's got no honour. No loyalty. No redeeming features at all. He's just a piece of shit.'

'You know, I've never heard that story,' Tania says, staring at the two-way mirror.

'That's because he's got a whole army of lawyers to keep everything out of the papers,' I tell her. 'We're not even meant to discuss it amongst ourselves because there's no incontrovertible proof it ever happened and it might prejudice any case against him. Roper's always had the establishment on his side. But tonight might be our chance to change all that.'

'I don't trust his daughter,' she tells me. 'She's hiding something.'

'She's hiding lots of things,' I say. 'But we'll get them out of her.'

Ten minutes later, DS Wild and I are back in the interview room with Kate and her lawyer. The lawyer looks irritated and Kate looks tired and ever so slightly anxious as we take our seats. I restart the interview for the benefit of the tape, apologising for the short delay in proceedings.

'So where were we?' I ask with a smile.

'My client is trying to tell you her story,' says the lawyer in a sharp tone, 'and we'd like just to get on with it.'

'Of course,' I say, 'but before we start, can I ask why you've been telling us you're pregnant when you're clearly not?'

20

Matt

I was on the A4 around Perivale, heading west out of London, trying to put as much distance as possible between myself and the scene of the crime, when the kidnapper's phone vibrated in my pocket again.

I knew I had to take the call, but the timing couldn't have been worse. As I went to pull the phone from my jacket, a police patrol car pulled level with me in the next lane. My first thought was that they had come for me – that someone had seen me flee the scene and called in the rental car's registration number – and I felt an immediate rush of panic. Somehow, though, I managed to keep my hands steady on the wheel. Staring straight ahead, I tried to see out of the corner of my eye what they were doing as we drove in tandem in the slow-moving traffic.

The phone continued to vibrate in my pocket. I knew I was going to have to take the call. I saw a side road up ahead and indicated while slowing down. The police car began to move ahead of me but the traffic was still too slow to put much space between us, and it was only when

I'd turned onto a residential street lined with a parade of shops that I finally grabbed the phone.

I was too late. It had stopped ringing.

Cursing, I took the slip road in front of the shops and managed to park in front of an empty unit at the far end.

I sat there for a full minute trying to regulate my breaths, slowing everything down, just as I'd learned in the yoga classes I attended several times a week at our hotel, pushing out all the panic and guilty thoughts I couldn't afford to have right now. Kate was being held captive. The man holding her had been trying to get hold of me. I needed to talk to him urgently.

I took out the phone. As well as the two missed calls from unknown numbers, there was also a text. When I clicked on the icon, I saw that once again the sender was listed as Matt Walters. It just said: *Answer the phone next time.*

No threat. No anger. Just a simple instruction. It struck me then that if I was arrested, no one would believe my story, for the simple reason that Kate's kidnapper had covered his tracks immaculately. I had no doubt the phone he'd given me was untraceable – as I'm sure were the numbers he'd called from. There were only two texts on the phone and both appeared to come from me. Neither one gave any credence to my story. I might be able to prove that Kate was missing eventually, but not that she'd been kidnapped, let alone by whom. If anything, the fact that I'd killed a man would make me the prime suspect in her disappearance. All it needed now was for the body of the woman to turn up downriver and it was unlikely I'd ever be a free man again.

There was, however, one thing that might bolster my story . . .

I opened up the Tor browser on the kidnapper's phone and found the link he'd sent that had shown Kate on the stage with the noose around her neck. If it was still live . . .

But when I pressed the button, it just said *Site not recognised* on an otherwise blank screen. I tried again with the same result, then, with a sigh, dropped the phone onto the passenger seat, realising in that moment that I couldn't handle this any more. My life, which only a few days ago – maybe even a few hours – had seemed so full of potential, was effectively over.

The rain started up again – a downpour like the one earlier, the raindrops clattering on the windscreen – and I hate to have to admit it, but I put my head in my hands and sat there sobbing my heart out, wishing there was someone – anyone – who could help me.

And then the kidnapper's phone was ringing again, that horrendous car horn noise that signalled that yes, I really was on my own, and no, things weren't over yet.

I wiped my tears away with a gloved hand, aware that there was still blood on the glove from where I'd been searching the pockets of a dying man. A little of it got on my face and I used my jacket to scrub it off before grabbing the phone.

I saw that this was a video call purporting to be from my supposed contact Matt Walters. A prompt asked me if I'd like to accept the call. I didn't like the idea because I knew there'd be a specific reason why he'd want to video-call me and it wasn't going to be good. But I pressed accept, and as I held the phone up to my face, I could see my own image – stressed and exhausted – in the top right-hand corner of the screen.

There was, however, no face staring back. Instead, all I could see was darkness surrounding a moving beam of very bright light. It took me a couple of seconds to realise it was a torch beam, and that the kidnapper was holding the phone the other way round so that I could see what he was seeing.

And what I was seeing was making my skin crawl. As I watched, the unseen kidnapper stepped inside a room and his torch illuminated the top half of Kate. She was sitting propped up against a toilet seat, the blindfold still over her eyes, her hands behind her back. She was now wearing a coat over her pyjamas and there was a blanket bunched up over her tummy.

I felt an intense yearning for her. If I could just get her back, everything else would be easier to face.

She squinted as she became aware of the light and turned away from it. I heard a chain rattle as she tried to move. 'Hello?' she called out, her voice remarkably calm. 'What's going on?'

And then something else appeared on the screen. A gloved hand holding a razor-sharp scalpel.

'Don't do anything,' I said desperately into the phone, my face amplifying the fear I felt. 'I'm here now. I've done what you asked. Leave her alone.'

But there was no answer, nor any response from Kate

to the sound of my voice. She was only a few feet from the phone now as the kidnapper crouched in front of her, holding the scalpel up to the screen. The bastard had muted me, and I had no choice but to stare as the scalpel moved ever so slowly towards Kate's face so that the tip of the blade was almost touching it.

'What's going on?' she said, fear in her voice now, even though she couldn't see the blade. 'What are you doing? Talk to me.'

The kidnapper angled the phone lower as he moved the scalpel slowly down Kate's body, the blade almost touching her silk pyjamas, moving inexorably towards her belly – and our unborn child.

The blade only millimetres away now.

My mouth was open. Nothing came out. I could no longer speak.

And then the footage cut out and the phone went dead.

21

Matt

The next five minutes were the longest of my life. With no way of contacting the kidnapper, I had to sit impotently in the car, wondering what he was doing to Kate. I couldn't believe that he'd physically hurt her, or our child. Why would he? That was what I kept telling myself anyway. But it made no difference. The fear was still there. It was like I was in a boxing ring, disorientated and alone, being dealt heavy blow after heavy blow from every direction.

When the phone rang again, I almost didn't pick up because I wasn't sure how much more of this I could take.

But I was simply going to have to be strong, and when I saw it wasn't a video call, I almost cried out with relief.

'Is Kate all right?' I said, before he could speak. 'If you've hurt her . . .'

There was silence on the other end of the line. I waited.

'Why didn't you answer my calls?' asked the heavily disguised voice.

'Is she okay? Tell me. Please.'

'What I showed you was a warning. That's what will happen if you disobey instructions.'

I felt relief, but it was tempered by the knowledge that Kate must be going through hell.

'I did what you instructed,' I told him, 'but I couldn't take your earlier calls because I was in the process of getting away from the house you sent me to.'

'Where are you now?'

I wasn't going to give him my exact location in case he decided to double-cross me and tip off the police. 'I'm not sure. Somewhere around Ealing.'

'Is the target dead?'

'Yes,' I said, closing my eyes, trying to block out the memories of his final moments. 'He's dead.'

'How did you kill him?'

It struck me that he could have been watching on a hidden camera. Was he testing me? 'The knife,' I told him, almost spitting out the words.

'And what about the master copy? Have you got that?'

I had to be careful. 'He said there wasn't one. I searched his body and didn't find anything.'

Silence. Then: 'The problem is, Matt, I *know* there's a master copy. So that means you've failed. Which means you're no longer any use to me.'

'I killed him, just like you instructed. Now for Christ's sake let Kate go!'

'I think we're finished here.'

He was washing his hands of me. Now that I had nothing

to bargain with, he was just going to leave me high and dry. I had to act.

'I know where it is. The master copy.'

There was a short pause on the other end of the line, but at least he was still there. 'So you were lying to me?'

I ignored the question. 'A woman came to the house and interrupted me while I was searching the man's body. She must have let herself in; she obviously knows him well. I chased her. There was a struggle and I saw she had a flash drive around her neck. It was black.'

'And did you take it?'

'No. She got away.'

'That was very foolish of you.'

'What the hell do you expect? I'd just killed a man. I'm not cut out for this. If you wanted him dead, I don't understand why you didn't just do it yourself. It would have been a lot easier.' Because that was the thing I couldn't understand. Why send a rank amateur like me to do a job that he was clearly better equipped for? It didn't make sense. Jesus, none of this did. 'The thing is,' I continued, 'I can find her.'

'How do you propose to do that exactly?'

'I have the man's phone. I can use that. I'll get her and then I'll get the drive. And this time there'll be no problems.'

The kidnapper was silent again. I had no idea how I was going to manage this task, but that really didn't matter. I needed to buy time. This was the only way.

'You've got until nine p.m.,' he said, and ended the call.

22

Kate

Okay, I'll admit it. I'm not pregnant.

I *was* pregnant, though, until very recently. And the truth is, Matt still thought I was. So when the kidnapper had come into the bathroom a few minutes earlier, shining a light in my face and refusing to speak, running something sharp down my body, all the way down to my tummy, I knew he was doing it for Matt's benefit.

I'd been absolutely terrified. It was the kidnapper's silence that got me the most. The fact that I couldn't reason with him. And I had no idea what he was going to do, and whether he planned to hurt me with the blade.

I didn't know why he had to involve Matt in this. It wasn't anything to do with him.

I love Matt. Deeply. I'd been single for the best part of fifteen years, and had pretty much given up hope of ever being in a relationship, when *bang*, one day he'd come waltzing into my life, gorgeous and smiling, like something out of a movie. It had been the classic whirlwind romance. He had it all. The looks, the teeth, the charm, the laugh. Maybe not the height. He was short – five foot eight (although he always claimed it was nine) – but at least he was all in proportion, and I wasn't going to quibble. The thing was, he was so damn likeable. You couldn't help but warm to him. He just had that authentic 'nice guy' vibe, which so many men try to put on but never quite muster. He also had just the right level of melancholy behind his eyes to suggest he'd lived a proper life, and that there was depth to his charm. Add to that the fact that he was only a year younger than me, and we really were the perfect match.

And it had all turned out so well. I got him to move in with me at the hotel. We became a team. I fell in love. So much so that after a year together I was the one who actually proposed to him.

Yes, before you say anything, I know that's not how it's meant to happen. But I've never been one to go down the conventional route. I did it one night when we were sitting alone beside the pool under a tropical star-filled night sky. Not on one knee. I just leaned over, kissed him softly on the lips and popped the question.

I caught him off guard, but then his face broke into one of his wide, infectious grins and he replied that yes, of course he'd marry me, and that was that. We were engaged. The future beckoned. We talked about kids. We both wanted them. Me especially. After the upbringing I'd had, I knew I could do a much better job than my mum had with me, and so we started trying straight away, because at thirty-seven, time was not necessarily on my side.

And then three months later, we got the news we'd been

longing for. I was pregnant. We were ecstatic. We were going to be a proper family.

It was my idea to come back to the UK for a few months. The April bombings in Colombo and Batticaloa had decimated our bookings that year, and even by November they were still extremely sparse, so neither of us was needed at the hotel. Even so, Matt hadn't been keen to come home. He loved Sri Lanka and had few ties to the UK – and no desire to be here just as we were heading into winter. But I'd persuaded him on the basis that healthcare for the baby would be better here, and after she was born, we could return to Sri Lanka as a family. There were other things happening in my life too. Things I wanted to share with Matt when the time was right.

A week before we were due to leave for England, when I was no more than seven weeks gone, I noticed some bleeding one morning. I knew instinctively that I'd lost the baby. I was so shocked I didn't say anything to Matt. I didn't say anything to anyone. I just carried on as normal, wondering how I was going to tell him, because I was terrified he might think I was infertile and leave me. I know it sounds totally irrational, but I wasn't thinking straight. I'm still not. And now I realise that I may never be able to tell him.

Poor Matt. He knew so little about me really. I'd kept my past from him as much as possible. I didn't want anyone to know the things I'd been through, least of all him.

He had no idea that my father was Sir Hugh Roper, the multimillionaire property developer, a man whose existence had haunted me for more than twenty years, ever since Mum had finally told me who he was.

Dad and I had met barely a handful of times over the years – our relationship could hardly be described as close – and yet it was because of him that I was in a makeshift cell, I knew that.

It was possible, of course, that this was a straightforward transactional kidnapping, with my father expected to pay the ransom. But I didn't buy that. The kidnapper had told me we were going to talk about my past, and I was certain that was what this whole thing was about. Unfinished business. Revenge.

Because, you see, there'd already been one attempt on my life. Sixteen years ago now. And it had come very close to being successful. My memory of what happened that fateful day is still a blank. I was in a coma for three weeks afterwards, and I still have recurring headaches even now, as well as a six-inch scar on my head where they'd had to operate to stop a bleed on the brain. But these injuries were nothing in comparison to the emotional loss I'd suffered, because another man I'd truly loved had died that day. And I knew exactly why we'd been targets then, and why I was the target now.

In the end, this was all about Alana. My half-sister.

The girl who some believed I'd murdered.

23

Matt

It had just turned 1 p.m. and was raining hard when I finally pulled into the driveway of our rental cottage. There were no lights on inside and it looked drab and uninviting in the gloom of the day, although right now it was about the only place I felt vaguely safe.

I exited the car fast and let myself into the house, shutting the door behind me and leaning back against it for a few moments. I was calmer now. In the two and a half hours since the death of the man called Piers the shock of what I'd become a part of had dissipated, to be replaced by the realisation that I had no choice but to deal with my new reality. That in order to get my fiancée back and come out of this ordeal as a free man, I was going to have to start thinking like a criminal. Because I only had eight hours left.

First things first. I needed to get rid of the bloodstained clothes, so I stripped naked on the doormat, shivering against the cold before taking a bin bag from the kitchen cupboard and shoving everything inside, including my expensive new trainers. There was a lot more blood than

I'd been expecting. As well as having large stains on the knees of my jeans, my trainers were splattered, and there were flecks all over me as if someone had been flicking red paint with one of those thin watercolour brushes.

I tied the handles and shoved the bag to one side, then went and took a long, hot shower, trying to scrub every trace of the last twelve hours off me. After I was done, and finally feeling slightly better, I switched on the heating and went downstairs in fresh clothes. I made myself a sandwich using some chicken in the fridge from a couple of days earlier. It was the first food to touch my lips in eighteen hours, and I ended up demolishing it in a few greedy bites.

I found an apple and a banana and wolfed them down too, then made myself a strong cup of coffee. While I drank it, I picked up the phone I'd taken from the man I'd killed. It was an oldish looking iPhone with a scratched screen. I pressed the home button and was immediately asked for a password. One way or another, I was going to have to unlock this phone, because it might lead me to the woman who'd seen me at the house. I looked at the clock on the kitchen wall and saw that I now had only seven and a half hours left. Time was ticking relentlessly away.

I knew there were shops where if you paid the proprietors enough money, they'd unlock a phone for you. Oxford was only twenty minutes up the road. I'd start there.

It was dangerous being caught with this phone – given that it was evidence that linked me inextricably to the murder scene – but I couldn't lose sight of it either, so I shoved it down the back of my jeans waistband out of sight, and put my own phone in my right pocket. With the kidnapper's phone in my left pocket, I now had three phones altogether, which was suspicious enough in itself, but at least I had a plan of sorts, and if I kept moving, it would mean I didn't have to dwell too much on the horrendous situation I was in.

I picked up the bag containing the bloodied clothes, which I intended to shove in a communal bin somewhere en route, and stepped into the rain.

Which was the exact moment I felt an intense electric shock like nothing I've ever experienced before somewhere in my side, followed immediately by a pain that seemed to rack me from head to foot. At the same time, my legs literally went from under me and I fell sideways against the cottage's outside wall, only dimly aware of figures closing in and grabbing me roughly by the arms.

Disorientated and unable to see properly, I felt myself being dragged roughly back into the cottage and heard the front door shutting. Still limp and helpless, I was tipped over onto my front, my face shoved into the carpet.

As I lay there, someone secured my hands behind my back, and then I was picked up again and manhandled over to one of the dining-room chairs and dropped into it. Everything was happening so fast, and I was in so much pain, that I had no idea what was going on.

And then it dawned on me: I'd been tasered by the police, who were arresting me for the killing this morning, and I felt a weirdly unexpected sense of relief that all the pressure to find Kate was finally being taken away from me. That other, better-equipped people were going to take over.

But then one of the figures suddenly marched forward, pushing a large gun directly between my eyes, and the relief evaporated immediately as he said: 'Where is she, you bastard? Tell me or you die!'

24

Matt

I'd never seen a real gun before. I'd seen plenty of fake ones during my acting career – and had even carried one during an episode of *Night Beat* where we'd raided the home of an armed suspect. It had looked cool in my hand. I'd liked the weight of it. The feeling of power it gave me. Unfortunately, it gives you absolutely no preparation for when you face a real one and can feel the cold hardness of the barrel being pushed against your skull. Knowing that one tiny pull of the trigger will end your life. Just like that.

The figure stepped back, still pointing the gun at me, and my vision cleared. The pain that had been surging through my body from the taser disappeared as my mind focused entirely on the situation I was in.

There were two of them, both men, although only one of them was armed. They were dressed in dark clothing, their faces covered by balaclavas. Straight away I knew they weren't police, and that made it a lot worse. As did the fact that the bin bag I'd been carrying – the one containing my bloodied clothes – was now sitting only a few feet away from them.

Instinctively I glanced towards it but forced myself to look away. Under no circumstances did I want them looking in that. But for an actor, I wasn't doing a good job of keeping a poker face, because to my horror, the man with the gun looked at the bag too. 'So what's in here then?' he said.

'Just some bits and pieces,' I answered, with a confidence I really didn't feel.

He clearly didn't believe me, because he tugged open the drawstrings and bent down to rummage inside, his hand emerging with one of my bloodied trainers. Even with blurred vision, I could see the blood splattered all over it.

'Well, well, well,' said the man inspecting the shoe, while the other one looked on impassively. 'This doesn't look good, does it?'

'It's not what you think,' I said, trying to calculate how much information to give them. 'Who are you? And what do you want?'

'Who we are is irrelevant, and I've already told you what we want,' he said, coming back over with the gun. 'We want to know where she is.'

'Who?'

'Your fiancée, Mr Walters. Kate. What have you done to her?'

Now I was completely confused. 'If you tell me who you are,' I said, 'I may be able to help.'

The blow caught me completely off guard and I felt a

searing pain through my nose as I toppled backwards with the chair.

My assailant grabbed hold of my shoulder to stop me going over entirely and brought his face close to mine. 'That was a warning not to fuck me about. Now where's your fiancée?'

I had no idea whether this was a trick question or not, so I gave him the truth. 'I don't know, I swear it.'

He hit me again. A hard slap round the face that rattled my teeth and sent the blood pouring from my nose onto the carpet. 'Don't lie to me or I'm going to keep hurting you. Do you understand?'

I nodded, feeling dizzy, confused and scared. I swore to myself that if I got out of here in one piece, I'd never set foot in this godforsaken house again. Or this country. 'I understand,' I said quietly.

'Good. That'll be better for all of us.' He sounded calmer now, more reasonable. 'Admit it,' he continued. 'You've killed her, haven't you?'

'God no,' I answered quickly, shaking my head even though the act of doing so hurt. 'I'd never harm Kate. I love her.' I tried to look over the man's shoulder towards the other one, hoping he might intervene. But instead he just stared back.

'I think you're lying to me,' said the gunman, an edge coming back into his voice.

I knew I was going to have to tell the truth. I didn't want to be hit again. 'She's been kidnapped. It happened last night.'

'And that's why you're trying to get rid of your bloodied

clothes, is it? Bullshit. You think I'm fucking about here, do you? You think I won't really hurt you?' Once again he shoved the gun barrel between my eyes, pushing hard until it seemed to cover my whole field of vision. I heard him cock the pistol and I swallowed hard.

'I'm telling you the truth,' I said, forcing myself to keep calm, knowing I was talking for my life now. 'She was taken from here last night while I was with friends in London. Her kidnapper gave me a phone and a link to the dark web to show where she was being held. But I think the link might be down now. The phone's in my left pocket.'

I realised how lame this all sounded, but you say and do pretty much anything if your life depends on it.

The gun stayed where it was for what felt like an interminably long time but which was probably no more than three seconds. Then the man stepped forward and fumbled in my pocket until he found the phone.

'If you're lying to me, you'll pay,' he said, glaring at me from behind the balaclava.

'I'm not,' I said, hoping I sounded desperate enough for one of them to believe me. 'The kidnapper's called me from an unknown number at least three times, and texted twice too. You can see it all on there. Along with the link to the Tor app.'

The second man took the phone and silently scrolled through it. I sat there waiting, my wrists cuffed tightly behind my back, the blood continuing to drip slowly out of my nose, wishing I hadn't just given away my only means of communicating with the kidnapper.

'The link's blank and the texts look like they're from you,' said the second man, speaking for the first time. He had a very deep voice and a local accent. 'You're not helping yourself here. Why don't you just admit what you've done?'

'Because I keep telling you, I haven't done anything.'

'Then whose blood is that all over your clothes?'

I hesitated. I didn't want to tell the truth, but I had to give them something. 'It's not Kate's. I swear it.'

The gunman released a frustrated sigh. 'This is going nowhere. We need answers. Now.' He reached into his jacket pocket and pulled something out.

At first I wasn't sure what it was, but when he started screwing it onto the end of the pistol, I realised with a jolt of fear that it was a silencer.

'I'm going to shoot you in the kneecap if you don't tell me the truth right now, and I'll keep shooting you in various joints until we get the answers we want.'

'I killed someone,' I told him quickly. 'The man who kidnapped Kate said I had to do it otherwise I'd never see her alive again. I have no idea who he was. I wasn't going to kill him, but there was a struggle and I stabbed him by accident.'

'So if that's the case, why isn't Kate back with you now?' said the gunman.

'Because the kidnapper told me I had to get a flash drive from the man before I killed him. I didn't manage to.' Even as I spoke the words, I realised how far-fetched my story sounded.

The gunman clearly felt the same way, because he stormed

over, clamping his shoe down on my right foot to hold it in place while he pointed the gun straight at my right knee. 'Don't give me that bullshit story. I know you killed her. I'm going to count to five and if you haven't told me the truth by then, it's goodbye to ever walking properly again.' He pushed the silencer into the flesh above the kneecap. 'One . . .'

'Please don't do this,' I pleaded. 'I'm not lying.'

'Two . . .'

I turned to the other man, tears filling my eyes, more scared than I've ever been in my life. 'Please help me. I'm not lying.'

He didn't move.

'Three . . .'

'I don't know what else I can say to convince you, but I'm telling the truth. Don't do this!' The words were tumbling out of my mouth now as my desperation reached new heights.

'You've got one fucking chance,' the gunman hissed, his mouth so close to me I could feel the hotness of his breath. 'Use it. Four . . .'

What could I say? My mouth opened again, but this time nothing came out. I looked down at the gun, then into the man's eyes. Saw the ruthless determination in them.

Saw his mouth begin to form the word 'five'.

'Oh shit.' It was the other man speaking. I could see him looking towards the window over the gunman's shoulder.

The gunman stepped back and turned. 'What is it?'

And then suddenly there was a distinct crackling sound

and the gunman was staggering blindly as his colleague tasered him, his gun hand jerking wildly, his finger squeezing the trigger as the barrel swung round in my direction.

I dived sideways off the chair, landing on the carpet with my teeth clenched in anticipation of the bullet.

But no shot rang out, and I saw him fall to his knees, dropping the gun. The other man fired the taser a second time, and this time the gunman keeled over, shivering frantically, his eyes wide behind the balaclava.

'Come on,' said my rescuer, crouching down beside me and using a knife to cut the ties binding my wrists before grabbing hold of my collar and pulling me to my feet. 'He won't be out for long. Have you got your car keys?'

I nodded frantically, up in an instant and half stumbling, half running as he guided me past his colleague and out the front door.

I pulled out my keys and almost felt like laughing out loud as we ran over to the car, the cold wet air hitting my face like a slap.

The guy jumped in the back rather than the front, which would have unnerved me if I'd had time to think about it. But right then I didn't, and as I switched on the engine and flung the car into reverse, I just had time to see the front door of the cottage fly open and the gunman appear, staggering slightly, in the doorway, and then we were out of there and heading God knows where.

25

Kate

When Mum told me the story of how she'd met my father, it did two things. It made me terribly sad for her. And it made me furious with him.

My biological father, Sir Hugh Roper, was married with very young children when Mum started working for the family as a cleaner and domestic help. According to her, the wife was rude, snobbish and generally unpleasant, while my father was a hard-nosed businessman involved in enough questionable activities to need bodyguards. But the pay was good for an eighteen-year-old, so Mum tried to keep her head down and get on with things.

In the end, it was the age-old tale. My father – successful, charismatic and ten years older – had started paying Mum attention. They embarked on a short, sporadic (and it seemed not very romantic) affair that came to an abrupt end when Mrs Roper told her she knew exactly what had been going on and fired her on the spot. Mum was given an hour to pack her things and get out.

But as you know, that wasn't the end of the story. A

month later, Mum realised she was pregnant. She'd hadn't slept with anyone else in the previous six months, which meant there could only be one candidate. She knew better than to contact Mrs Roper, but she was determined that my father should know what had happened and do something to help, so she'd waited for him outside his London office and, after several fruitless attempts, finally confronted him with the news. At first he hadn't believed her, and had even accused her of extortion, but for once in her life Mum stood her ground, and eventually my father agreed to pay her a monthly income to help bring me up – in return for her signing a non-disclosure agreement that also forbade us from having any future contact with him.

But I was never going to leave it at that. When Mum died a few weeks after telling me the story, leaving me all alone in the world, I knew I was going to try to build some kind of relationship with the man who'd rejected me all these years.

And so I came up with a plan.

My father had two other children. A son, Tom, four years older than me, and a daughter called Alana, eighteen months older.

Alana, oh Alana. I can still picture her now. Short and petite, with a round little face beneath a spiky cloak of dyed black hair. Like a goth fairy, with twinkling green eyes that promised adventure, and a deep bass laugh that shocked everyone when they first heard it because it emanated from such a pale, small thing.

God, she had such charisma. Even now, all these years later, I still missed her.

When I'd first found out I had a half-sister growing up barely fifteen miles from me in vastly different circumstances, I'd felt a mix of excitement and anger. I'd never enjoyed being an only child, and was perpetually jealous of children from big, loving families. I would have loved a sister to confide in growing up – a role Mum had never adequately fulfilled – and to realise I'd always had one but had never been told felt like a terrible injustice.

I began researching everything I could about her. It wasn't hard. In 1999, the Internet, though not the all-encompassing Big Brother it is today, was still far enough advanced that you could mine it for information if you were prepared to look hard enough.

It turned out Alana hadn't had it easy either. Her parents had divorced acrimoniously in 1990, when she was only nine years old. There'd been a court case and accusations about our father's adultery (which came as no surprise to me), and Alana and Tom had remained with their mother in the family house. At the age of eleven, Alana had been sent away to a girls' boarding school, from where she'd been expelled four years later, but had still managed to get into Bristol University, where she was studying politics.

I remember finding a photo of her online for the first time. It wasn't a particularly good shot – a reproduction from a local newspaper showing her and a friend who, at the time, were raising money for a school in Malawi. The friend looked dumpy and dour, but you could see the magnetism coming out of Alana as she gave the camera a sly, knowing smile. Even then, she was effortlessly cool and wise beyond her years.

I'd stared at that photo for a long time, trying to find resemblances between her and me but unable to see any obvious ones. No one would ever guess we were sisters. There was a gulf between us, not only of breeding, but of something else I couldn't put my finger on. A vague feeling that while I was somehow empty, she was somehow full.

The photo made me jealous. Everything about her made me jealous, I'm sad to admit now. But at the same time, I decided that I was going to meet her and she was going to be my friend. She would be my introduction to my father and a new life beyond.

I'd just turned eighteen, and Alana was beginning her second year at university, when I moved to Bristol. By that time, thanks to some prudence on my part, as well as my father's 'generosity', I had close to five thousand pounds in the bank, so had no problem finding a decent place to live. It all felt like a big adventure, the first I'd ever had. A new life where I could reinvent myself as whoever I wanted to be.

It took a couple of months before I first saw Alana in the flesh. It was at a bar called Basement 45, where they often had live bands, and the place was busy. I recognised her instantly. Her hair, spiky and wild, bordered her white face with its bright green eyes, and she wore the kind of short black cocktail dress that would have been perfect in Paris in the fifties yet still managed to look just right in a sweaty student club. There was something unique about her that stood out a mile, and for a moment, I couldn't speak.

Here I was looking across the room at my half-sister, barely ten feet away, and she didn't even know of my existence.

Well, that was going to change, I thought, as I watched her join a large group, holding a drink precariously in one tiny hand, the sound of her raucous laugh reaching me across the room. From the energy she was exuding and the way she wasn't quite steady on her feet, I thought she was drunk or stoned, and I noticed she spent quite a bit of time clinging on to a good-looking guy with long dark hair, who appeared to be a couple of years older. I asked the girl I was with if she knew Alana, but she just shook her head, and I remember her saying that she looked like trouble.

I won't bore you with all the details about how we became friends, but I worked out pretty fast that Basement 45 was Alana's hangout of choice, and so the logical way forward was to get a job working the bar there, which I duly did.

Yes, of course I'm conscious that it might look like I was stalking her, but what else was I meant to do? I couldn't walk up to her and tell her that I was her long-lost sister, not without coming across like some kind of nutjob. The whole thing had to be done slowly and methodically, so that when I finally broke the news, it would have the desired effect.

And we did become friends. Great friends. Though we might not have been that good for each other: she got me into drugs. Not just dope, which I'd had a few times before, but other stuff too. Coke, ketamine, Ecstasy, but especially coke. I taught her how to be harder, how to get rid of hangers-on. And how not to be so . . . vulnerable.

It could have been so different. It could have been wonderful.

But it wasn't. And that was why all these years later I was trapped in a dark, cold place, with no idea what was to become of me.

And that was also why I couldn't just sit here waiting. I had to try something. My options were limited, but I did have some. I was certain the kidnappers were no longer in the vicinity. I hadn't heard anything from them for several hours now, which meant I wasn't being closely guarded. My first priority was to get out of the plastic restraints round my wrists. They were the cheap, easy-to-get-hold-of kind, and the material was probably no more than half a centimetre thick. I'd tried brute force – leaning forward, then yanking my arms up in the air behind me – hoping to break the plastic. But that hadn't worked, so I'd moved on to using the limited freedom the chain afforded me to explore the room, searching for a sharp surface to rub the cuffs against, hoping to create enough friction to wear away the material.

I struck lucky. The bath still had an intact Perspex shower screen above it, and so for an hour or two – it was impossible to tell how long – I sat on the edge of the tub running my wrists up and down its edge until it felt like every nerve ending from my shoulders down to my hands was on fire. But when I ran my fingertips along the edge of the cuffs, I could feel the plastic thinning.

Occasionally I tried to use brute force again, before having a couple of minutes' rest. The fact that I was actually doing something was finally giving me some hope. I can be very determined when necessary and there was no way I was giving up without a fight. I ignored the pain. I ignored my raging thirst. I ignored the fact that I couldn't see; that my wrists were so sore they were probably bleeding. I just kept going because I was on my own. Like I'd been for most of my adult life.

The plastic began to fray as the edge of the screen cut into it. It was close to breaking and I felt a sudden surge of elation.

And then I heard it. The sound of a door shutting downstairs.

Someone was back, and as I stood there, very still, I could hear footsteps coming my way.

Fast.

26

Matt

'Who the hell are you?' I demanded, breaking the silence in the car.

I'd been driving for about ten minutes, following the barked instructions from the man in the balaclava in the back seat. To be honest, I was still pretty shell-shocked, but somehow I managed to keep my hands steady on the wheel, conscious that we were on the main road to Oxford.

'Well, right now it seems like I'm the only person who believes your story,' he replied evenly. 'No one lies when they're about to get kneecapped. Especially if they're a civilian like you. You might be an actor, but you're not that good.'

'How do you know I used to be an actor?' I asked.

'I remember you from *Night Beat*,' he said, and I thought I detected a hint of humour in his voice.

It's incredible. Even at that moment, after all that had happened, I was still flattered. 'Really?'

'Yes. I thought they wasted your character. And I did wonder what had happened to your career after it ended.

I guess I know now. You landed on your feet, Matt, didn't you?'

I didn't like the way he said that. 'I don't feel like I've landed on my feet right now.'

'No, I bet you don't,' he said, pulling off his balaclava to reveal the face of a black man in his thirties, with a strong jaw and a confidence in his eyes that told you he wasn't the sort of person to be messed with. 'All right, pull over,' he ordered.

We were travelling along a rural stretch of road, and there was an empty bus stop up ahead, so I did what I was told, wondering what on earth was coming now.

He told me to turn off the engine, then reached forward and removed the keys from the ignition before pulling out a walkie-talkie-style contraption from his jacket. It made a low humming sound as he moved it round the interior of the car. He then stepped outside and crouched down on the passenger side so he was out of sight of anyone driving past.

It took me a few moments to realise what he was doing, and when he stood up a few moments later and threw something into the bushes, my suspicions were confirmed.

'That was a tracking device, wasn't it?' I said as he got back in the car.

He shot me a knowing half-smile. 'Well done, Sherlock.' He threw the keys back and told me to drive. 'And put your foot down. They might be following already and we need to put some distance between us.'

'Who's "they"?' I asked, pulling out into the road and accelerating away. I figured that right now it was best to do what I was told, and to find out all I could from the man sitting behind me.

'My colleagues,' he said. 'Including the one who just threatened to kill you.'

I was totally confused. 'If you people aren't anything to do with Kate's kidnapping, then please can you just tell me who you actually are?'

The man regarded me with what I'd describe as professional interest. 'How much do you actually know about your fiancée?'

'I thought I knew a fair amount,' I said wearily. 'But obviously I know less than I thought.'

'I'm assuming an intelligent man like you is aware of who her father is, though?'

'Only that he's some businessman Kate hasn't had much to do with over the years. I know she was brought up by her mum, who died some time ago. She was talking about the possibility of me meeting her father while we were in the UK, but there was nothing in the diary.'

'He's not just some businessman, Matt. His name's Sir Hugh Roper and his net worth is around two hundred and fifty million pounds. He's a very powerful man and definitely not one you want to cross.'

That caught my attention. Jesus. Two hundred and fifty million pounds. The number was so big it didn't even sound real. And I was sure it couldn't be right either. I knew Kate had some money. She effectively owned the hotel in Sri Lanka, even though there was a nominal Sri Lankan co-owner, and it had to be worth a few hundred grand at the least. Even when the place wasn't doing well, there always seemed to be cash in reserve. But this was something else entirely, and for the first time since this nightmare had begun, I felt real fury. It seemed like I was being manipulated by everybody. Even my own fiancée.

'I didn't know he was worth that kind of money,' I said bitterly. 'She never said anything about it. And I suppose you work for him, do you? The dad?'

'Well I did. I don't think I've got a job now.'

'Why did you rescue me?'

'Because I'm not prepared to see someone get shot. I'm employed to provide security for Kate's father. The job sometimes requires some strong-arming of people, but not that. My colleague, on the other hand, is less discerning. I believe he would have shot you. We were instructed to find your fiancée and to take whatever steps were necessary. The bonus for finding her is a hundred thousand pounds in cash. And that's just for me. My colleague is head of security for Kate's father, so he's going to be on course for a lot more. People will do some extreme things for that amount of money, especially if they're that way inclined, as my colleague is.'

'How did you people even know Kate was missing?' I asked him.

'Because a firm of private detectives have been watching the two of you from the moment you came back into the country. Apparently the one on duty last night was meant to check in by phone just before the end of her shift. When she didn't, the alarm was raised.'

Something struck me then. 'Jesus, was she a brunette in her thirties with glasses?'

'I never met her, but I do know she was a female freelance private detective. Why? Do you know what happened to her?'

It was a huge risk telling this stranger anything, especially if it incriminated me. But for some reason, I trusted him, and right now he was the only person in the world I could talk to. So I told him how I'd come back after an evening in London and discovered a woman's body in our bed, and then how the whole nightmare had panned out. 'I know how it all sounds,' I added, 'but you've got to believe me. I had nothing to do with Kate's disappearance. She's my fiancée. She's pregnant with our child.'

'I do believe you, Matt. As I said, no one's that brave when they're about to get kneecapped. But you're also a killer, and it doesn't matter whether it was self-defence or not, because that presents me with a very real problem.'

I looked at him in the rear-view mirror. 'Why?'

He stared right back at me. 'Because,' he said, 'I'm a police officer.'

27

Matt

I didn't say anything, because really, what was there to say to that?

'I've been working undercover for the last eight months,' continued the man in the back. 'And you've just blown the whole thing.'

'I'm sorry about that,' I said, looking at him in the rear-view mirror, 'but since I don't know what the hell's going on, forgive me for not feeling too guilty. And anyway,' I added, sceptical now, 'I thought you said her dad was some rich businessman. And a "sir" too. So what on earth are you investigating him for?'

'He might have got a "sir" before his name, but Hugh Roper is a real lowlife. And I think your prospective wife knows more about his crimes than she's letting on.'

'What's that supposed to mean?'

'Just keep driving, Matt. You'll find out everything in due course.'

I didn't like the sound of that. 'Where am I driving to, exactly?'

He shot me a confident smile. 'Where do you think? You've killed one person, and unlawfully disposed of the body of another. I've got no choice. I'm going to have to take you in.'

I froze, then stared back at him, desperate. 'If you take me in, my pregnant fiancée dies. It's that simple.'

'If I don't take you in, I won't just lose my job, I'll end up charged with assisting an offender. I'll do prison time. And even if I did decide to go rogue and help you, there's absolutely no guarantee we're going to get your fiancée back. We're going to have a lot better chance of finding her with police resources. I mean, how were you planning on tracking her down?'

I debated telling him that I had the phone of the man I'd killed and was going to use that to find the flash drive Kate's kidnapper wanted so badly, but stopped myself. He might have had a point about the police being in a better position than me to locate her, but I had my doubts about their abilities. Anyone who's watched documentaries showing how they really solve cases knows that it's nothing like *CSI*. The police work steadily and methodically. They go for the obvious leads, and Kate's kidnapper wasn't leaving any. The police weren't going to catch him quickly – and certainly not before the 9 p.m. deadline.

Something else stopped me too. If I went with this guy now, I'd be going straight to a prison cell and there was a good chance I wouldn't be getting out of it any time soon. And if Kate was killed, or worse still, simply made to disappear forever, then no one was ever going to believe my story. I'd probably end up charged with her murder, spending the rest of my life in prison.

'I don't know how I was planning on finding her,' I told him. 'I was just hoping I might be able to convince the kidnapper to spare her life. So far, I've done what I said I'd do for him.'

'So how come he hasn't released her then?' For the first time, I noticed a hint of scepticism in his tone.

'I'm waiting for his call.'

'On this phone?' He took it out of his pocket and examined it. 'Don't worry. We'll be able to trace his location when he calls. We can do it in real time.'

I knew that this sort of thing was possible, but I doubted the kidnapper would make such an elementary mistake. 'Are you sure there's no way he could disguise his location? This guy's no fool.'

'It's possible, but very few criminals have got that sort of expertise. Look, we can help you, Matt. There's a service station up ahead. I want you to pull in there and we're going to wait for my colleagues, okay? And don't try anything. It won't help. It's going to be a lot better for you just to cooperate with us. We'll get your fiancée back.' He was speaking more calmly now, like I'd expect a police officer to do. As he did so, he took another phone from his pocket, pressed a button and put it to his ear.

The service station appeared up ahead, a riot of bright yellow and green against the dull backdrop of the day.

'It's Astra. My cover's been blown,' he said into the phone, gesturing me to make the turn into the service station. 'I've got a potential murder suspect with me and I need to file an urgent missing persons report.'

A potential murder suspect. That was how he saw me. I glanced in the rear-view mirror. He still had the kidnapper's phone in his left hand as he gave our location to the person on the other end of the call. He was watching me carefully as he spoke, the expression in his eyes telling me not to try anything stupid. He was a big guy and his look told me in no uncertain terms that he'd come down on me hard if I did.

I indicated and slowed down. There was a car just ahead of me also making the turn, and I followed it onto the slip road.

I'm not the kind of man who makes snap decisions. I've always preferred to take my time. Look at the pros and cons. But sometimes life doesn't work like that.

An idea hit me then, and before I'd worked out whether or not it was a good one, I acted, slamming my foot down hard on the accelerator. The car in front – a mud-caked Land Rover – was doing no more than twenty miles an hour as it decelerated onto the station forecourt, and I rammed into the back of it with a loud smash and enough force to send me lurching forward in my seat, but not enough – thank God – to set off the airbags.

The man in the back jolted forward too. He wasn't wearing a seat belt so he almost went straight through the gap between the front seats, and it was only his bulk that stopped him. In one of those strokes of luck I'd been sorely missing so far, the kidnapper's phone flew out of his hand, bounced off the dashboard and landed in the passenger-side footwell.

I was already reacting as the car stopped, simultaneously releasing my seat belt and pulling the keys from the ignition before scrabbling in the footwell for the phone.

As I came back up with it, a powerful hand reached through the seats and grabbed the collar of my jacket, dragging me backwards, while its owner yelled into his own phone, telling his colleagues to get here as fast as possible because I was trying to escape.

I'm not proud of what I did next. But desperate times call for desperate measures, so I yanked my head round and clamped my jaws down hard on his hand like a dog. He shrieked and briefly let go. That was enough. I was out of the door like a shot and bolting up the slip road away from the service station. The driver of the car in front, an angry-looking gamekeeper type in Barbour jacket, flat cap and hunting regalia, leapt out and demanded in a loud and thick West Country accent that I come back immediately.

Clearly there was no way I was going to comply. Unfortunately it was already dawning on me that I had another major problem on my hands as I ran back towards the dual carriageway: namely that I had no idea where I was going, and with just my feet for transport I wasn't going to get very far before police reinforcements arrived.

I would have cursed my stupidity but there was no time for that because I could hear heavy footsteps coming up fast behind me, and as I glanced over my shoulder, I saw the undercover cop only feet away, his face a mask of anger.

I don't know what made me do it – maybe something I'd once seen on TV, possibly even on an episode of *Night Beat* – but I immediately slowed, and as he grabbed me round the midriff in a high rugby tackle, I swung round and slammed my elbow into the side of his head.

He grunted and relaxed his grip, but momentum drove us forward and I hit the concrete hard with him on top of me. Over my shoulder, I could see the man in the Barbour jacket striding towards us with a confidence I wouldn't have shown.

'Help me!' I yelled, still struggling violently. 'I'm being kidnapped! Call the police!'

Barbour jacket man looked momentarily confused but he kept coming anyway. 'All right, leave him be, come on now,' he said, addressing my attacker in a voice that suggested he was used to giving orders. He then grabbed him by the scruff of the neck, pulling him away.

'I'm a police officer, let go of me!' yelled my attacker. 'This man's a murder suspect!' Unfortunately for him, he didn't look much like a police officer, with his aggressive demeanour and all-black gear. And with the terrified expression on my face, I wasn't looking a lot like a murder suspect either. So Barbour man kept pulling, and luckily he was no small man either. At the same time, seeing an opportunity, I launched a sneaky punch into my attacker's balls, and this time he let go of me completely.

I was back on my feet in an instant, thanking God that I'd managed to rear-end one of the few people around willing to intervene physically in a stranger's dispute. As if to prove the point, a car coming onto the slip road veered round us, slowing down long enough for the woman in the passenger seat and a round-faced, sociopathic-looking kid in the back to have a good look at what was going on before immediately accelerating away again onto the forecourt.

As the undercover cop continued to shout at Barbour man, I made a dash back to the rental car, fishing out my keys and jumping inside. As I put the key into the ignition and shoved the car into reverse, I could see both men running back towards me with furious expressions on their faces.

But there was no way I was hanging round now. I reversed fast, straight at them, forcing them both to jump out of the way, then cranked the car into drive, mounted the low bank separating the slip road from the dual carriageway, and rejoined the traffic, accelerating away and watching the two of them become tiny dots before disappearing altogether.

I was still free. But for how long?

28

DCI Cameron Doyle

And that's my problem with Matt Walters' story. He's got an excuse for everything. He claims he had no alternative but to do the things he did because he couldn't trust the police to find his fiancée. But what on earth made him think *he* was capable of finding her? He's a half-arsed actor who by his own admission has never been in a fight in his life. And yet he felt he could pit his wits against a hardened criminal?

Something's not right and my gut tells me to treat his account with extreme caution. He's not the good man he's making himself out to be. He's trying too hard. And he's hiding something. Maybe more than one thing.

DS Tania Wild and I have already had a thorough debriefing with our undercover operative, DC John Obote, who I've had planted within Hugh Roper's organisation for the past eight months (a highly expensive operation that sadly has yielded no evidence of Roper's litany of wrong-doing beyond the usual hearsay). Obote told us that he believes Walters is telling the truth about the kidnap and the fatal stabbing of the man in London – given the fact that Clint Thomson, Roper's chief bodyguard, was pointing a gun at him at the time. I can see Obote's point, but it still seems a stretch that the stabbing was an accident.

But what is Walters' motive for lying? Indeed, what would his motive be for killing this man if not to get his fiancée back? This is what I've got to find out. There's a lot more to this than he's admitting. I'm a little concerned that maybe Tania, and even Obote, is actually veering towards believing him.

No way. He's a liar. All three of them are. And before tonight's out, I mean to prove it.

29

Sir Hugh Roper

Hearing about my daughter's disappearance had terrified me. And that, I can tell you, is not something I find easy to admit.

I'd spent the last five minutes coughing up blood into a handkerchief that was now almost drenched in it, and yet, somehow, that wasn't my biggest problem.

As the coughing fit subsided, I threw the handkerchief into the bin, no longer bothering to conceal it from the staff, who all now knew that I was on my last legs, and resumed my incessant pacing of the study, ignoring the pain that seemed to come from every part of my body. The doctors had said that stress wasn't good in my current state, and that it could make my symptoms worse, although how I was meant to remain calm and relaxed while dying painfully from cancer was anyone's guess.

More importantly, how was I meant to react to my only living daughter going missing? I was angry with myself. I should have known that something like this might happen: the threat to Kate had always been there. But the truth was, I'd wanted her back here with me for these last few weeks of my life. And yet even that hadn't worked out as planned. We'd only seen each other once since she'd returned. I'd avoided a second meeting until I had proof that this new fiancé of hers was the gold-digging fraud I knew he was. I mean, let's face it. A broke, not-very-successful former actor who'd been travelling alone somehow bumped into Kate at the boutique hotel she ran in the hills of Sri Lanka? There's no way that wasn't some sort of con. Now I had proof of it in the shape of the photos Burns had shown me this morning. The problem was, it was too fucking late.

My mobile rang. It was my chief bodyguard, Thomson.

I sat down heavily in my chair as the rain battered against the window. 'What's going on?' I asked him. 'Have you found Kate yet?'

'We've got a problem,' said Thomson, which was not what I wanted to hear.

'I know,' I told him. 'My daughter's missing and it's a problem I'm paying you a very large amount of money to solve.'

'We apprehended the fiancé, Matt Walters, back at the house. He had a bag of his bloodstained clothes with him.'

I felt like I'd been punched in the gut and had to grab the desk for support. 'The bastard. I knew I couldn't trust him. Did he ... did he hurt her?'

'We don't know.'

'Well find out, for Christ's sake!' I snapped. 'Torture him if you have to, I don't care.' And I'll be straight with you.

157

I honestly didn't. If he had killed Kate, I wanted his head on a platter.

'That's our problem,' said Thomson. 'I had him tied to a chair and was aiming a gun at his kneecap, getting answers out of him, when Obote tasered me.'

This was getting worse. 'What the hell did he do that for?'

'I don't know,' said Thomson helplessly. 'But he took off with Walters in Walters' car and now I can't get hold of either of them.'

'Hasn't Walters' car got a tracker on it?'

'Not any more. They must have removed it.'

I had to force myself not to blow a gasket. The problem was, Thomson was a bodyguard, not a head of security like Nigel Burns had been. Good for muscle work but not much else. 'You said you were getting answers out of him. What did he say?'

'He claimed that Kate's been kidnapped, and that he had nothing to do with it. That the kidnapper told him that if he wanted her back, he had to kill someone. That's why he said his clothes were bloodied. It sounds like bullshit to me but he was sticking to his story even with a gun pointing at him. People don't usually do that. They break.'

Walters' story sounded like bullshit to me too. More worrying was why Obote had disappeared with him, but I didn't think I'd get any useful insight into the reason for that from Thomson. 'Keep looking for them,' I told him. 'And think about that quarter of a million I promised you for finding Kate alive.'

I ended the call, not confident I'd be paying him his bonus

any time soon, and phoned Burns. He might be wanting to take a back seat on this, but I needed his help urgently.

Unfortunately, he wasn't answering.

There was a time when he'd have taken a call from me even if he was humping the Duchess of Cambridge, but those days were long gone. He might still have been on my payroll, but with each passing day my power was waning. Soon I'd be gone. Which meant I was no longer a man to fear. It was an indignity I found harder to accept than the ravaging decay the cancer wrought on my body.

I left a message telling him to call me back urgently, then sat back with a sigh. For the first time in my adult life, I felt completely helpless. And full of regret for the way my life had gone. I wanted to cry. To break down and let the tears take hold. But something inside stopped me, as it had always done.

My phone rang again. It was Burns.

So there was still some vestige of my authority left.

'I missed a call from you,' he said. It sounded like he was outside somewhere.

I told him Thomson's story. 'You hired Obote, Nigel. Why would he take off with Walters like that?'

'I didn't hire him, Hugh,' the bastard replied testily. 'I recommended him to you because he came recommended to *me* as a good bodyguard. *You* hired him. But there's a big difference between guarding you and threatening civilians with a gun, especially if he thought Thomson was going to shoot Walters. He probably bailed because he didn't want to be involved in that kind of violence.'

'I didn't want someone soft,' I growled.

'Obote's ex-military and police. He was thrown out of the Met for violently assaulting a suspect, so he's not soft. But nor is he a lunatic. It was dangerous to send him and Thomson after Walters.'

'My daughter's missing, Nigel. What choice do you think I have? If Walters knows something, I have to find it out.' I stifled a cough and stared up at the ceiling. 'Do you think he killed her?'

Burns sighed. 'The kidnap story sounds far-fetched, but there are two things that support it. One: Walters would be unlikely to lie when he's about to be shot. Two: what's his motive for killing her? Even if he doesn't love her, as we both suspect, I still don't see what use she is to him dead. In fact, he's far more likely to want to keep her alive, especially if there's a possibility she'll inherit some wealth from you ...' he paused, 'when the time comes.'

When the time comes. It was coming very soon. Too soon. I thought about this. 'If she's been kidnapped, then who's holding her? It's definitely not someone after a ransom, because I haven't heard anything.'

'She has enemies, Hugh. You know that. You might have to start looking closer to home.'

'That's what I've been thinking. I have an idea that you can help me with.'

'I'll do what I can, but I told you earlier, I'm not going to get involved in violence. I want to enjoy my retirement, not spend it in prison.'

'This doesn't involve violence.' I briefly told him what I wanted him to do.

'Okay. I'll do what I can, and if I find anything out, I'll let you know immediately, but I'll be straight with you. My advice is to go to the police.'

I'd already thought about that more than once, but I was loath to involve them, knowing that it could well open a very large can of worms.

I ended the call and sat staring into space for a long time, trying to think who might wish Kate, or indeed myself, harm. And who had the necessary organisation and ruthlessness to abduct her from under the nose of the private detectives Burns had organised. I've made numerous enemies over the years and I have no doubt there were plenty of people out there raising a glass in celebration when they'd heard I had terminal cancer. But being pleased about someone's misfortune and doing something radical to bring that misfortune about are two very different things, and there was no one I could think of who might be going after my daughter to target me. Very few people even knew of her existence or our relationship. And no one bar my lawyer of thirty years, Ivan Stransky (who would never breathe a word to anyone), knew that I intended to leave her the vast bulk of my fortune, including my thirty-five per cent stake in Peregrine Homes.

So there had to be another motive for going after her, and the problem was, I was fairly certain I knew what it was, even though I'd been trying hard not to think about it since hearing the news of her disappearance.

But now it was something I could no longer ignore. It was time to dredge up the past.

I reached for the phone and dialled one of the few numbers I'd always known off by heart.

'You need to come over right away,' I said the moment it was picked up.

30

Kate

I'd just sat back down again in my usual position leaning against the toilet when I heard him outside the door. He'd been hurrying through the building – and it was just one of them now, not two – as if he somehow knew that I'd been trying to escape. But as he was turning the lock, I heard the distinct buzz of his phone vibrating, and he moved away from the door, going back through the building and out of earshot.

I stayed where I was, breathing slowly, trying hard to ignore the cold seeping into my bones. It struck me that there might be a hidden camera somewhere with night vision that had recorded me trying to get out of the restraints. If there was, then all that effort would have been in vain, and it would also mean that I was probably going to be trussed up even more to prevent any repeat of it.

That scared me. The longer I was here, the weaker I would become and the less likely it would be that this would end well for me. I told myself not to panic. There *will* be a way out of this. I just had to stay strong.

He was coming back again. I could hear him, his foot-fall moving steadily through the building, and then he was directly outside and I felt myself tensing. I knew that even if I broke the cable now – which I was pretty sure I could do – I was still essentially helpless with a chain round my ankle.

I noted once again that there were two locks on the door, suggesting they'd deliberately reinforced it before bringing me here.

He came inside and I turned my head towards the door. I felt vulnerable and played to it. I'm no psychologist, but I could tell the man holding me wasn't a complete monster – which meant it was possible I could reason with him, even if he had seen me on camera trying to escape. 'Hello?' I said, my voice laced with fear and uncertainty. 'Is that you? Would it be possible to have some more water?'

'I'll give you some water in a moment,' he said. 'Stay exactly where you are and don't move.'

I complied as he crouched down and unlocked the pad-lock holding the chain to my ankle. I thought he was going to let me out of the chain completely and felt a twinge of hope. But then he unlooped it from whatever it had been attached to and wrapped the slack round my other ankle before relocking the padlock. I was now effectively in shackles and going nowhere. The only thing that made me feel slightly better was that if he was planning to kill me, he probably wouldn't have gone to all this trouble.

Probably.

But at least he hadn't seen that I'd come close to breaking out of the restraints, which meant there wasn't a camera in here.

He lifted me to my feet and led me slowly out of the bathroom, then through the other room and into the hallway, my chains rattling and dragging on the hard floor. I could smell smoke again. And the damp, mildewy odour of neglect. I asked him where we were going.

'We're going to have a little talk,' was all he said.

He led me into a different room and sat me down on a hard chair, pushing it forward until I was pressed against the edge of a table. 'I'm going to release your hands at the back, then retie them at the front,' he continued, almost gently. 'You're not going to misbehave, are you?'

'Look, I just want to get out of here,' I said. 'And I'm not going to risk doing anything that puts my baby in jeopardy.' He didn't need to know I was no longer pregnant.

He didn't say anything and I knew I'd touched a nerve. It takes a particular sociopath not to have sympathy for a pregnant woman, and his hesitation meant he was feeling something.

'If you do what you're told, you'll get out of here,' he said, coming round behind me and cutting the zip tie binding my wrists without, it seemed, looking at it too closely.

It felt incredibly liberating having my hands free, and I flexed my fingers, trying to get the circulation going.

He told me to put my hands out in front of me, palms facing outwards.

'Please,' I said, 'can't I just hold them out normally? It's so much more comfortable like that, and it helps with, you know, the other stuff.'

He hesitated, and I thought he might agree, but instead he said a simple 'no'.

I didn't push it, especially as I now knew I was capable of getting out of the restraints myself. I rested my elbows on the desk with my hands out in front of me. He leaned down close, and it briefly crossed my mind to launch myself at him. He was clearly on his own here this morning, and if I could somehow stun him and get the keys to the shackles . . .

But you only have a moment to make those decisions, and mine passed.

Instead, as he applied the new zip tie to my wrists, I moved them ever so slightly apart so it wouldn't be so tight. He didn't seem to notice, applying it quickly and expertly before moving away from me.

I heard him rummage round in the room and pick something up from somewhere, then put whatever it was down on the table, and I wondered what he was up to. It occurred to me that he might be putting me at ease before finishing me off with a quick bullet to the head, and I tensed behind the blindfold as he came close to me again.

But there was no bullet. Instead he placed what felt a lot like a blood pressure cuff round my left arm, pumping it tight before making me lift my arms up as he attached two thick rubber tubes round my body, one above my chest, the other just below.

He asked me if it was comfortable.

'Not really,' I said. 'I've been in pain since I got here. What are you doing?'

Ignoring me, he lifted my forefinger and wrapped some tape around it. He then did the same to my middle finger. Now I knew exactly what he was doing. I'd seen a film once where a man was hooked up to a lie detector and questioned about a murder he was suspected of committing. The man had lied through his back teeth and it had all shown up on the machine.

I heard him sit back down again on the other side of the table. Then the tap-tap-tap of his fingers clicking on a keyboard.

'I'm going to ask you some questions,' he announced, 'and you're going to answer them truthfully. I'll know if you're lying. And lying isn't going to help you.'

I swallowed. I felt I knew what was coming, and that my answers might well decide whether I lived or died. 'Okay,' I said uncertainly.

'First question: what's your full name?'

'Katherine White.'

'How old are you?'

'Thirty-seven.'

These were just the introductory questions, the ones that he would know the answers to, used simply to test that the machine was working.

'Katherine White isn't the name on your birth certificate, though, is it?'

'No,' I said. 'My birth name was Nicola Donohoe. Nikki for short.'

'Were you a friend of Alana Roper?'
Here it was. What I'd been expecting.
And dreading.
'Yes,' I said.
'Next question: did you kill her?'

31

Kate

Did I kill Alana Roper? The big question. One I'd been asked many times in the past. But not for a long time.

I took a deep breath. 'No.'

There was a pause.

'Tell me what happened on the night she died. You were there, weren't you?'

There was no point denying it. 'Yes, I was there. What do you want to dredge all this up for? It happened eighteen years ago.'

The twenty-third of June 2001. A date I'll never forget.

'Tell me exactly what happened, from the beginning of the evening until the moment of her death. Do you remember everything?'

Again, there was no use pretending. Not with the lie detector. And anyway, that night was etched in my memory forever. 'Yes,' I said. 'I remember.'

'Then begin.'

And so I told him. How I'd met Alana, her boyfriend David and a couple of their friends for drinks at Alana's amazing penthouse flat on the fifth floor of a converted warehouse building not far from the old docks, then how we'd all headed out to dinner at Loch Fyne. I could even remember what I'd eaten. Salmon sashimi to start with, which they always seemed to do well there, followed by the haddock-and-chips special for main. Then sorbet for dessert. All washed down with a white Rioja that Alana and I ordered whenever we were in Loch Fyne. By that point we'd been friends for almost a year, and in all that time I'd resisted saying anything about how we were related. I'd come close a few times, always when it was just the two of us, and we were wrecked at her place and lying on the huge cushions she used to have in front of her big TV, chatting about this and that. But my courage had always deserted me. I didn't want to risk spoiling what we had, because what we had was good, and it was exactly the same on that night. I wasn't going to say a word.

From Loch Fyne, drunk by now, we'd headed to Steam Rocks, a bar we'd discovered near the old docks. A woman was singing with her acoustic guitar, but the atmosphere was too laid-back for us that night. Alana, David and I snorted some coke in the toilets, then left the other people we were there with and headed to a club, where we'd snorted some more coke, taken half a tab of Ecstasy each, danced a lot, and finally got a taxi back to Alana's place when the club had shut at three.

That was the thing about that night. It had been so much fun.

Back at her place Alana had cracked open a bottle of

champagne. We'd still been flying – or me and Alana had been anyway. David had drunk about half a glass of his then crashed out on the sofa.

I remember that it was an especially warm night, and Alana's flat had a tiny roof terrace you reached from a step-ladder in her bedroom, so the two of us took the bottle and went outside and stood there, looking out across the city.

I paused. I didn't want to relive the next part.

'Go on,' he ordered.

I'd been feeling a tension growing in my belly as I recounted the events of that last evening, and now it seemed to be all-encompassing. I felt sick. 'It's hard to talk about it,' I told him.

'But you're going to have to,' he said.

'I need water.'

He put a bottle to my lips, letting me drink a few gulps.

I took a deep breath and pictured the scene on Alana's roof terrace, surprised by how well I remembered it all these years later.

'We sat out there for a while, finishing off the champagne, and Alana rolled a joint. She said it was to bring us back down after everything we'd taken that night. And so we sat on these two deckchairs she had out there smoking it, and afterwards we got up and stood looking over the city, just enjoying the moment. That was when she turned to me and said: "I love you, Kate. You're my best friend." And, you know, she'd never said anything like that to me before. She'd said nice things, but not something like that.' I could feel the tears coming now, wetting the inside of the blindfold, as everything I'd tried so hard to repress came flooding back to me. 'And I remember feeling incredibly emotional, and it just came out then and there. I told her we were sisters.'

'How did she react?' he asked gently.

'She thought I was joking. But by that point it was too late to take it back, so instead I blurted out the whole story, about how Mum had been their cleaner, how her dad had got my mum pregnant but had never had anything to do with us. I knew she didn't get on that well with her dad so I thought she'd be okay hearing that.'

'And was she?'

'No,' I said. 'She wasn't. I could see her face darkening as I was telling her all this. I remember thinking: Kate, you've got to stop talking. This is not going to end well. But I just couldn't. It was like I had to get it all out then and there.

'And then she slapped me. Hard. Right round the face.' I paused, back in the moment for the first time in years. I'd suppressed this memory for a long time, but I could recall everything with perfect clarity.

'I was shocked. It was so unexpected. And it hurt. The slap really hurt. I was staring at her and her face was contorted in this angry, wild snarl. She called me a lying bitch, said she couldn't believe I'd do this to her. That she thought I was her friend. That everyone did this to her eventually. And then she went to slap me again and I managed to block her this time, and I was apologising. I was saying, I'm so sorry, I didn't mean to upset you, because in my head all I wanted to do was bring back that moment we'd had just before, when we had that bond. And yet I knew we'd never have it again. Never. So now I just wanted to calm her down, but she was having none of it.

'She started crying, these great heaving sobs. She was hugging herself tightly and shaking her head. And she was muttering to herself too, and I remember thinking then that I was really worried about her. So I went to her, and tried to put my arms round her, but she wouldn't have any of it. "Get your fucking hands off me!" she hissed. "I thought I knew you. But you're a sick little bitch, you fucking liar!"'

I paused again as those words – delivered slowly and with utter venom – came back through the years and hit me once again like hammer blows to the heart.

'And then she pushed me away, and I stood there on that little roof terrace, shocked and shaking, and crying too. And I remember it like it was happening in slow motion. She looked at me, and the anger left her and it was replaced by something worse. Sadness. She looked so sad. And she said . . . she said something like "everyone fails me in the end" and then she turned away, walked to the edge and before I had time to say or do anything, she just . . .' I took a deep breath, 'she just jumped.'

I exhaled and lowered my head, utterly deflated. 'That's what happened.'

I heard my kidnapper move in his seat. 'At the inquest, you said she slipped. Not jumped.'

'I know,' I said. 'That was a lie. I thought people wouldn't believe me if I told them she jumped.'

'Did she jump? Or did you push her?'

'I told you,' I said quietly. 'She jumped.'

There was a long pause. 'And was David there with you when she jumped?'

'No. He was asleep on the sofa. The first he knew about it was when I ran back inside to tell him what had happened.'

'Death follows you around, doesn't it?'

'What do you mean?' I asked wearily, though I knew exactly what he was getting at.

'We're going to take a break now. But when I come back, we're going to talk about David and the day he died. Because you were there then too, weren't you?'

32

Sir Hugh Roper

'Follow the herd. End up in the abattoir.' That's always been my motto. Right from a young age, I wanted to make it – and making it for me meant being a millionaire. When my primary school teacher had asked me what I wanted to do when I was older, that was exactly what I'd told her: 'I want to be a millionaire, miss.'

I didn't have the best of starts, but I'm honest enough to admit that I didn't have the worst either. I came from a lower-middle-class family, with a father who worked away a lot as a travelling salesman, and a domineering mother who seemed to be permanently stressed with my dad. But I had one thing that so many of the herd haven't. Ruthlessness. I bought my first house – a tumbledown wreck in Ilford close to where I was brought up – in 1971, aged twenty-one, after securing a mortgage with an application that I'll readily admit was lies from start to finish. I begged, borrowed and stole to keep up the repayments, and then shafted all those who worked to do it up by delaying their payments, or in some cases not paying them at all. I sold the house on within a year at close to double what I paid for it, having already bought two more properties with similarly fraudulent mortgage applications.

It's true. I'm no saint. I never have been. And I don't feel guilt for my actions either. I always knew that I had to be hard if I wanted to get ahead in business. If people were naïve and stupid enough to fall for my patter, well, that was their problem. Weakness is a trait I despise more than any other.

And yet now, for the first time in my adult life, I felt weak and fearful, unsure of who to trust. I knew it had been a mistake not to replace Burns with a proper head of security when he'd gone into semi-retirement. Because Burns had taken his eye off the ball. I'd taken on Thomson as my chief bodyguard, because I knew he was as tough and as merciless as Burns, and at that point in life a hard man was all I felt I needed.

Unfortunately, I also needed someone who was resourceful enough to know where to start looking for Kate, because I had no doubt she was in terrible danger. And as I stood at the study window, watching my first wife get out of her Range Rover Evoque and walk towards the front door, I wondered again if she had anything to do with it. She'd always been a hard woman and, in all the time we'd spent together, I don't remember ever seeing a softer side. There was no weakness about her, which had been one of the things that had caused my initial attraction to her. They sometimes say you marry your mother. I think I did. And I'd loved her too. More, I'm sure, than she'd ever loved me.

Even at seventy years old, she still had that striking, almost regal air about her. She walked purposefully, with shoulders back and chin up, looking down at the world around her, daring it to take her on.

Unbreakable. That was the word that best described her, and I had a sudden, unexpected frisson of excitement as I remembered those times in our very early days when she'd got out the riding crop and administered a beating.

Unfortunately, someone like Diana was never going to put up with my infidelities. I hadn't done it as often as some like to make out, and I'd generally been very discreet. Except for Kate's mother, that fucking cleaner! That had been insane – one of those things you do in life that you know can never end well, but which you still do anyway because you can't see past the pussy. My excuse to myself was that Diana hadn't been showing me any attention and consequently fucking the cleaner was both forbidden and exciting, especially as the dirty little minx had been the one who'd as good as instigated it.

Although if I'd had the remotest idea how it was going to turn out, I wouldn't have gone anywhere near her.

I remembered Diana's rage when she'd found out, and I'd known that I'd never get away with anything like that again. Even so, that had been nothing in comparison to the rage she'd exhibited after the death of our daughter.

By the time of Alana's death, we'd been divorced eleven years. I wouldn't pretend my daughter and I had had the best of relationships. I hadn't seen enough of her when she'd been growing up, and in her teenage years she'd been difficult and hadn't wanted to spend time at my new house. But losing a child so suddenly and so young is the kind of blow that hits you as hard as anything can.

But I had taken it, and though it had unbalanced me, it hadn't knocked me down, even when the details of Alana's drug-taking had emerged. According to the pathologist, her body had contained traces of cocaine, Ecstasy and marijuana, as well as a substantial amount of alcohol. She'd been with her boyfriend and another friend on the night she'd fallen from the roof of her apartment building, and the boyfriend, a twenty-two-year-old called David Griffiths, who I'd never met, had admitted supplying the drugs that had been in her system when she died, and had been sentenced to fourteen months in prison.

I'd been mortified by the pathetically lenient sentence he'd received, a feeling made worse by the fact that he was released after only seven. But my disappointment was nothing compared to Diana's. She'd been furious. She'd wanted Griffiths to suffer properly for what he'd done. I'd felt like making the bastard pay as well, but I also knew that you should only ever use violence in business. The moment you let your emotions get involved, you make mistakes, and if anything had happened to Griffiths, it wouldn't have taken the police long to come straight back to me.

But Diana hadn't been prepared to let it go, and it was when she'd hired a private detective to look into the background of both Griffiths and the other girl with Alana that night, and had discovered that the girl was none other than my illegitimate daughter, that the cat had really been put amongst the pigeons.

With Thomson out looking for Kate, and the housekeeper finished for the day, the house was empty. I answered the front door myself. It was raining hard and Diana marched straight inside without waiting for an invitation.

'You wanted to see me,' she said brusquely. 'What's so important that it can't be done on the phone?'

'Can I get you a coffee?' I asked, wanting this to be as civilised as possible.

She gave me a look. 'I haven't drunk coffee in fifteen years. Do you have green tea?'

'I have no idea.'

'Well you don't look in any state to go hunting round to find out, so let's leave it,' she said, removing her gloves and coat and handing them to me to hang up.

That was Diana in a nutshell. A woman devoid of human sympathy and who kept her bitterness safely stored away and regularly topped up. The only feelings she had for me now were unpleasant ones, even after three decades of keeping out of each other's way.

I led her back through to the main study and sat down in my chair while she took the seat opposite. She still looked good in that stern way of hers. I'd heard she'd recently taken a lover almost twenty-five years her junior, and I had no doubt she was giving him a run for his money. I immediately felt jealous. Not so much of him, but of her. She looked the picture of health, and I remember thinking then that she'd still be fucking her younger lovers and drinking champagne long after I was in the ground.

'I was sorry to hear about your cancer,' she said.

'So was I.'

'At least you're still moving around.'

I sighed, not wanting to show my weakness to her. 'I'm not sure for how much longer.'

She nodded slowly, putting on a vague expression of sympathy. It was clear she had nothing else to add to the conversation.

I tried to gauge from her overall demeanour whether she had anything to do with Kate's disappearance. She wasn't giving any signs, but then she'd always been a cunning operator.

'Did you want to talk to me about the company?' she asked.

I'd been forced to give her a ten per cent stake in Peregrine Homes as part of the divorce settlement, but, having sold off chunks over the years, she now held less than two per cent. I couldn't see why she thought I'd want to talk about that. Unless, of course, she was trying to throw me off the scent.

'No,' I said. 'I wanted to talk to you about Kate.'

'Kate who?'

'You know very well which Kate, Diana. My daughter.'

Diana's eyes narrowed and she fixed me with a cold stare. 'I don't want to talk about that person. Not now. Not ever.'

'She's back in the country and she's missing.'

'I fail to see what that has to do with me.'

I decided it was best to ask her straight out. 'Are you

responsible for her disappearance, Diana? Because if you are, and you let her go now unharmed—'

'What on earth are you talking about, Hugh? I'm seventy years old. I don't go around kidnapping people. Might I suggest that rather than accusing your former wife, who divorced you almost thirty years ago, you call the police and get them involved. That would seem to me to be the sensible option.'

I stared at her and she returned the stare, hard and angry. If she was involved, she was doing a very good job of hiding it. But then if she was part of it, she would have been prepared for this meeting.

'I'm not saying you were the one who actually made her disappear, but—'

'But what? That I hired someone to do it? You really are living in a fantasy world, aren't you, Hugh? Rattling around in your mansion, waiting to die. And if you've invited me here just so you can accuse me of kidnapping your little bastard girl, then frankly I've got better things to do.'

She sprang to her feet with an agility that belied her age, and I was all too aware how cumbersome I was by comparison as I pulled myself up.

'I'm asking because you've got form,' I told her, failing to stifle a cough that I managed to control before it turned into a full-scale fit.

She gave me a withering look. 'What do you mean?'

'You know exactly what I mean. David Griffiths. I remember when you came to me not long after he was released from prison, demanding that I make him pay. You wanted him dead. Those were your exact words. "I want him dead." And you wanted me to organise his murder. But I refused to do it. And then three months later, lo and behold, he's murdered in his home, and my daughter – my *daughter*, Diana – is found in a coma in their back garden. She almost died too. She was in that coma for three weeks. They didn't think she'd make it.'

With an effort, I raised myself to my full height. 'Now,' I said, 'I had nothing to do with that. And as far as I'm aware, you were the only other person in the world who had a motive.'

We glared at each other like two boxers, and it was Diana who spoke first. 'Do you know, Hugh, for a man who's been very successful in life – at least financially – you're not very perceptive. Yes, I was furious. Yes, I was full of grief. Especially when I found out that it was your daughter who was with Alana on her last night. Who was with her, in fact, when she supposedly slipped and fell. And I wanted answers. I have always believed that David Griffiths was withholding information. I told you that I wanted him to tell us the truth of what happened that night, and if he refused to do that, then yes, I wanted you to take action against him, to give us justice for Alana. And I'll be honest, I thought it was you who'd had him killed. After all,' she added with a barbed smile, 'you've done that sort of thing before, haven't you? Used men like Burns to do your dirty work for you.'

I shook my head. 'I've never committed murder, Diana. Or had anyone else commit it on my behalf.'

'That's not what I've heard.'

'Then you've heard wrong. I would never have done that to Kate. I'd already lost one daughter. It would have been too much to bear to lose another.'

'But as I recall, you admitted to me that you had no relationship with this other daughter of yours at the time. And as I recall further, the police theory about the David Griffiths murder was that your daughter returned home unexpectedly and disturbed the killer, and that she suffered her injuries when she jumped from a second-floor window to escape him. So it could still easily have been you behind it. Making Griffiths pay for Alana's death but protecting your bastard daughter. Or trying to, at least. You know the police always suspected it was you who was ultimately responsible.'

I did know that, which proved my earlier point. They'd questioned me twice, although I was never formally arrested (mainly because there was no evidence linking me to it), and both the questioning itself, and my relationship to Kate, were kept out of the newspapers by my lawyers.

'You have a remarkable memory for the case considering it happened sixteen years ago,' I told her.

Diana gave a contemptuous snort. 'Are you surprised? The two individuals involved were responsible for the murder of our *real* daughter. Because I have never believed that she slipped. I think she was pushed. And the person most likely to have pushed her is your bastard daughter.'

'Bullshit. Why on earth would she have done that? They were friends.'

'Didn't it ever surprise you that she took up with Alana's boyfriend as soon as he was out of prison? They were living together when he died, remember? She was jealous of Alana. She wanted to take what Alana had. And she did, too.'

Diana's words silenced me, because the relationship between Kate and Griffiths had always bothered me, even though Kate and I had since made peace. She'd told me that the two of them had got together because neither of them had anyone else, and because of Alana, whom they'd both adored. I'd chosen to believe her. It seemed a plausible enough story if you didn't look at it too closely, and I suppose I hadn't.

In truth, I'd had something of a road to Damascus conversion regarding Kate when I'd learned that she'd been horrendously injured in the same incident that had left David Griffiths dead. Believe me when I say that it made me realise for the first time that, having lost one daughter, spent more than two decades pretending another didn't exist, and in the meantime seeing my son go completely off the rails, it was time to act before I lost everything. It had been me who'd paid for Kate to recuperate in a private hospital, and me who'd organized security so that there was no further attempt on her life. And it had been me who'd been there when she'd finally woken up in her hospital bed. The relationship that had followed had built up very slowly, and very awkwardly, and for most of the intervening time, the two of us had lived on different continents, but at least it was something I'd actually done right.

I looked at Diana now, still unsure about her involvement.

'There's no evidence whatsoever that Kate pushed Alana. And as for Griffiths' death, I never had a thing to do with it, as the police rightly concluded.'

'Well neither did I,' said Diana. 'Whatever *you* may have concluded. And nor have I had anything to do with what may or may not have happened to Kate now. From what I remember, she's more than capable of getting herself into trouble. What's she doing back in the country anyway? I thought she was over somewhere in Sri Lanka.' She waved a dismissive hand, as if she couldn't imagine why anyone would want to be in such a place.

'How did you know she was in Sri Lanka?'

Diana gave me another of her scathing looks. 'I'm not a complete fool. It's not exactly a trade secret.'

I didn't like the fact that she knew so much about Kate. I was about to say something else but felt a cough coming up fast from deep in my lungs. I doubled over as it racked me, swift to get a handkerchief to my mouth before I produced any blood. Diana might have known I had cancer, but I didn't want her to see how low it had brought me.

The fit passed quickly, thank God, and I stood back up straight, clearing my throat and swallowing something thick and viscous. I wiped my mouth as casually as I could under the circumstances, replacing the handkerchief in my jacket pocket.

Diana was watching me carefully, and there was a knowing look on her face. She'd always been one of those calculating types, measuring people's strengths and weaknesses. 'So,' she said, stretching out the word, 'are you going to hand over your share of the company to your bastard daughter now that you're stepping down?'

'Stop calling her that. And it's none of your business.'

'While all the time you ignore your son. Your real son.'

The last thing I wanted to do was talk about my 'real' son, whatever that meant. 'I don't ignore him. But too much water has passed under the bridge for us to ever have a relationship again.' I knew how this must have sounded to Diana, given that I'd managed to form a relationship with Kate after all that had happened with her, but there was no way back for Tom and me. Diana resented me because of it, which also gave her another motive to hurt Kate.

'So you're going to give her everything, are you? And leave Tom destitute?'

'He's hardly destitute. And he can live perfectly well without my money.'

Diana shook her head dismissively, her features hard. 'You know, I almost feel sorry for you stuck alone in your big palace, but then I remember that all your life you've always done exactly what you wanted, and fuck everyone else along the way. And now finally you have to sit down to a nice big banquet of the consequences. And I'll tell you this – not just from me, but from all the other people out there who can't stand you, and I can assure you there are plenty of them – it's not before time.'

And with that, she turned on her heel and strode out of the door, her head held high with a perfect finishing-school posture.

I suddenly felt terribly weary, and as I heard the front

door close, I sat down, wondering what I'd got from our meeting. Diana had a motive for Kate's disappearance, but she hadn't come across like someone with anything to hide. And even though she looked remarkably fit and healthy for her age, she couldn't have done it on her own.

Yet it was eminently possible that she'd used someone else to carry out her dirty work. She certainly had the financial resources. But if she *was* involved, I'd find out. I might have been dying, but I was no fool.

When I heard her car accelerate away up the drive, I called Burns. Again it sounded like he was outside. 'She's just left,' I told him. 'Did you get inside her house?'

But Burns didn't have good news either. 'No. I went over there, but there's a younger fellow there. I think it might be her boyfriend. Did she say anything that makes you think she's involved?'

'She denied everything. It was hard to tell whether she was acting or not. I don't know how I'm going to find out either way.'

'I can follow her if you like. See if she goes anywhere. But I doubt she'd have involved the boyfriend.'

I sighed, stifling a cough. 'Hold back for now. I need to think.'

I put the phone down on the desk and sat back again, wondering if I could even trust Burns now. We'd never been friends. Just close business associates who shared some potent secrets. His loyalty to me was based on money, and if someone was paying him more, then it would disappear immediately.

I looked round at my beautifully furnished office: the

expensive paintings; the Persian rug worth ninety-four grand; the industry awards on the mantelpiece; the photo of me with the Queen as I accepted my knighthood ... and none of it mattered. I might not have followed the herd, but I was still heading for the abattoir.

And it looked as if I was going there alone.

33

DCI Cameron Doyle

I was wondering if Roper would try to deflect blame from himself over the murder of David Griffiths while he was giving his version of events to my two colleagues, DI Webb and DS Sharma. And, of course, he did, very conveniently blaming his ex-wife.

But let me tell you something, it wasn't Diana. She may have been a hard-nosed battleaxe, but she's not the kind who's got the connections to organise a murder, whatever Roper might claim.

Roper, though, *he's* got the connections. And he's done it before. We were certain he was behind the 1986 murder of Ronnie Welbeck, a fellow developer with links to organised crime, who he'd fallen out with over a property deal in Spain, and who'd ended up riddled with bullets outside his Marbella villa. Roper might not have pulled the trigger (we were sure it was his head of security, Burns, who'd either been the triggerman or had organised the logistics), but we knew he was responsible. We just couldn't prove it.

It was the same with Martin Bymer, the council planning

officer who was about to blow the whistle on a huge bribery scandal involving – surprise, surprise – Peregrine Homes. He vanished in 1992, never to be seen again. Not only did Roper have a compelling motive to get rid of him but, more damningly, a witness positively identified Burns as the man he'd seen near Bymer's home the night he went missing. Unfortunately for us, the witness later retracted his statement, so again we couldn't prove anything. But the fact was, we *knew* who was behind it, even if we couldn't make it stick in a court of law

Jesus, you must be thinking, how can a man like that, someone who's so obviously a serious criminal, end up being knighted? There's a simple answer to that. Lawyers. Roper's got plenty of very aggressive ones on his books, the sort who'll sue the shirt off your back if you so much as hint that the bastard isn't whiter than white.

But as any police officer will tell you, when you've killed once and got away with it, it's a lot easier to kill again. Easier still when you've done it twice.

I'd bet my life Roper ordered Griffiths' killing. Of course, he had a cast-iron alibi that day (he was at a board meeting), and the investigating officers were pressured from on high not to arrest Burns (who didn't have an alibi). Burns eventually submitted himself for questioning and denied everything. There wasn't any physical evidence tying him to the scene, so that was the end of that. Case unsolved. Just like the others.

I strongly suspect that Kate realises it was her father who ordered the murder of her boyfriend and the attempted hit on her. And that's got to hurt. The two of them may have made up now, but who knows? She might have been planning her own revenge on him for all these years. She may even be using her fiancé to help carry it out.

Because as I've said before, Matt Walters isn't whiter than white either.

34

Matt

It was 4.30 p.m. and already getting dark as I parked up a couple of hundred metres down the street from the pub in Camden where we'd been drinking last night – a time that might as well have been a thousand years ago. The front of the car was mangled where it had gone into the back of the Land Rover, and one of the headlights was out, but somehow it had made it. The car was finished now, though. I had no doubt that every cop within a fifty-mile radius would be looking for it, which was why I'd left it a long way down the road from where I was going.

Okay, I've got a confession to make here. The friend I'd spent the previous evening with was Geeta Anand, my police mentor from my days on *Night Beat*. Geeta had also once been my girlfriend. We'd fallen in love during the time she'd been mentoring me and we'd been together for close to four years, the longest relationship I've ever had. Even after we broke up we'd remained close and I counted her as possibly my only real friend in the world.

That was another reason why I hadn't wanted to involve

her in this. Because I knew she'd feel pressurised to help, and as a former high-ranking officer in the Met, who'd made detective inspector before she'd left, it would have put her in too much of a precarious position.

To be fair, I should have done the honourable thing and left her alone, given that the charges against me seemed to be mounting almost by the hour. But I no longer had the strength to keep fighting this battle alone and I was painfully aware how little time I had to locate Kate. On the drive here, which had taken the best part of an hour and a half thanks to the appalling traffic, I'd been listening to the radio to find out whether my name was in the public domain yet. Thankfully it wasn't, but on the local London news they had the first report about the man I'd accidentally killed this morning. They hadn't named him but said that an individual, believed to be in his fifties, had been stabbed to death during a suspected burglary, and that the police were looking for a white male who'd been seen running from the scene.

By now, though, the police knew about my involvement, thanks to the undercover officer I'd inadvertently confessed to. They were probably dredging the river too, looking for the woman with the glasses. Either way, I was finished. It was just a matter of how long I could drag things out for.

It's not over till it's over, I kept telling myself as I walked down the street, head down and collar turned up against the driving rain. But I didn't believe that. Maybe, with hindsight, I should have just given myself up. My kidnapper wouldn't necessarily have known, and it would have been much easier to hand responsibility over to those with experience of this sort of thing. Perhaps my confession to the undercover cop – arguably given under duress – would prove inadmissible, and a decent lawyer might still get me out of this.

I told myself all these things as I walked past the pub, looking through the brightly lit windows at the small clusters of late-afternoon drinkers inside. A TV was on showing the football and, even from the street, I could hear their laughter, the clink of glasses, the sounds of normality. The contrast with my own situation made me feel nauseous.

Geeta lived in a third-floor flat above a Thai restaurant another hundred metres down the road. As I came close, I could see the light in her living room was on.

She was in.

Taking a deep breath, I silently apologised to her for what I was about to do, then called her number.

She answered quickly. 'Matt? I wasn't expecting to hear from you today. Is everything okay?'

'Not really. Are you on your own? Can I come round?'

'Sure,' she said, uncertainly. 'When were you thinking?'

'Now. I'm right outside your front door.'

'Okay,' she said, stretching out the word, clearly not entirely comfortable with my appearance, which didn't really surprise me. Because – another confession here – we might not have been lovers for close to two years, but there was still something of a frisson between us.

I should never have gone to meet her the previous night. It was just putting temptation in the way of both of us, and

194

yet, in truth, I didn't have many friends left in London. I'd wanted to see her if only to tell her how well things were finally going for me. And it had been a good evening, full of easy chat. She'd seemed happy for me, right up until she asked me back to her flat for coffee and I'd said no. I knew what would happen – I could see the glint in her eye – and I didn't want to put myself in that situation, because maybe I'm not a total angel. Geeta had nodded, smiled, said she'd understood and wished me luck for the future

But then, as we'd gone in for the final goodbye peck on the cheek, she'd kissed me on the mouth. Hard. Her scent was heady, and I felt something rising within me. I kissed her back, just as passionately, already beginning to get lost in the moment . . .

And then I'd thought about Kate. The life we had. The future in front of us. The guilt I knew would haunt me if I went ahead, and I pulled back.

'I've still got feelings for you,' Geeta had said quickly, going to kiss me again, but this time I gently pushed her away and told her that I was sorry but I couldn't do this.

The whole thing suddenly felt strange and awkward, and I thought I even detected relief in her eyes as she realised this was a bad idea too. Then I'd turned and walked away to the car, and in that moment, I'd known that we'd probably never see each other again.

And now, less than twenty-four hours later, here I was.

The buzzer sounded and I stepped inside, closing the door behind me to shut out the wintry cold. Climbing the narrow, winding staircase up to the third floor, it struck me that Geeta lived in fairly chastened circumstances for a woman who'd risen as high as she had in the Met and now worked as a consultant for TV programmes. But that's London for you. A spacious one-bedroom flat this close to the centre was probably worth the same as our ten-acre Sri Lankan hotel, with its infinity pool and glorious views across a peaceful forested valley. I knew where I'd rather be, though whether I ever saw it again was anyone's guess.

Geeta was already standing in the doorway as I mounted the last steps. She was dressed in a black T-shirt and garishly coloured leggings – like she'd just been doing yoga – and her feet were bare, the toenails painted bright red. She was good-looking, slim and gym-fit, her hair cut in a short, spiky bob that somehow made her look far younger than forty-two. Once again, I was amazed that she was single.

'My God, Matt,' she said. 'You look like shit.'

I'd checked myself in the car's rear-view mirror on the drive here and could attest to the fact that she was right. I'd already developed the haunted look of the fugitive and seemed to have dropped half a stone since I'd got home last night. There were exaggerated bags under my eyes, and a big red mark on my cheek where I'd been struck earlier. 'I know,' I said wearily. 'It's a long story.'

'Is it anything to do with last night?' she asked, ushering me inside and shutting the door.

That caught me off guard. 'What do you mean?'

'I mean, is it anything to do with you meeting me last night?'

Geeta's front door led directly into her small open-plan

living area, and I stood there now staring at her, getting a feeling that something was off here. 'Why would it be anything to do with that?'

She shrugged. 'I don't know, I just wondered.' She was trying to act casual, but she looked uncomfortable.

'Is there something you're not telling me, Geeta?' I asked.

She didn't say anything.

I waited. Staring at her. Knowing that she was going to admit to something, but with no idea what it was.

And then she said it, and my whole world took yet another blow.

35

Matt

I stared at her aghast, unable to take it in, and when I finally spoke, my voice was little more than a croak. 'You were paid to meet me? By whom?'

Geeta sighed and turned away, no longer able to meet my eye. 'I don't know his identity,' she said quietly. 'I was contacted via email by a man claiming to be from a TV production company. He said they were looking for someone who was ex-police to front one of those real-life cop shows. I always need the work and I liked the sound of it, so we agreed to meet for coffee at the Landmark Hotel in Marylebone. This older man turned up – well dressed in a suit and tie, white, probably early sixties – and before we'd even sat down, he told me he'd got me there under false pretences. He said he was offering me five thousand pounds in cash for a one-off job. To set you up in a honey trap.'

'Me?'

'Yes, Matt. You.'

'When was this?'

'About three weeks ago.'

I thought about it for a moment. Three weeks ago, I'd only just found out about the baby. We hadn't even decided to come back to the UK. And yet it seemed I was being set up from thousands of miles away.

'So, right about the time you got in touch?' I said, remembering the WhatsApp message Geeta had sent me, seemingly out of the blue, and how pleasantly surprised I'd been to hear from her after all this time. Yes, I was happily in a relationship with Kate, but that didn't mean I didn't want to remain friends with Geeta.

'Yes,' she said. 'Look, I'm not proud of doing it, and if it's any consolation, I wanted to see you anyway.'

'It's not a consolation,' I said. 'So, how did it work exactly?'

Geeta turned away again and began pacing the room. I remembered this was a habit of hers when she was confronted by things she didn't want to discuss.

'He told me to get in contact with you. He said you'd be coming to the UK soon and would have some time on your hands. He wanted me to set up a lunch or a drink. I was to ask how you were, to find out whether you were in love with your current girlfriend, and then at the end of our date—'

'It wasn't a date, Geeta. It was a drink between old friends.'

'Okay. At the end of our drink, I was to tell you I still had feelings for you, and to see how you reacted.'

'Were we being watched the whole time?'

She shook her head. 'No. I was recording everything on

a miniature camera. As far as I know, it was being fed back live to the man who hired me.'

I felt physically sick. 'You know, I really wanted to see you.'

'And I genuinely wanted to see you too.'

'But you had to be paid to do it. And you tried to set me up. I can't believe you'd do that to me.'

'Come on, Matt. You've got form. You were unfaithful to me, for Christ's sake.'

'Once. Just once.'

'It only needed to be once to destroy everything we had.'

I lowered my head in shame. 'It was a stupid mistake. I regret it.' And I did. Bitterly. A drunken one-night stand with a radio producer I was doing some voice-over work for. It should never have happened, and I ought to have known that Geeta was always going to find out about it.

We were both silent. She'd stopped pacing now and she put her hands on her hips and sighed. 'It seems your fiancée doesn't trust you either. Oh, and you neglected to mention that she was your fiancée when we were chatting last night. You kept referring to her as your girlfriend.'

It was true. I hadn't mentioned it. I wasn't sure why. Maybe because I hadn't wanted to upset Geeta, given that I'd never asked *her* to marry me, even though we'd lived together for the best part of two years. I hadn't said anything about the pregnancy either. I knew that Geeta had wanted children and it had always been me who'd demurred. And at forty-two, her window of opportunity had probably passed.

'We only just got engaged,' I said by way of explanation.

'Ah, that's interesting,' said Geeta.

I didn't like the tone of her voice. 'What do you mean?'

'Well, your girlfriend – sorry, fiancée – has obviously got very deep pockets to set up a honey trap like that. Not only hiring me, but hiring someone else to hire me. If she's just a part-owner of a small hotel halfway round the world, it suggests she's got family money behind her – and perhaps they're not that keen on you.'

That was why Geeta had risen so fast through the ranks. She had a detective's brain, which was what I needed right now. I'd have been a lot better off if I'd come to her earlier. But it worried me to think that Kate might have been the one who'd set this up. Did she trust me that little?

'So what happened?' asked Geeta. 'And why are you here? It's not like you wrecked your relationship by begging to sleep with me. You were remarkably well behaved.'

I sighed. 'I don't even know where to start.'

She sat down in one of the room's two armchairs. 'Try the beginning.'

So I told her, everything, and when I finished, she was back on her feet, staring at me with a mixture of anger and bewilderment.

'This is insane,' she said, resuming her pacing. 'I can't believe you've killed a man.'

'It was an accident,' I told her, desperately.

'Matt. Please. You were threatening him with a knife. I know you were operating under duress, but even so, calling it an accident won't wash. You've got to give yourself up before this gets any more out of hand.'

'I know. I know, and I will. But I don't trust the police to find Kate before the deadline. You said yourself that they don't move anything like as fast as they do on TV.'

Geeta stared at me aghast. 'But how the hell are *you* going to find her, Matt?'

'The man this morning. The one I killed. I took his phone. If I can use it to trace his girlfriend,' I continued, ignoring her disgusted look, 'then I can get the flash drive from her and exchange it for Kate.'

'Even if you do manage to trace her, what makes you think this woman will talk to you after what you did to her boyfriend?'

'Precisely because of that. She'll be scared. I'll make her hand over the drive, then I'll leave.'

'You know how that makes you sound? Like a predator.'

I took a deep breath and ran a hand down my face, removing a thin sheen of sweat. 'I'm not a predator, you know that. But I've got no choice.'

'You know, don't take this the wrong way, Matt, but I've always thought that the most important person in your life was you. I didn't know you could love anyone so much that you'd risk everything for them like this. You certainly wouldn't have done it for me.'

She was right. I wouldn't have. But I didn't say that. How could I? I needed her help desperately, and desperation can make you do some awful things. 'I like to think I'd have done it for you, Geeta. I really do.'

'Sure you would,' she said dismissively.

I didn't say anything, and she stared at me appraisingly. 'Are you really telling me the truth?'

'I wouldn't lie about something like this.'

'I don't understand it. Why would someone kidnap your fiancée, then blackmail you to commit murder? It just doesn't make sense.'

'She comes from money, that's what the undercover guy told me. Big money. He said her father's name is Sir Hugh Roper.'

'I know that name,' said Geeta. She grabbed her laptop from the coffee table, and a few seconds later she was nodding sagely. 'Just as I thought. I had the dubious pleasure of meeting him at a charity bash about ten years ago. He was a lech and an arsehole. He asked for my number, and when I wouldn't give it to him, he tried to grope me, and called me a stuck-up bitch when I threatened to floor him.'

She scrolled down the page she was reading. 'It seems he's a major-league property developer and CEO of a big house-building company. Estimated seven hundred and ninety-second richest person in the UK according to the *Sunday Times* Rich List.' She whistled through her teeth and looked at me. 'Maybe he was the one who wanted to check you out and make sure you were good enough for his daughter, although it's ironic that he hired me after what happened between us. Either way, it looks like you could end up being a rich man, Matt, if you ever get out of this.' There was a sarcastic edge to her voice, but also something else. Excitement. She'd suddenly been presented with a mystery to solve.

'I don't want any money,' I said. 'I was happy before all this began.' I looked at her. 'I'm out of my depth, and I need your help. Just to track down the man's girlfriend. Would you do that for me? Please.'

Geeta didn't say anything, but I could tell she was contemplating it.

I pushed my advantage. 'Last night you said you were planning on writing a book. A crime thriller. Well, now you've got an idea and I'll help with it.' Geeta had told me she'd been approached by a literary agent to write a fictional crime series on the back of several articles she'd written for various newspapers and magazines, so I was hoping I could tempt her.

She looked at me sadly. 'This is a lot more important than writing a book, Matt. Hand yourself in.'

I shook my head. 'Not until I know Kate's safe. Then I'll gladly hand myself in.'

Her expression softened, and I knew then – just as I think I'd always known – that she still had strong feelings for me. 'God, you always manage to complicate my life.'

I looked straight back at her and realised I still had feelings for her too, and that I probably always would.

She took a deep breath. 'Okay. I'll help you.'

36

Sir Hugh Roper

I was travelling in the back of my chauffeur-driven Tesla on a visit I'd hoped I would never have to make when I had an idea where Kate's errant fiancé might be. Matt Walters was the key to finding Kate. Even if he hadn't killed her, I had no doubt the bastard knew what had happened to her and who was responsible.

As soon as I'd found out about his background and circumstances, I hadn't trusted him an inch, which was why I'd paid Burns to set him up using his old girlfriend, the glamorous Asian ex-Met detective. I knew that if he was given a chance to get back in her knickers, he would, and the photos Burns had shown me this morning of the two of them kissing had proved me absolutely right. Those photos had been taken last night. That was when Kate had gone missing.

It was possible that Walters was still with my erstwhile employee Obote, but if he wasn't, there would be very limited places he could run to. Thanks to Burns's research, I knew he had a mother and sister up north somewhere, but if I'd been in his shoes, I'd have gone to my ex's. She was closer, and if the photos were anything to go by, he was still very keen on her.

I sat back in my seat and called Thomson. It was time he made up for his earlier mistake.

'Where are you?' I demanded.

'I'm watching the cottage,' he told me. 'Waiting to see if Walters comes back.'

This is what I meant about Thomson not being the brightest of sparks. 'He's not going to come back,' I told him, 'but luckily for you, I think I know where he is.'

I gave him the ex-girlfriend's address and told him to do whatever he needed to.

A few minutes later, Jonathan, my chauffeur of fifteen years, pulled up opposite the expensive chrome and glass apartment block in Kensington that my son Tom called home.

Tom. I'll be blunt. What a fuck-up. I'd fallen out with him years ago, and although the prospect of imminent death has taught me that I'm not infallible, and that some of the decisions I've made in this life might possibly have been questionable, I wasn't to blame for what happened between us.

Tom was handsome and headstrong, always had been. A lot like me at his age, except he'd never had any of my determination. His mother had always spoiled him, and I hadn't been around enough in his formative years to act as a counter-balance and instil some values in the boy. The results had been predictable. He went off the rails

as a teenager (expulsion from school and drugs at university, just like his sister), and in the end, he never got
back on them. Against my better judgement, I'd tried him
briefly in the family business, but that hadn't worked out.
Career-wise, nothing much else had worked out for him
either. I've fought for every penny I've earned, so I thought
that if I stopped giving him money, things might change.
Unfortunately, Diana – indulgent to the last, especially after
the loss of Alana – had continued to give him an allowance,
indulging his pointless and hedonistic lifestyle.

I could have lived with all this, but the problem was,
being a handsome, rakish socialite, Tom's many misdemean-
ours (a drink-driving conviction; a fight with a doorman at
Chinawhite; a stand-up row in the street with an ex-model
girlfriend in which he'd slapped her on camera) seemed to
have a habit of ending up in the press, and that was just
plain embarrassing, especially as I'd recently been given a
knighthood.

And finally there was Tom's business venture, with a
couple of shady characters for partners, building a luxury
spa resort in Fuerteventura that predictably enough never
actually got built and which left many small investors badly
out of pocket. Tom broke the cardinal rule of business: if
you're going to fuck things up, always make sure someone
else carries the can. Which he most assuredly didn't do. He
was lucky to avoid charges, and when I was asked in a
Sunday Times interview a few weeks later what I thought
about his antics, I'd been characteristically blunt. 'I tried to
bring my son up to appreciate the values of hard work and

honesty. Unfortunately, he decided it was easier to ignore both of them.'

I'd meant the words to be hard-hitting – and they had been. The night the article was published, Tom had phoned me in a tearful fury and unleashed a torrent of foul abuse, until I'd told him, without raising my voice, that he was disinherited, and hung up.

That had been nine years ago now, and we'd only spoken twice since. Once when Tom had swallowed his pride long enough to come to my home cringingly asking for money, to which I'd given the weak fucker a simple two-word reply. The other time had been at the funeral of a long-standing Peregrine employee. Neither of us had expected the other to be there, but we couldn't avoid each other, so I'd said: 'Hello, Tom.' He'd said hello back. And that had been that. We'd gone our separate ways.

And now here I was.

I hadn't called ahead. It was possible he wasn't even here, which meant that I would have had a wasted journey, but it felt good just to be out of the house. I'd spent too much time at home in the last couple of weeks, rattling around in my prison, as Diana had once described it, with more accuracy than I cared to admit. My house no longer felt like a home. In some ways it never had, even when Ellen had been there with Edward. It was as if I'd tried to create the illusion of family, fitting it to my own selfish ends, and had ultimately failed.

I felt a painful twinge of regret that it had come to this. Visiting my firstborn child for the first time in years – no, actually it was the first time ever – to ask him if he'd had anything to do with the disappearance of a half-sister he'd never once been introduced to, because I'd never allowed it.

I sighed and propped myself up against the outside wall with an unsteady arm, my finger, thin and bony like an old witch's, wobbling above the buzzer.

After a few moments, a voice came over the intercom. 'Well, well, well, this is a surprise.'

I looked up at the security camera. 'Can I come in?'

There was a pause. 'It's a little bit inconvenient.'

'Please,' I said. 'It's important.'

The lock on the tinted-glass door clicked and I stepped inside. Tom hadn't bothered telling me which apartment he lived in. He assumed I knew. I did. We might not have spoken in nine years, but that didn't mean I hadn't kept tabs on him.

A fast ride in a spotless elevator took me to the eighth and top floor of the building. Apartments in this block started at eight fifty for one bedroom. Tom's was worth 1.3 million in the current market. Not that he owned it. His mother paid the five-grand-a-month rent, which must have been hurting her. Although neither of them was short of money, they weren't rich, and they weren't going to be getting any richer with my demise either, which at least provided me with a minor sense of satisfaction.

So there was no financial gain to them in Kate's disappearance or death.

Tom had already opened his front door by the time I reached it. He was barefoot and dressed in a pair of jeans and an open-necked shirt, wearing the kind of smile that I immediately felt like wiping off. At forty-one, he was still strikingly handsome in a superficial way. Like a catalogue model. He was just the right height at six foot three, with broad shoulders, a full head of natural blond hair only just beginning to fleck with grey, and the air of a man who'd made it in life without too much of a struggle. Tom had always been a good salesman. He had bundles of charm, and he could have ended up highly successful on his own terms. Instead, his vanity, laziness and inability to plan had always sent him down the road to cheap con-artistry.

We looked at each other for a moment, then he moved aside to let me in, ushering me towards the sofa in his huge open-plan living room with its views out over the city.

I sat down on one end while he took a chair opposite. Before I could start speaking, I heard a noise behind me and saw a young man – also strikingly handsome – walk by in the direction of the front door. It looked like he'd only just got dressed. He nodded at me and smiled at Tom.

Tom smiled back. 'I'll call you, Jav,' he said. Then, when the young man was gone, he turned back to me, a smug look on his face, as if he hoped I'd disapprove of him sleeping with a man, even though I'd known for years he was bisexual.

I didn't rise to the bait. 'It's good to see you, Tom.'

That caught him out. 'Why are you here? Is it because you're dying and you want to make peace after all this time?' He didn't look comfortable with the prospect.

Neither was I.

'I'd like to make peace with you, but that's not why I came.'

'Then why *are* you here?'

Nothing in his demeanour suggested he knew the answer to that already.

'I've never discussed your half-sister with you,' I said.

'You mean the little bitch who was the by-product of you and the cleaner? No, you haven't. Believe it or not, I've never felt the need to discuss it. Not with you, anyway.'

'Who have you discussed her with?'

'With Mother, of course. We'd both like to know what happened between her and my sister – my real sister – on the night Alana died.'

'Kate has always maintained that Alana slipped and fell after they'd both been taking drugs.'

'Well, to paraphrase someone, she would say that, wouldn't she?'

'She had no motive for killing Alana. They were friends.'

Tom sat forward in his chair, glaring at me. 'Of course she had a motive. Jealousy. She was the one who grew up the daughter of a cleaner. I can't believe a cynical old bastard like you would have fallen for her lies. Alana was your daughter, for Christ's sake.'

'And I loved her!' I shouted, the effort almost starting a coughing fit, which somehow I saw off. 'I loved her,' I repeated quietly.

'You never showed it. With either of us. But according to Mother, you've made up with the little bastard girl and now she's your favourite. I gather you even financed her hotel in Sri Lanka. And I suppose you'll be leaving all your money to her as well, won't you? How do you think that's going to look if it turns out she did push Alana? You'll be laughed at even beyond the grave.'

I felt like telling him that once I was beyond the grave – all too soon now – I'd cease to care. But I ignored the jibe, focusing instead on the fact that Tom and Diana had been discussing Kate, and that they knew about the hotel in Sri Lanka, even though I'd made huge efforts to keep her presence there under wraps.

'Did you know Kate was back in the UK?'

Tom met my eye with confidence. 'No. Why's she back here?'

'To see me. She arrived a few days ago. And now she's disappeared. Off the face of the earth.'

'I'm sure she'll reappear. She'll want to keep buttering you up, won't she?'

'I think she's been kidnapped. She may even be dead. So far I haven't involved the police. But I will if I must. So if you have anything to do with it, tell me now. If Kate is alive and you let her go, I'll consider that to be the end of it.'

Tom looked at me with disgust. 'Are you serious? Of course I don't have anything to do with it. I'm here, aren't I? With company as well. And she's definitely *not* here. Or would you like to search the place, just to check?' He waved his arm in a gesture of invitation.

I didn't move. 'You have unsavoury friends. People you could have used to do it for you.'

'But why? You've disinherited me anyway. You made that

perfectly clear many years ago. You want to leave all your money to her, be my guest. You can leave it to Battersea Dogs' Home for all I care. I really don't give a fuck.'

'Someone's taken her. And they're not demanding a ransom. That tells me it's something to do with Alana.'

'How do you know she's even been abducted? She might have just gone off somewhere.'

'No,' I said. 'She's been taken.' I wasn't prepared to give him any more details, in the hope that if he *was* involved, he might let something slip by mistake.

Tom sighed theatrically and got to his feet. 'Well, it's nothing to do with me.' He walked behind the long chrome kitchen counter and produced a beer from the fridge, without offering me anything. 'Is she still with that man?' he asked, cracking the lid on the bottle.

'Which man?'

'You know, the actor guy.'

I tensed. 'How do you know about him?'

He took a gulp of the beer, an amused smile on his face. 'Because I was the one who hired him.'

37

Sir Hugh Roper

I hadn't expected Tom's confession, and yet it made perfect sense. I'd never trusted that actor's motives, which at
least showed that my instinct for identifying liars hadn't
entirely disappeared. Although it wasn't good that Kate,
my only surviving daughter, could fall for such an obvious
deception.

Tom looked triumphant, clearly enjoying his moment of
power. He'd wounded me and he knew it. I was never the
last person to know something. I felt manipulated, which
was deeply unpleasant for a man who'd always considered
himself a master manipulator.

However, the important thing was to find out everything
I could.

'So what did your man discover then?' I asked him,
working hard not to display emotion.

'He didn't,' said Tom, taking another slug of the beer.
'Not a thing. Or nothing that he told me anyway. But that
wasn't why I hired him. I wanted your daughter to fall
in love with him, and then, when I was certain she was

completely infatuated, I'd pay to take him away again.' His face hardened. 'I wanted to hurt her.'

'Why, for God's sake? What did she ever do to you?'

'You still don't get it, do you? You're so fucking blinkered. She killed my sister. She may not have pushed her, but she was there. She was part of it. She still has questions to answer. I told Walters to find out all he could about her past. I wanted her to share all her intimate secrets with him, so that he could report them back to me.'

'And did it work? Has he done what he was meant to do?'

'No. You'll be pleased to know he's been an utter failure. He was paid five thousand upfront and he sent me some photos of them together two months later, along with a report saying he was living at the hotel full-time. He was sent some more money, but I never heard from him again, even though I repeatedly tried to make contact.'

'You went to a lot of trouble to hurt her and it failed. So that makes you a prime suspect as far as I'm concerned.'

'My plan may have failed, but it required someone else doing the hard work. I'm not into taking huge risks, like organising a kidnap or a murder. Especially when there's no obvious financial gain.'

I watched him carefully, trying to ascertain whether he was lying. But that's the problem with con men: it's very hard to tell. I didn't like the way he still had that cocky air about him, as if he was the one pulling the strings, and I briefly considered bringing Thomson in to force some answers from him. But even after everything, I couldn't stomach doing that to my own flesh and blood.

'Was there anything else?' he asked, still standing with his beer.

Slowly I got to my feet, using the arm of the sofa for support. It seemed such a huge effort, and Tom – whom I'd held in my arms as a newborn baby – made no move to help me.

We looked at each other, and in that moment I really did want to make peace.

His expression softened and he nodded his head slowly, as if he understood what I was thinking. But then I saw it. The calculating glint in his eye. He couldn't quite hide it and I knew that any rapprochement he made would simply be a lie. The bastard had no feelings, and never had had.

'If Kate isn't returned to me and I find out that you had anything to do with her disappearance, I'll have you killed,' I told him, turning and walking as steadily as I could to the door. I didn't look back.

'I fucking pity you,' I heard him snarl.

I pity me too, I thought, and walked out of there knowing that we'd never speak again.

Once I was back out on the street, I put another call in to Thomson.

'I'm on the M40, sir, heading into town,' he told me. 'The traffic's clear and I've got an ETA of twenty-six minutes.'

'Walters was paid to start a relationship with Kate,' I said. 'Find out from him what's happened to her and I'll double what I offered you this morning. I want answers and I want them now.'

'You'll have them,' he said.

38

Matt

'I'm not going to do anything that puts you at risk,' I told Geeta as she sat on the floor trying to break into the iPhone 7 of the man I'd killed. According to her, there was a security flaw on that model that made it susceptible to hacking. Apparently the flaw utilised Siri, the World Clock in Settings, and the Apple Store, and for the last fifteen minutes she'd been using instructions from Google to break into it. She'd already failed twice, but unlike me, Geeta had always been persistent. It was another reason why she'd made such a good detective.

'You've already put me at risk, Matt, just by coming here,' she said, 'but I'm a big girl and can make my own decisions. Now do me a favour and get me a coffee. You remember how I take it, I assume?'

Despite everything, I managed a smile. It was comforting to be with her. She was a strong, reassuring presence. 'Yeah,' I said. 'I remember. Two scoops. Strong white. No sugar.'

'Brew for four minutes.'

'Of course.' She was, I thought, remarkably calm, considering the story I'd just told her.

Maybe even too calm.

As if she already knew it.

As I made the coffee, I told myself I was being paranoid. Why would Geeta be involved? And yet she was. She'd been hired by someone to set me up in a honey trap. Whichever way I looked at it, it was an act of betrayal. Could she have deceived me further? I didn't buy it. Geeta wasn't the sort to get involved in murder. And I couldn't afford to be choosy about my friends.

When I came back with the coffees, she was on her feet, looking at the iPhone.

'Okay, we're in,' she said, handing it back to me. 'It's unlocked.'

I thanked her and immediately went into Settings. I saw straight away that the phone belonged to a Piers James MacDonald. There was a picture of the man I'd killed next to the name, smiling at the camera. The sight of it made me feel sick. I rapidly scrolled down to the Display and Brightness panel, where I changed the Auto Lock function to Never so I could keep the phone open.

I'd been working out what I needed to do if I managed to break into it. Piers MacDonald had clearly been very close to the woman I was looking for. After all, she'd been the one with the flash drive round her neck, so it stood to reason that they were in regular contact. A quick look in the phone records located seven calls to and from a contact called Laura over the past three days. I scrolled through the contacts until I found her. There was a photo attached of the woman who'd confronted me this morning. Like Piers, she was smiling. She was also topless. Unfortunately, there was no address for her.

Undeterred, and conscious of the way Geeta was watching me closely, I scanned the phone for the Life360 app, which I knew some people used to keep tabs on where their loved ones were. I didn't know how possessive Piers was, but I hoped he'd be the type to have the app – and thankfully, he was. There were three contacts listed on it, including Laura, and I immediately zoomed in on the location of her phone. She was on a street in Wembley, barely a mile from Piers's house.

My heart sank. 'Shit.'

'What is it?' asked Geeta.

'It looks like she's in the police station.'

She gave a hollow laugh. 'Are you surprised? Her partner's been stabbed to death. They'll be questioning her. She's probably given them a good description of you too. And they'll be checking CCTV footage of the whole crime-scene area. It's only a matter of time before they come for you, Matt. That's why you need to hand yourself in.'

I looked at my watch: 5.03 p.m. 'In just under four hours, if I haven't found the flash drive this woman was wearing round her neck, the mother of my unborn child dies. I've got to do whatever I can to get her back.'

'But you can't do anything if the woman's in a police station. That's why you've got to get help. The police can help you.'

I put the phone down, ran a hand through my hair, tried to think. 'You know,' I told her, 'I just wish I had some idea what was going on here.'

Geeta took a sip of her coffee, looking at me calmly. 'You were told to kill this man to get your fiancée back, right? So he must be connected to this somehow. You need to find out who he is. Or was.'

Now I had his name, and the help of Google, it didn't take me long. 'That's him,' I said, having used Geeta's laptop to scroll through photos of various Piers MacDonalds in image search. You don't forget the faces of men who've died in front of you. It was an upper-body shot, sideways on. He was wearing a suit and had his head bowed as if he was trying to avoid the attention of the photographer. I clicked on the link attached to the photo and was directed to a newspaper article from a November 2011 edition of the *Bristol Evening Post*. I quickly skimmed it.

Geeta looked at me. 'Well?'

I frowned. 'It seems Piers MacDonald was a psychiatrist from Bristol who was struck off eight years ago for making inappropriate advances to two female patients while threatening to blackmail them, and for being under the influence of alcohol and drugs during some of his sessions. He got a suspended prison sentence because he promised to do a drug rehabilitation course. And that seems to be all there is on him. I've never seen this man before today, and I have absolutely no idea what connection he could possibly have to Kate. As far as I know, she's never even set foot in Bristol.'

'But that's your problem, Matt. You really don't know anything about her, do you? You seemed very vague about her past when we were talking last night. Before today, you didn't even know she had a hugely wealthy father. And frankly, there's got to be a lot more to her than meets the eye, otherwise why would all this be happening?'

Which was the big question. I used my own phone to google the name 'Sir Hugh Roper' and was immediately presented with a slew of images of a man in his sixties with silver hair and a lean, hard but not unattractive face. There wasn't an immediate likeness to Kate.

Roper had his own Wikipedia page and I raced through it quickly. 'It says here that he's the father of two children, a son and a daughter. But the daughter died in 2001, although it doesn't give any further details.' I shook my head in confusion. 'This whole thing gets stranger and stranger.'

'So we're going to have to keep trawling the Internet, trying to connect the dots.'

I looked at my watch again: 5.12. Time was running out. I thought about the flash drive, wondering what significance it had, then checked Piers's 360 app a second time. The flashing red dot on the screen signified that Laura's phone was moving. And moving fast. It stopped at the end of the road and then turned right, speeding up.

'There may be a quicker way,' I said. 'Our woman's not in the police station any more. She's in a car.'

39

Kate

When you're incarcerated and unable to move, it gives you a lot of time to think.

My captor had been gone for a while. Forty minutes, an hour. Something like that. Although I couldn't hear him, I was certain he was somewhere near, because I hadn't heard his car driving away as I had before. I had no idea what he was doing, or why he'd left me in this room, attached to the lie detector with my hands and feet still bound.

I simply sat there staring into space from behind the blindfold, travelling back in time.

Alana's death had been a huge blow. To witness her suicide and know I was the reason for her death was a hard cross to bear.

I was already on the phone calling for an ambulance when I rushed back inside the flat and woke David. But it was too late. Alana was pronounced dead at the scene. I remember her body being taken away under a blanket while the police questioned David and me – first at the flat, and then at the police station. I'll be honest, I didn't tell them the whole truth. I didn't want them to know Alana's true relationship to me, so I said we'd been drinking and taking drugs and that Alana had slipped and fallen while standing too close to the edge. They'd asked what kind of drugs and who'd supplied them. I didn't want to get David in trouble but I was terrified about what might happen if someone in the Roper family worked out who I was, and I knew that that would be a lot more likely if I didn't cooperate. So I told them the truth.

I was released without charge. David was less fortunate. He was charged with supplying class A drugs. Because Alana came from a wealthy family, there was a lot of publicity, and although the coroner concluded that her death was an accident, her parents demanded that justice be done for their daughter. The result was that the CPS threw the book at David and he was found guilty and sentenced to fourteen months in prison, a sentence that Alana's mother described in the press as 'a travesty', although it seemed like a long time to me.

In the end, because of good behaviour, he was released after serving seven months, and that should have been the end of it.

But of course, it wasn't. David had been a good friend of mine too, and I felt guilty about what had happened – particularly as none of it had really been his fault. Alana and I had willingly bought the drugs from him, as we'd done plenty of times before, and he'd had nothing to do with what happened on the roof. And yet he'd taken the rap for everything without complaint and, like the police and the coroner, he believed my story that Alana had simply slipped and fallen. I didn't like having to lie, but I could hardly tell the truth.

The fact that Alana was my half-sister never came out. I remember being in the coroner's court, giving evidence in front of my stony-faced father and his equally stony-faced ex-wife, and thinking how these people didn't have a clue who I was. The man who'd fathered me nineteen years ago had never even bothered looking at a photo of me. I was nothing to him. In fact, I was worse than nothing. He hated me for leading his beloved Alana astray. I could see it in his eyes. And hers.

But if I'm honest, I was thankful they didn't know who I was. After all that had happened, I just wanted to be left alone. My father had become as dead to me as I'd always been to him. And I was terrified about losing my monthly allowance, which I'd come to rely on far too much.

Anyway, the upshot of it all was that I moved away from Bristol to a cottage in rural Gloucestershire, not far from the prison where David was being held, and began visiting him regularly. I won't bore you with the details, but to cut a long story short, I was there to collect him when he was released, and he came to stay at the cottage on an open-ended basis, because, as he told me, he had no desire to go home and face his family. In the end, we only had each other and I think that's why we fell in love.

It was an idyllic time. The past was behind us and we'd both made the decision to move on. I started working as a teaching assistant at the local primary school, while David got a job as a gardener on the country estate to which our cottage was attached. We lived simply and kept ourselves to ourselves, although occasionally we'd go for a drink in the local pub and exchange pleasantries with whoever was in there. No one knew who we were. No one bothered us. Thanks to our jobs and my allowance, we had no money problems. One time we even took our car – an old Renault Clio – on a three-week road trip round the UK, and ended up swimming with dolphins in freezing crystal-clear seas off the coast of western Scotland. It was as if, for the first time in my life, the cards were truly falling in my favour.

And then it happened. Just like it always seems to do with me. About a year after David had got out of prison.

The incident.

I was suddenly brought back to the present by the sound of footsteps coming towards me down the corridor, moving purposefully, and I felt a tightness in my chest, wondering what my kidnapper planned to do next.

I soon found out.

'We're going to talk some more,' he said, sitting opposite me and tapping away on the keyboard. There was a severity to his tone. A cold professionalism that unnerved me. I knew he'd been talking to whoever he worked for – presumably going through the details of the conversation we'd had earlier and the results from the lie detector. I knew I'd told the truth but that didn't mean the lie detector wouldn't get it wrong. If it had, it was possible that the man had been told to kill me.

And yet he wanted to talk.

'What about?' I asked.

'David,' he said. 'I want to know what happened on the day he died. Tell me everything you remember, starting from the beginning.'

There was no way I wanted to talk about that day – it was too painful – but clearly not talking wasn't an option. 'It's all very vague,' I said. 'I remember leaving home that morning, kissing him goodbye and telling him that I'd see him later.' I'll always remember that. Our last goodbye. 'I think I recall working at the school that day . . . but that's it. After that, nothing, until I woke up in a hospital bed three weeks later.'

'Do you remember coming home that day?'

I didn't pause. 'No.'

'The polygraph says you're lying.'

I sat back in the chair, exasperated. 'Then it's wrong. I was in a coma, for Christ's sake. That's a matter of public record. Comas give you amnesia. I have amnesia. And why the hell are you so interested anyway? What does it have to do with anything?'

'I don't think you realise,' he said, 'how important your answers are, and how important it is that you tell the truth. Because any failure to be completely honest means you won't leave here alive.'

His words were delivered carefully and with the utmost seriousness. And yet he wasn't telling me anything I didn't already suspect. You don't abduct someone – keeping them blindfolded and tied up in a dark, isolated building – unless you're prepared to kill them.

And I'll be honest. The fact is, I *was* holding back.

For a long time, it was true, I couldn't remember. A head injury followed by a three-week coma does that. And I hadn't wanted to think about it either, because in many ways it was the day that my life was irreversibly destroyed.

But slowly, ever so slowly, tiny snippets have come back to me over the years. Not much, and very vague. Sometimes I wasn't even sure if it was anything more than a dream I'd had. But then, a couple of years ago, I'd forced myself to read an old newspaper article about what had happened to David and me. It said that the police theory was that I'd come home unexpectedly, having finished work early because I wasn't feeling well, and had disturbed the killer as he murdered David in our bedroom. The killer had then chased me and, while fleeing, I'd either jumped, fallen or been pushed from the window in the first-floor spare bed-room (which I suppose was ironic given what had happened to Alana), striking my head on the patio below.

This version of events seemed to fit with my gradually returning memories, and that was what made me conclude that they were probably real. And it was why the lie detector was finding me out.

The kidnapper's words broke the heavy silence. 'You remember coming back home that day, don't you? Tell the truth.'

I knew I wasn't going to get away with another lie, but still I paused. I just didn't want to go back there. For years I'd been able to suppress it, but somehow, like formless ghosts, the memories had slipped through the cracks of my consciousness.

'Vaguely,' I said at last. 'I remember going upstairs and thinking how quiet everything was. I might have called David's name but I can't say for sure. Our bedroom door was shut, but I think I heard a noise, a kind of faint moan, and I knew ... I knew it was David, and that he was in pain.' I paused, swallowing. I could hear that moan now. It was the last sound I ever heard him make. The man who'd been the love of my life. 'I went to open the door, and then all I remember is seeing him lying there on the floor, covered in blood ... blood everywhere ... and a figure standing over him with his back to me.'

I stopped, my mouth dry. Reliving the scene.

Or was I? I couldn't be sure.

'I think ... I think I remember the figure turning round, and then I was running, running for my life, through the house, just trying to get out, like I was in some kind of nightmare. And then ...' I exhaled slowly. 'That's all I can remember.'

'Why did you lie to me before?' asked my captor.

'Because,' I said with a long sigh, 'I wanted to forget it.'

'Is that the only reason?'

'Yes.'

'The polygraph says you're lying. There's another reason why you lied, isn't there? And tell me the truth this time. Because there'll be consequences if you don't.'

His voice was hard. I knew what he was getting at.

'Is there another reason why you're lying to me?'

'Yes.'

'What is it?'

'I've always been afraid of remembering too much because they never caught the killer.'

There was silence. 'Do you think I was David's killer?'

This was the question I truly hadn't wanted him to ask, because it had been in the back of my mind ever since I'd been brought here. I'd always believed that David's death, and my attempted murder, had been organised by someone in the Roper family. Just as this kidnapping had been. Unfortunately, there was no way I could avoid answering the question now. 'Possibly,' I said.

'Did you see the killer's face?'

'If I did, I have no recollection of it.' Which was true. He'd been a blur.

'And do you remember anything else about him or her?'

'No,' I said, with confidence.

I heard him get up from his seat and come over.

That really scared me. Because as he came in close, it occurred to me that he could be holding a knife and this could be it – the end of my life.

'I can put your mind at rest,' he said as he began removing the blood pressure sleeve from my arm. 'I didn't kill David. And before last night, I'd never set eyes on you.'

Which begged the obvious question – why was he so interested in my recollection of the murder?

'We're finished now,' he said, cutting the zip ties round my wrist and telling me to put my hands behind my back.

Once again I kept my wrists as far apart as possible as he retied them.

'Is that too tight?' he asked, his voice gentler.

'No,' I said. 'It's fine. But why can't you let me go now? I've answered all your questions, and if it's money you're after, I've got plenty. I can pay you.'

'You just need to stay calm for a few hours longer, and then you'll be able to go.'

But there was something in his voice that didn't sound quite right. I don't know whether it was a change in his demeanour, or purely my instinct, but either way I had this awful nagging feeling that he wasn't planning on letting me leave here alive.

40

Matt

'I can do this alone,' I said to Geeta as she drove us through the largely deserted London streets. We were in her car, as my rental would definitely be on the police's radar by now, and closing in on Laura's phone. It had stopped five minutes ago at a residential street in Harrow, which I was hoping was her home address. 'I don't want to put you at any more risk.'

Geeta turned to me. 'I'm involved now and I have been ever since I accepted that money to meet you. And I don't like being manipulated, so I want to find out what's going on too.' She sighed. 'And believe it or not – even after all our ups and downs – I still care about you. And I also know that deep down you're a good man.'

'Thank you,' I said, touched.

'Okay,' she said as we approached a junction, 'where do I go now?'

I told her to turn left. 'We're only a few minutes away.'

'I don't want you doing anything stupid, Matt,' she said. 'From now on, we do things my way, okay?'

'Sounds like a plan to me,' I said, happy to let someone with expertise take over. 'Take the next right.'

Geeta made the turning onto a road of tall, narrow old town houses, lined on both sides by cars, and with a succession of speed bumps, forcing her to slow right down.

'Her phone's pinging from down here on the left,' I said, examining the app.

'I think I can see where,' she said. 'There's a squad car double-parked just up ahead.'

I looked up and saw the squad car with its hazards on outside one of the town houses. The house had a For Sale and a To Let sign from two different companies out the front. That meant it was almost certainly divided into flats, which complicated matters.

Geeta drove past and I glanced across, careful to shield my face. The squad car was empty. She found a spot about thirty yards further up the road marked *Residents Only* and pulled in, turning off the engine.

'What do we do now?' I asked. For some reason, I hadn't expected the police to be here, and yet it stood to reason that they'd be looking after a witness to what they believed was a murder. And that, of course, was my big problem. I might have managed to track this woman's location, and the location of the flash drive, but I had no idea how to get it from her. I was simply winging it, allowing myself to get carried along on the wave of events, trying hard to keep focusing on finding Kate and not think too much about all the trouble I was getting both myself and Geeta into.

But Geeta seemed remarkably calm as she looked in the

rear-view mirror. 'We wait,' she said. 'If they were staying with her, they wouldn't have their hazards on. I think they'll go.'

'Don't you think they'll leave someone behind?'

'I doubt it. The police are stretched to the limit these days, and if they don't think there's a direct threat to her, she won't be offered protection.' She settled back in her seat and looked at me. 'Do you know what's bugging me about your story?' she said. 'If your fiancée's kidnapper was so desperate for this flash drive in the first place, why not kill Piers MacDonald himself and take it? It's a totally unnecessary risk to use someone like you, a man who's never killed before.'

I wasn't sure if I imagined it, but I sensed scepticism in her voice, as if she had doubts about this part of my story. 'I've asked myself that question dozens of times today,' I said. 'And the only thing I can conclude is that he's setting me up.'

'If he just wanted to set you up, he could have done that with the body in the bed last night. It still doesn't feel right using you for the killing.'

'None of it feels right. Maybe we can get some answers here.'

'Well, now's your chance,' she answered, looking once again in the mirror, 'because I can see two uniforms coming up from the basement flat, and it looks like they're leaving.'

41

Matt

As soon as the police had passed us and disappeared from sight, we were out of the car. The wind had picked up. As had the rain.

'Stay well back and out of sight,' said Geeta as we hurried down the street. 'I'll knock on the door, show my old warrant card, and then you appear when she lets me in.'

'What if she doesn't let you in?' I asked.

She gave me a look from under the hood of her coat. 'I'll get us in, don't worry.'

I believed her. And not for the first time, her confidence unnerved me. Could I trust Geeta after what she'd done?

A slippery set of stone steps led down to the front door, and I hung back as she pulled out a warrant card and rang the doorbell.

A few seconds later, the door was opened a few inches. I heard the rattle of a chain as I leaned back out of sight.

Geeta was as smooth as I expected. 'Hi, Laura, my name's DCI Anand. I need to ask you a few quick questions about today.'

I immediately recognised Laura's voice as she spoke. 'It's not a good time right now.'

But Geeta was insistent. 'It'll only take a few minutes.'

Laura muttered something inaudible under her breath, but I heard the chain being removed ... and then Geeta was inside, with me following closely behind.

'What the hell's going on?' said Laura, taking a step back as I shut the door behind me, flicking the chain back on and pulling my hood off. 'He's the one who killed Piers.' She looked rapidly from me to Geeta and back to me again, clearly thinking we'd come to do her harm.

'It's okay, Laura,' said Geeta, putting both hands up in a semi-passive, unthreatening stance that she'd once told me all cops use to defuse dangerous situations, as she walked further into Laura's cosy lounge. 'Let's all just calm down.'

'He killed Piers.' Laura pointed at me accusingly. 'I saw him. So no, I'm not going to calm down. And you're not really the police either, are you?'

'No, I'm not. But I'm not here to hurt you either.'

'What happened this morning was an accident,' I told her, taking a step forward to see if she was still wearing the chain with the drive attached. It didn't look like she was. 'I didn't mean to hurt Piers,' I continued, willing her to believe me, 'but they have my pregnant fiancée, and they will kill her unless you give me the drive you were wearing round your neck this morning.'

She shook her head firmly. 'I don't know what you're talking about.'

'You know exactly what I'm talking about,' I said, raising my voice in frustration.

Geeta gave me a look. 'Keep your voice down.' Then, to Laura: 'Look, please. We just need that drive, then we're gone.'

Laura looked like she wanted to believe Geeta, and I could tell she was wavering. 'How do I know you won't do to me what you did to Piers?' She was staring straight at me as she said this, and it made me feel awful that someone could be so scared of me.

'I'm not a killer,' I told her, 'I promise. It was an accident. All I wanted was that drive and my fiancée back. I've got until nine p.m. tonight or they'll kill her.'

'The people who have his fiancée are the same people who wanted Piers dead,' said Geeta. 'Maybe we can work together to deal with them. Otherwise you're likely to be in danger. Do you still have the drive?'

Laura looked at us both in turn. I knew that if she'd given the drive to the police, I was doomed. But then she nodded, and I let out a sigh of relief.

'I was going to get rid of it,' she said, 'but I've been at the police station all day. Whatever's on it, I don't want to be a part of it.'

'Do you know what's on it?' asked Geeta.

She shook her head. 'No. Piers only gave it to me this morning, for safe keeping. I haven't looked. As far as I'm concerned, the less I know about it the better.'

'Did Piers give you any idea what this was all about?' I asked her.

'I know he was negotiating a deal with someone. He had

236

some information from his time as a psychiatrist that he was trying to sell. We hadn't had much luck of late, and we were going to use the money to go away together. I knew that whatever it was wasn't strictly legal, but I didn't think it would get him into the sort of trouble where someone would kill him.'

'Do you have any idea who he was trying to sell this information to?' asked Geeta.

'No, but I had the feeling he might be dealing with different parties, playing one off against the other. He had two meetings and I'm certain they were with different people.'

'How do you know?' I asked.

'Because he took me along both times. The meetings were in public places and my job was to stay out of sight and make sure no one tried to hurt him. Both times he was collecting money. The first meeting was three days ago with a woman at a café. The one today was at Brent Cross, and it was with a man.'

'Can you describe either of the people he was meeting?' asked Geeta.

'I can do better than that. My job was also to take photos if possible, and I got shots of them both. But the ones of the woman are much better, because she and Piers were sitting together in the café window for a few minutes and I was parked almost opposite.'

Geeta took a step forward. 'Can we take a look?'

Laura produced a phone from her pocket, pressed some buttons and handed it to Geeta, who stood there staring at it. Then, without a word, she handed it to me.

237

The first photo – the one from today's meeting – was of an older man in a thick coat and a flat cap. It was clearly taken from a distance and wasn't good quality. I knew for a fact that I hadn't seen the man before.

But the woman from the other meeting was a lot easier to recognise.

Because it was Kate.

42

Matt

'It's your fiancée? It's Kate in the photo?' Geeta looked at me incredulously. 'Are you sure?'

I was just as shocked. I genuinely didn't know what to make of it. 'I know what my fiancée looks like,' I said. 'It's definitely her.' I stared back at the photo. Kate was standing up in the café window, a box file under her arm, an inscrutable expression on her face as she turned away from the man sitting at the table. And that man was Piers MacDonald, who appeared to be putting something in a briefcase on the seat next to him.

'Can I have my phone back, please?' asked Laura, who was staring at both of us.

Feeling sick, I handed it to Geeta, who gave it back to Laura. 'You said that meeting was three days ago,' I said.

'That's right,' said Laura. 'The date's on there.'

'Where was it taken?'

'Gerrards Cross.'

Where Kate had gone supposedly to meet her friend. And

239

where she'd been followed by the woman who'd ended up dead in our cottage.

I suddenly had an overwhelming urge to get out of there. 'So,' I said to Laura, 'can I have the drive?'

Her eyes narrowed as she looked at me. 'Piers collected some money this morning. Five thousand in cash. The police never said anything about it, which means it wasn't there when they found his body. Which means you have it.'

'I don't know anything about any money,' I said, truthfully.

'I need that money. I don't want to hang around after what's happened to Piers. You're going to have to give me five grand for the drive.'

This was the last thing I needed. I thought about forcing Laura to give it to me, but I'd tried that this morning, and not only had I failed, it had made me feel sick with shame.

'I'm sure we can come to an arrangement, Laura,' said Geeta smoothly. She fished out her car keys and turned to me. 'My purse is in the car, Matt. In the boot under a blanket. There's a thousand in cash in there. Go get it and I'll stay here.' She turned back to Laura. 'That's all we've got and it's our best and final offer. Enough?'

Laura nodded. 'Okay.'

I caught the keys as Geeta threw them to me, momentarily perplexed. Why would she have a thousand pounds in cash? And why would she leave her purse in the car when she was the most security-conscious person I knew?

Then I realised. She was going to get the drive from Laura by force and didn't want me to see it.

I felt bad, but with barely three hours to go until my deadline was up, I wasn't going to argue.

I turned towards the door, unsure whether I even wanted to know what was on the drive. Or what I was going to say to Kate if I ever saw her again. Because it was clear she was a total stranger to me. And whatever her connection to the disgraced psychiatrist Piers MacDonald was, it wasn't likely to be pleasant. The photos of them together didn't give the impression of two old friends catching up. They looked more like a blackmailer and his victim. And now the blackmailer was inadvertently dead at my hand, leaving a lot of unanswered questions.

I opened the door, immediately letting in cold air, and by the time I registered there was someone standing there, the blow had struck me right on the bridge of the nose, sending me crashing backwards onto the living-room carpet.

43

Matt

The pain was excruciating and I could feel blood running down my nose and onto my upper lip. Even so, I sat up fast, blinking hard as my vision blurred and darkened then finally cleared. As I wiped my face with the back of my hand, staining it bright red, I saw the same man standing there who'd waylaid me at the cottage earlier. He was still wearing the same balaclava and holding the exact same gun, which he pointed at us as he closed the door slowly behind him.

'All right, everyone stay calm,' he growled. 'I only want to talk to *him*. You ladies, sit down on that sofa and stay quiet, and all will be well.'

'Please don't point that thing at me,' said Geeta with her customary calm, adopting the same hand gesture she'd done with Laura earlier. 'If it goes off, you're looking at a murder charge.'

'I know exactly what I'm looking at,' said the gunman. 'But I'll also tell you this. I'm being paid a lot of money to get answers out of this piece of pond scum as to where his fiancée is. Enough to pull the trigger if I have to.'

'Look, this has got nothing to do with me,' said Laura, unable to take her eyes off the gun.

'I'll be the judge of that,' said the gunman. His whole bearing was composed and authoritative, as if holding three civilians at gunpoint was part of his everyday routine. Which for all I knew it was. He waved the gun at the sofa and Laura sat down uneasily.

'And you,' he said to Geeta, who was staring at him defiantly. I'd always liked that about her. She was strong, even in the face of real danger, and I remembered how she'd once won an award while off duty for rugby-tackling then disarming an armed robber who'd held up a convenience store. When reinforcements arrived, they'd found her sitting astride him, his confiscated knife between her teeth, holding him in a tight armlock. Which was Geeta all over. Fearless.

But this time she did as she was told, moving slowly over to the sofa under the gunman's watchful eye, while I used the opportunity to crawl out of his line of fire and get unsteadily to my feet.

The gun moved back in my direction. 'You. Stay exactly where you are.'

I stopped dead, swallowed. Told myself to keep calm. Perhaps I could enlist this man's help rather than antagonise him, since it seemed clear we were both after the same thing. 'Listen, I wasn't lying earlier,' I said. 'I don't know where Kate is. I'm desperately trying to find her. That's why I'm here.'

'Is that right? And have you told your friends here that you're a failed actor, hired to supposedly spontaneously meet the woman who is now your fiancée, then pump her for information while she fell in love with you?'

Out of the corner of my eye, I saw Geeta pause in a half-crouch as she sat down next to Laura, her eyes widening with surprise, then almost instantaneously narrowing in anger.

'That's bullshit,' I said firmly. 'Whoever told you that is lying. I'm in love with Kate. She's pregnant with my baby, for Christ's sake. The man you're working for – Sir Hugh Roper – knows that.'

'I haven't heard anything about her being pregnant, except from you. And you've spent your career being paid to lie. So no, I don't believe you. It's time to start back where we left off. Wasn't I just about to shoot you in the kneecap?'

My heart jumped as he lowered the gun to my knee. And this time I had no one with a taser to rescue me.

But something struck me. When this man had been tasered earlier, his finger had definitely squeezed down on the trigger, and yet the gun hadn't gone off. Was it even loaded? Because it was the same gun, I was certain of that, having been on this end of it only a few hours earlier.

'Where's your fiancée?' he said. 'Just tell me. We'll go and get her, and if she's all right, I'll hand you over to the police.'

'How many times do I have to tell you? I don't know. She's being held hostage.'

'I'm going to start counting to five again.'

The gun was steady in his hand as I furiously worked the odds. My guess was there was a seventy-five per cent chance it wasn't loaded. They were good odds, but not so much if the twenty-five per cent meant death or life-changing injury. But if I did nothing, I was probably never going to walk properly again anyway, and the thought of that filled me with terror. I loved walking the forests and hills that surrounded our hotel, with the smell of a thousand different spices filling the warm, fresh air. I didn't want to limp for the rest of my life. I didn't want to die either, but I knew I had to do something.

Anything.

Geeta was still in her half-crouch, as if waiting for an opportunity, and the gunman could see this. 'I told you to sit down,' he said, turning his gaze – and more importantly, the gun – away from me for just one second.

I'm not a brave man. You know that by now. But right then I was a desperate one, and that was enough.

We were only ten feet apart, and I charged him.

The problem was, I was never going to make it. This man was a professional and he'd already turned the gun back in my direction so that I was staring straight at it just before we collided, knowing I'd made the wrong decision . . .

But the gun never went off, and with a howl of rage, fear, exhilaration and who knows what else, I hit him front-on, trying and failing to wrap my arms around him as he twisted away from me. I kept going, slamming shoulder-first into the front door and bouncing off it before landing in a heap on the floor.

The gunman had somehow stayed on his feet – but then he was a big guy – and he was already coming back round to face me, still holding onto the gun, when he was suddenly pitched forward as Geeta jumped on his back, scratching at his face and yanking up the balaclava so it covered one eye. He cried out and stumbled, kicking me either by accident or design as he tried to stay upright and fight her off, the gun waving round all over the place but still largely aimed at me. And still, thank God, it didn't go off.

But I wasn't hanging about. I half crawled, half scrambled across the floor and out of range, then jumped to my feet as the gunman lurched backwards, deliberately slamming Geeta against the front door in an effort to dislodge her.

At the same time, I saw Laura get up from the sofa and run into the kitchen.

I knew I had to go after her, but there was no time. The gunman rammed Geeta into the door a second time and with a lurching twist freed himself from her grip, sending her sailing over a glass coffee table and into the sofa, which flew back with her momentum.

The gunman was hurt, with one eye bloodied, but he was still upright and holding the gun. But everything was happening so fast that it was too late to stop and I charged him again, certain now that the gun wasn't loaded. This time I caught him off guard and managed to get him in a bear hug, keeping my body low. We both hit the front door together, bouncing back off, and then, just when I thought I might be winning the battle, he broke free of my arms with far too much ease and punched me in the side of the head, sending me back to the floor.

And then he was right above me and I was looking straight up at the end of the gun barrel.

'You piece of shit. I'll make you pay for that,' he snarled, and this time I was certain he would pull the trigger. But then I heard Geeta howl with rage, and the next second there was a loud smash as she hit him over the head with something, and I was covered in a spray of broken glass.

This time the gunman finally did go down, toppling sideways like a felled tree, his head cracking off the wall before he finally hit the carpet and lay there groaning.

There was no time to feel any relief or satisfaction. I had to get that flash drive, and the only person who knew its location was Laura.

The whole fight had probably lasted a dozen seconds at most, but already I could hear a door slamming shut at the back of the property.

Panting with exertion, and without even acknowledging Geeta – who was holding what was left of a vase – I took off out of the living room and through the long, narrow kitchen towards the door Laura must have gone through, flinging it open and rushing out into the cold, wet air, where a short flight of stone steps led up into a patio garden.

I scrambled up them, banging my shin on the edge of one in the process and slipping at the top, but I kept going because I could see her now at the end of the garden about fifteen yards away, clambering onto the roof of a shed that backed onto the fence, only just visible in the rain-lashed gloom.

I ran across the cobbles towards her, blinking the rain out of my eyes, knowing there was no way I could catch her before she disappeared down the other side. 'Stop, please!' I called as she scrambled across the roof. 'I need that drive. It's to save my fiancée.'

I slowed down and stopped, looking up at her with a pleading expression as she turned back towards me, and we stared at each other through the rain. And then her face softened and she reached into the pocket of her jeans, pulling something out and throwing it towards me.

I tried to catch it – even in the darkness, I could see it was the drive from this morning, still attached to the chain – but it flew over my head and landed somewhere behind me, clattering on the paving stones. I was down on my hands and knees in an instant, using the faint glow from the window of the ground-floor flat to locate it next to a plant pot.

The moment I had it in my hand, I felt a strange foreboding. Whatever was on this drive was extremely important to someone. Important enough to kill for. It also had something to do with the woman I loved, and I wasn't at all sure I wanted to find out what.

Placing it round my neck, I turned round to see that Laura was gone.

And that was when I heard it. Loud and unmistakable, coming in my direction, only a few streets away.

A siren.

Ignoring my exhaustion, I ran back down the steps and into the flat. 'I've got it, I've got it!' I called out, racing into the living room.

But there was no Geeta. And no gunman either.

The room was empty.

44

Matt

If it wasn't for the mess in the room – the glass on the floor, the sofa askew, the divot taken out of the wall where the gunman's head had clocked it – I would have thought I'd been hallucinating the fight. It was hard to believe that, having taken the beating he had, the gunman himself was anything other than unconscious.

However, right now, all that was academic. Because the important thing was to get the hell out of there before I was discovered alone in the house of a witness to a murder, surrounded by signs of a struggle, and the police put two and two together and worked out that I was the suspect they were looking for.

Still pumped up with adrenaline, my face on fire from the shock of the blows I'd taken, I made a rapid decision to go out the front rather than the back. But as soon as I opened the door, I could hear the siren again, even closer now. It didn't stop me. I raced up the steps – saw no police car or blue lights, but knew they'd be here any second – and took off down the street in the other direction, just as

Geeta's car pulled out of its parking spot, heading away from me.

I sprinted into the road waving my arms, hoping she'd see me.

She slowed down over a speed bump, and I got to within ten yards of her, but then she sped up again, taking a right turn, and I followed her, staying in the road, running as fast as I could now, knowing that if I was left out here alone there was no way I'd avoid arrest.

I knew why Geeta was leaving me here, of course. Because she believed what the gunman had said about me seducing Kate for money. Geeta and I had only split up a few months before I'd left on the travels that had led me to Sri Lanka and Kate, so it clearly hurt. And now she was making me pay for it.

I kept running. She kept driving. My lungs felt like they were about to burst, but fear kept me going. I could still hear the siren, although it no longer seemed to be moving, and I guessed they'd stopped outside Laura's place.

And then, thank God, Geeta slowed the car right down and I ran round to the passenger side and half jumped, half climbed in, slamming the door shut as she accelerated once again.

'Jesus,' I panted. 'Why did you do that?' Even though I knew the answer.

She turned to me, her face alive with anger. 'You lied to me, you bastard. You've lied to me all along. You were paid to get together with her. And don't try to deny it. Because I

250

know when you're lying by now. God knows you've done it to me enough times.'

I didn't say anything. I was still trying to get my breath back.

'Well?' Her eyes burned with fury, and I could understand why.

'No,' I said. 'I wasn't hired by anyone.'

'And yet you had enough money to buy a ticket to Sri Lanka, intending to go round the world for a few months? I remember wondering at the time how you could afford it.'

'And if you'd asked me, I'd have told you. I borrowed some, and I made some more from selling most of my stuff. What he was saying was bullshit, I promise you.'

I sat back in the seat, still panting, too tired to argue, but calming down as Geeta turned the car into the traffic on a main road with no sign of any flashing blue lights behind us. My face was beginning to hurt as the adrenaline faded, and I used my sleeve to clean up the blood around my nose.

She was watching me closely. 'Do you swear on your unborn child's life that you weren't hired to meet her?'

I didn't hesitate. 'I swear it.'

'If you're lying about this, or anything else, then I'll fucking kill you myself. Do you understand that?'

I nodded. 'I understand, and I'm not.'

We were silent for a few moments, then something occurred to me. 'I can't work out how the hell the gunman found us. He definitely didn't follow me to your place. There was a tracker on the rental car but the undercover guy removed it.'

'Maybe they used me to find you.'

I looked at her. 'What do you mean?'

'The man in the photo on Laura's phone. The one Piers met today to sell the flash drive to. It wasn't a good photo of him, but that was the man I met at the Landmark Hotel. The one who hired me to set you up.'

'Jesus. I was thinking the man today must be Kate's kidnapper. Because the kidnapper knew about the meeting; he knew what time Piers left and when he'd be getting home. And most importantly, he knew that the drive he'd handed over wasn't the original, so he had to have been there when it was delivered. So why on earth was he setting me up in a honey trap? I don't understand it.'

'Neither do I,' said Geeta. 'This is the kind of mystery I spent my whole career wishing I could get involved with.'

'Except this time my pregnant fiancée's life is at stake.'

She looked at me. 'Do you really love her?'

I took a deep breath. 'I know I'm flaky, I know I'm fickle. And I know I haven't always been truthful. But yes, I love her.' I looked at my watch. 'And right now, according to the kidnapper, she's got less than three hours to live.'

'Did you get the drive from Laura?'

I nodded and showed it to her.

'That's what he wants, isn't it? In return for her life? Whatever's on it is the key to everything.'

'It looks that way,' I said, feeling a weight begin to sink down on my shoulders. Because I knew what Geeta would say next.

And she did. 'Then we'd better take a look at it.'

45

Sir Hugh Roper

Put bluntly, the meeting with Tom had been a disaster, and had left me in a foul mood. I was no further forward in locating Kate, and at this point, so near to the end of my life, it was painful to see at close quarters how much my son truly hated me.

My mood wasn't helped by a call from Edward, that pain-in-the-arse stepson of mine, who seemed to have an uncanny knack of phoning at the exact times I least wanted to speak with him, like he had some kind of app for it. He apologised for being pushy earlier in the day, and before I'd even had a chance to accept his apology, he'd opened fire with a spiel about the costings for the Rickmansworth project, specifically the prices our boutique kitchen designers were charging. Like I gave a fuck. He wanted me to put pressure on their MD, Mike 'the Prowler' Fowler, who was a personal friend and former golf buddy of mine, to drop their prices by ten per cent, which I knew for a fact 'the Prowler' would never do. I felt like telling Edward just to fuck off and sort it out himself, but I couldn't tolerate yet another falling-out right now. So instead I said I'd see what I could do and ended the call before the bastard could blather on about something else.

I'd got Jonathan to drive me round the streets of the West End so that I didn't have to go home. It gave me time to think while I sat in comfort and watched people milling about under the bright lights of a city where I'd spent plenty of nights eating in the best restaurants, attending parties, drinking, having fun. Good times. But it all felt like such a long time ago now.

I tried Thomson's number twice, but he wasn't answering, which frustrated me still further, and then, as we were driving down Old Street, meandering towards the City – the place where I'd had some of my greatest triumphs – my phone rang.

I didn't recognise the number but decided that, given the circumstances, it was worth taking the call.

'Good evening, Sir Hugh,' said a growling male voice, which unfortunately I recognised immediately.

'DCI Cameron Doyle,' I answered, only just managing to keep the contempt from my voice. 'What do you want?'

'I want to talk to you about your daughter, Kate. I understand she's gone missing.'

I tensed involuntarily. 'Who gave you that information?'

'That's not the question I'd have expected you to ask.'

'Because whoever it was is wrong. My daughter is fine. I spoke to her yesterday.'

I'd been considering getting the police involved in this incident for a while now, especially as we were no closer to finding Kate, but the one person I didn't wish to discuss it with was Cameron Doyle, a man who'd spent his career determined to destroy mine. He'd tried to tie me to various serious crimes he believed I'd committed, including the attempted murder of Kate and the murder of her then boyfriend, David Griffiths. And he almost certainly had an underhand motive for calling now.

'Why don't you give me her number so I can ring her and put my mind at rest?' he said, with typical slyness in his voice.

'I don't give a fuck about putting your mind at rest, Doyle.'

'Your daughter's in danger and you don't seem to be too worried about it. Which is a surprise to me, given that you've already lost one child.'

I was tempted to cut the call, but I needed to know where he was getting his information. 'How do you know my daughter's in danger?'

'We have reason to believe she was kidnapped last night. During the course of that kidnap, a woman we suspect was a private detective employed by you was killed. We've just fished that woman's body out of the River Thames two miles south of the cottage where your daughter and her fiancé have been staying for the past week, and her car's been recovered thirty metres from your daughter's rental cottage . . .'

As he droned on in that supercilious way of his, I tried to work out how on earth he knew all this. Only a handful of people were aware of the existence of the PI.

Me, Burns, Thomson and possibly Obote, the bodyguard who'd absconded with Matt Walters. Perhaps that was why Obote had run off. He was a police informant. Or worse, an undercover copper working for Doyle.

But I've been around far too long to walk into this particular trap. 'I don't know what you're talking about,' I said, trying to determine how much Doyle had on me.

It didn't take long to find out.

'My understanding is that you offered a sizeable payment to one of your bodyguards, Clint Thomson, to threaten to kill Kate's fiancé, Matt Walters, if he didn't reveal her whereabouts as you were, and presumably still are, convinced that he's involved in her disappearance. And please don't bother repeating that you don't know what I'm talking about, because we both know you do. And if your daughter's in danger, I suggest you cooperate with us right now.'

But cooperating with Doyle wasn't going to get Kate back and would just lead me into a lot of trouble. I needed to contain the situation, and the best way to do that was to get off the phone fast.

'If you're worried about Kate, I suggest you talk to Walters.'

'We would, but we can't find him. Do you know where he is?'

'I'm afraid I don't. Goodnight, DCI Doyle.'

I cut the call, then put a block on the number so he couldn't reach me again. I wondered if they'd got Thomson. I hadn't spoken to him in over two hours and, if they had him, it was possible he'd talk and implicate me. But clearly he hadn't done so yet, otherwise I'd have been arrested.

I sat back in my seat and closed my eyes. It was all beginning to fall apart.

When I'd first married Diana, and Tom was born, I'd genuinely thought it was the beginning of a family dynasty. I'd wanted him to be part of a thriving business that stretched forward into time, becoming the most successful building company in the UK. And look how it had turned out. All the money I'd made had brought me nothing of use. I was dying. My precious daughter Alana was long dead. My son was an utter waste of space who'd spent a lifetime specialising in disloyalty and hadn't even managed to provide me with an heir. The only flesh and blood I had left was Kate, and now she too was gone. And someone in what I would almost laughably call my inner circle had taken her. But who? Tom and Diana had both denied it vehemently, and yet they were the obvious suspects.

I've always been a man able to make quick decisions, but I was in a genuine quandary here. If Kate was being held because her kidnapper suspected she was responsible for Alana's death and hadn't been telling the truth about it all these years, then they would spend time interrogating her. That was what I would have done. But she'd been taken sometime the previous night, which meant the interrogation would surely have finished by now. It was a question of what they did with her next. Ordinarily my bet would have been that they'd let her go – for all their flaws, I didn't believe that either Diana or Tom was a killer. Except

257

one of them had almost certainly been behind the previous attempt on Kate's life, and though they might not be killers themselves, it was possible that they'd hired someone who was quite capable of doing their dirty work for them.

But what could I do? Calling the police wasn't going to help Kate. If Tom and Diana were behind it, they wouldn't admit to anything. And I could no longer rely on any of my own people to find her, even with the promise of almost unlimited money.

But I had to do something. I'm not the sort of man who waits for events to overtake him. I almost picked the phone up again then and there and called Doyle to ask for his help. Almost.

But I didn't. In the end, I broke my own rule and did nothing.

And that's something I bitterly regret.

46

DCI Cameron Doyle

By the time I called Roper that evening, we were building up a picture of what had happened. We knew from Obote that Kate was missing – either kidnapped or dead – and we'd tentatively identified the woman whose body we'd recovered from the Thames as thirty-three-year-old Caroline Seed. Even though she'd been carrying no ID, the car we believed she'd been using was traced back to a London-based firm of private detectives, who'd verified her name. The firm's MD confirmed they had negotiated a private contract with Roper's former head of security, Nigel Burns, to provide twenty-four-hour surveillance on Kate and her partner, Matt Walters. It was clear that someone had killed Ms Seed and abducted Kate, but the problem we had was that we couldn't get hold of either Walters or Burns.

Which was why I'd taken the decision to call Roper and urge him to cooperate. And it would have saved lives if he had. But he'd chosen to deny all knowledge of Kate's kidnap, and you can draw your own conclusions from that. *My* conclusion was, and still is, that he had other reasons for holding back. Perhaps he was the one who was actually behind the kidnap. I can't say for sure, but he has as solid a motive as anyone else. It would be a way of finding out once and for all whether Kate had been responsible for Alana's death. He was clearly ruthless enough. Whatever he's been telling my colleagues, I know that Hugh Roper is a narcissistic psychopath who doesn't have a decent bone in his body. This definitely wouldn't have been beyond him.

We're back in the interview room with Kate now, Wild and I, ready to resume her version of events, but before she begins, I chuck her another of what the Americans like to call curveballs.

'So,' I say, we've suspected for a long time that your father was the man behind the murder of your partner, David Griffiths. We don't think he planned to hurt you, but what happened was that you came home unexpectedly and disturbed the killer, who had no choice but to try to silence you. Your father's involvement must be something you've considered?'

Kate's lawyer is on this like a shot, demanding to know what this has to do with anything, but I just give her my stock answer to such things: 'We're just trying to build up a picture, that's all.'

The lawyer keeps complaining, but Kate hushes her with a hand and makes it clear that she's willing to answer all our questions.

So I sit back and wait for her to start talking.

47

Kate

After my kidnapper had put me back in my bathroom cell, he'd driven off somewhere, leaving me chained, cuffed and blindfolded – and that was when I started to think very seriously about the people who could possibly be behind my kidnapping, knowing that it was almost certainly the same person who had been behind David's murder.

The most obvious suspect was Diana, my father's first wife. A hard-faced bitch who'd never believed my denials of responsibility for Alana's death, and who I remembered staring at me with dagger eyes as I'd given evidence in the coroner's court. She'd be ruthless enough to come after me, I was sure of that. Then there was Tom, Alana's brother. He hadn't been in the coroner's court, and in truth I knew very little about him, other than that he and my father didn't get on and hadn't done for many years. He had to be a suspect too, but less of one than Diana.

And then, yes, there was my father himself.

He had the means to do it. And I knew as well as anyone that he was callous enough. And although I'd looked into his eyes and told him more than once that I'd had nothing to do with Alana's death, it was possible that he still didn't believe me and had decided on this as a make-or-break attempt to make sure he knew the absolute truth before he died and left me money in his will.

But in the end, I didn't buy it. I was still my father's flesh and blood. Whatever his faults – and by God he had enough of them – I didn't think he'd do this to me. And I didn't think he'd killed David either.

Before David's murder, I'd never spoken a word to my father. After his death, though, when I'd woken up from my coma, disorientated and alone in my own private hospital room with a guard outside, he'd been my first visitor.

I'd only seen him once before in the flesh, almost two years earlier in the coroner's court. Then his expression had been cold and unyielding. Now it had softened, and he was looking at me with genuine pity in his eyes. He cared for me, I could tell.

We'd talked. It had been awkward. He'd sat by the side of the bed but kept his hands down by his sides, as if he wasn't sure how much affection he should give. He was the first person to explain what had happened to David and to me, because at that time I really couldn't remember. I recall him promising solemnly that it had been nothing to do with him, and that my near-death experience had made him realise that it was time to start afresh.

I was distraught at David's death, but pleased to have my father come out and say for the first time that he was actually interested in developing a relationship with me.

As I slowly recovered, he visited me regularly in hospital. We talked more frequently. We even spoke occasionally about Alana, and I shared my memories of her, saying how distraught I'd been at her death. I always assumed he'd believed me.

Because David's killer hadn't been caught, my father made sure that I was guarded by private security during my stay, and when I was finally well enough to be discharged, several months later, he paid for me to stay in a hotel in Knightsbridge, again providing security.

But I was never going to live like that for long. After everything that had happened, I realised that I wanted to get away from England, to travel. And when I'd told my father this, he'd agreed that it was the right thing to do and that it would be safer for me as well.

So I'd gone. I'd seen the world for the first time, spending the best part of a year circumnavigating it, immersing myself in adventures in a bid to assuage the grief that burned within me, until finally I arrived in Sri Lanka and realised that this was the place I wanted to call home.

That had been fifteen years ago now. Life had been good, if a little empty. My father had visited once but hadn't really enjoyed it. He wasn't a huge fan of the heat. I'd visited him over the years a handful of times too, but there'd always been a distance in our relationship, as if we both knew the events of our past were never going to be fully resolved.

And now, with our time finally running out, I'd walked straight into a trap. Both my father and I should have known that my homecoming was going to cause ripples among those who'd always wished me harm. But we'd underestimated the threat, and now here I was at their mercy, which meant I had no choice but to try to escape before my kidnapper came back.

So it was with a sense of déjà vu that I sat back on the side of the bath again, and rubbed the plastic restraints frantically up and down the Perspex shower screen to wear them down.

I worked fast. It's incredibly motivating to know that if you don't do something, there's a good chance you're going to die, and soon I could feel the plastic fraying fast. I accelerated the pace of my rubbing, conscious of a bead of sweat running down my face, knowing I was nearly there. I paused, stood up, and yanked my arms up behind my back in a single rapid motion, as if trying to hit someone behind me, driving my wrists apart at the same time. I felt the cuffs give but not go completely. I also pulled a muscle in my shoulder. I was weak. I needed to stop. But I was close, too, I could feel it, and now was not the time for weakness.

I tried the same yanking motion a second time. It didn't work and my shoulder spasmed painfully. I wanted to cry. This was all getting too much, and once again, as so often in my life, I was utterly alone with no one to help me. But I wouldn't let the tears come. I'd been through too much for that. Instead I waited until the pain subsided. Then I took three deep breaths and tried again, putting everything into it.

The cable snapped and suddenly my hands were free. It was an ecstatic feeling and I almost cried out with pleasure as I pulled the blindfold up over my eyes, finally able to see again.

The room was so dark I hardly needed to blink. There was no natural light in there at all. I could only just make out the bathtub and the radiator. But I didn't care. I could see. My wrists were sore and stripped of skin where the cables had been cutting into them, and I blew cool air on them before going down on one knee to examine the chain.

It was wrapped several times round my left leg and kept in place by a heavy padlock, while the other end was looped tight round a pipe leading to the valve of a standard radiator, which was attached to the wall, and again held in place by a padlock.

I sat back against the toilet seat and grabbed the chain in both hands, pulling hard as if I was in a one-woman tug of war, hoping to wrench the pipe away from the wall. It didn't budge a millimetre. There was only one way I could escape and that was by getting the chain free of the radiator, but as I crouched down in the near-total darkness and felt around the pipe, I realised that that would mean pulling the whole radiator from the wall, and there was no way I had that kind of strength.

But then, as I felt further along the pipe, I found the fat plastic thermostat valve at the end. I began unscrewing it, and a few seconds later it fell off and landed on the floor. This was too good to be true. The chain was still tightly wrapped round the pipe, but slowly, ever so slowly, I was able to move it along. It was a hard job and made my forearms burn with the effort, but eventually there was only an inch left to go.

And that, unfortunately, was when I heard the car pulling up outside.

48

Matt

'I don't want to look at what's on it,' I said.

Forty-five minutes had passed since we'd fled Laura's basement flat. Geeta was concerned that her own apartment might be compromised, so we stopped there only briefly to pick up her laptop and were now in the car park of a Burger King just off the A40. The flash drive was plugged in and ready to be opened.

'Don't you want to know what this is all about?' she said. 'Because I do.'

I took a deep breath. 'I do, and I don't. Piers obviously wasn't just selling this drive. He also sold something to Kate – it looked from the photo like an A4 file. If the information on this drive is the same, then it's obviously something she wants to keep secret.'

'It seems like all you two have is secrets,' said Geeta. 'You knew nothing about her meeting with MacDonald. You didn't know that her father was a multimillionaire who clearly cares enough about her to send a gunman after you. Right now, Matt, it just looks like you're a pawn in this whole thing. And if you want to move beyond that, then the key to your survival is information. And I'm betting there's information on here.'

She was right. She always was.

Even so, I was hoping the drive was encrypted so we wouldn't be able to read what was on it. Unfortunately, it was not to be. When Geeta opened it up, a dozen or so audio files appeared on screen. They were all entitled *Session, Client 271*, followed by different dates. The first was dated 28/11/01, with each subsequent one roughly a week, or in some cases two weeks, apart, with the last one dated 07/03/02.

Without looking at me, Geeta double-clicked on the first one and we waited the few seconds it took for the file to load before pressing play.

There was a long pause, with the slow crackle of background noise, then the sound of a door opening and shutting, and a chair scraping.

'Hello, Nikki, pleased to meet you, I'm Dr MacDonald,' said the man I'd killed this morning.

'Hi,' said a nervous female voice that I immediately recognised as a younger version of Kate. 'Pleased to meet you too.'

So it seemed I didn't even know my fiancée's real first name. 'That's Kate,' I told Geeta.

She paused the file. 'Are you sure?'

I nodded slowly, wondering where this was going. 'Absolutely.'

Geeta resumed the recording. Dr MacDonald offered

Kate a seat and then asked what he could do to help her. His tone was calm and reassuring, just as you'd expect a psychiatrist's to be, and so very different to his demeanour this morning when I'd confronted him with a knife. It felt both strange and depressing to listen to him now, knowing that I'd killed him only hours before. I would have to live with that knowledge for the rest of my life, whatever happened in the coming hours.

Kate took a long time to answer MacDonald's question, but when she did, I felt a pang of pure emotion that made me shiver. Whatever anyone might accuse me of, I loved this woman.

'I've been having terrible, terrible nightmares, and I feel suicidal,' she said, in a soft voice. 'I feel so alone. I feel as if the whole world's grinding me down and I don't know what to do about it.'

'Well, you've done something about it already by coming to me. And that's a very positive thing because I'll be able to help. Tell me what the nightmares are about.'

And so it went on. She described her nightmares, which seemed to vary, but included a recurring one where she was being chased through a forest before coming to a cliff edge, knowing she had to jump or face whatever it was that was pursuing her. Occasionally Dr MacDonald would make a comment or ask a question, but in general he just let her talk, which Kate seemed to be happy to do, and it was clear she was unburdening herself. But nothing she was saying was in any way incriminating, either to her or to anyone else. I said as much to Geeta.

'No,' said Geeta, pausing the recording, 'but it's inter-esting what you read about Dr MacDonald earlier. That one of the reasons he was struck off was because he was blackmailing clients. Because he should never have been recording them like this. It's a complete breach of the patient–doctor relationship.'

I stared down at the laptop screen. 'I don't understand why he would have recorded his sessions with a woman barely in her twenties for blackmail purposes. Unless he knew that her father was Sir Hugh Roper. But how would he have known that? Even now, his Wikipedia page says that Roper only had one daughter and she died in 2001.'

'The same year as this recording,' said Geeta.

I nodded. 'Then there's got to be some connection.'

She closed the audio files screen and went back to Roper's Wikipedia page. 'So the daughter who died was called Alana,' she murmured, clearly thinking aloud as she googled *Alana Roper death*. A long string of articles came up, as well as a photo of a young woman of about twenty with short, spiky black hair and a pretty elfin face. 'I remember reading about this at the time,' she said, opening up one of the stories, 'but I didn't realise it was Roper's daughter. Alana fell to her death from the roof terrace of her flat in Bristol in June 2001 when she was off her head on booze and drugs. You said earlier that MacDonald practised his psychiatry in Bristol?'

'That's right,' I said, watching as Geeta started putting things together.

'Alana's death was ruled an accident,' she continued, 'but

there was some controversy about it. She was at the flat that night with her boyfriend, who was convicted of supplying the drugs, and another friend ...' she continued scrolling down the screen until she found what she was looking for, 'a nineteen-year-old girl called Nikki Donohoe.'

She turned to me, and there was sympathy in her dark eyes. 'This isn't a coincidence, Matt. Your fiancée and Nikki Donohoe have to be one and the same ... which means she was there when Alana died.'

I didn't ask if she was sure. I don't believe in coincidences that big either.

Geeta's fingers continued to rattle across the laptop's keys while I stared out of the window into the night, feeling like a fool. I'd fallen in love with a woman I didn't know at all and suddenly, out of nowhere, her past was causing my whole world to collapse. Everything could have been so good. If we'd just stayed in Sri Lanka, none of this would have happened. I opened the window a little, breathing in the cold air, wishing I could get out of the car and start running, and never stop.

'This is interesting,' mused Geeta, her fingers easing up on the laptop keys. 'David Griffiths – the man who supplied the drugs to Alana – was murdered two years later, in August 2003, during a suspected home invasion. His girlfriend at the time, one Nikki Donohoe, was seriously injured in the same attack. The case remains unsolved, but it doesn't take Sherlock Holmes to guess that it had something to do with what happened to Alana, and that it was likely her family were behind it.'

I shook my head, trying to take in this last twist. 'Jesus Christ. But if the police think her dad had something to do with that, then why is he trying to find her now?'

Geeta shrugged. 'I really don't know. But either way, there appear to be people out there who still wish her harm. And who want to get hold of these audio files.'

'So you think there's a confession to Alana's murder somewhere on one of them?'

'All I can say is someone wants to get hold of them pretty badly.'

'It would explain why MacDonald was blackmailing her,' I said uneasily. It was still hard to believe that kind, gentle Kate, the woman I loved, who treated our staff with generosity and respect, who was proud of all she'd achieved, could have killed someone. But then again, it was obvious that I didn't really know her at all.

Geeta sighed. 'From what Laura told us, MacDonald was touting this information to other interested parties. And if these other interested parties already blamed Kate for what happened to Alana, and they found the confession on here, then they're not going to let her go, are they? They're going to kill her.'

I took a deep breath as I considered the ramifications of this. 'So the minute I deliver this drive, I effectively seal her fate. But that still begs another question. MacDonald handed over a copy of this flash drive to the man he met this morning, so why does that man want the master copy? He only needs one drive if he's looking for a confession, and he should already have it.'

'I don't know, Matt, but we're both out of our depth here. It may be best just to go to the police now. I've still got friends in the force who could help.'

I looked at my watch. 'It's too late, Geeta. It's eight thirty now. He's given me until nine at the latest to get hold of the drive. I wouldn't even have time to explain the story to the police before the deadline passes.'

'It's your funeral, Matt.'

This was probably true. But in that moment, I made a decision. 'I'm going to get her back, Geeta.'

She looked at me sceptically. 'How?'

'By standing up to him for once.'

This time she didn't say anything and we sat there in silence with our Burger King coffees as the car's heating blasted out warm air. It was strange. Like the calm before the storm. I almost felt myself drifting off to sleep.

And then the car horn ringtone of the kidnapper's phone started.

I looked at my watch: 8.40 p.m. He was early. I pulled out the phone, staring at the words *No Caller ID* on the screen. 'It's him,' I said.

'Don't agree to do anything until you've spoken to Kate. It's essential you make sure she's alive and unharmed. And when you deliver the drive, you do it as a straight swap. Her for it. Understand?'

I nodded, suddenly terrified, knowing the endgame was approaching fast.

I took a deep breath and hit the green button.

He started speaking immediately, the voice disguised. 'Are you alone?'

I wasn't expecting that question, but I didn't miss a beat. 'Yes.'

'Have you got the drive?'

'Yes, I have.'

'Have you looked on it?'

This time I didn't lie. 'I took a quick look.'

'And what's on there?'

'Audio files.'

'Have you listened to them?'

'No. I was going to, but I'm not sure I want to find out what's on them. Sometimes it's best not to know.'

'Very wise. So now it's time for you to deliver it.'

'Not until I've spoken to Kate. I need to know she's still alive.'

'Log on to Tor browser link in fifteen minutes.'

'That's not good enough. I need to speak to her.' I looked at Geeta, and she nodded in encouragement.

'No,' said the kidnapper just as firmly. 'The Tor link. Take it or leave it.'

The moment of truth. Did I capitulate once again or finally stand up to the man who'd tormented me all day? Instinctively, and uncharacteristically, I chose the latter. 'Put her on the phone to me or the deal's off,' I told him. 'Because if you can't do that, I've got no choice but to believe she's dead. And then there's no way in hell you're getting hold of this drive.'

'Then the deal's off,' he said, cutting the line.

I stared at the dead phone, riddled with self-doubt.

'You did the right thing,' said Geeta. 'You've got to stay strong.'

Five minutes passed. Then ten. Still he didn't phone back.

And as I sat in the heavy silence, I had a truly terrifying thought. One that seemed to creep up out of nowhere and strike me right between the eyes.

Was it possible that somehow Kate had set this whole thing up herself, using me as the killer?

But I dismissed the idea just as quickly. She didn't need to do something like that. She could have just told me about her past and I'd have helped her get through it, whatever it took. I was the father of her child, for Christ's sake. I loved her.

More importantly, she loved me.

And yet somewhere deep down in the recesses of my mind, a niggling doubt persisted. Because the person who clearly benefited most from having the master copy of these audio files, which might contain her confession to murder, was Kate.

49

Kate

I could hear at least one person coming through the building in my direction, so I moved fast, knowing that if I was discovered with my blindfold off, I was in real trouble. Feeling around desperately, I found it on the floor and pulled it over my face, then screwed the thermostat back onto the radiator just as he unlocked the door and came inside, shining the light into my face.

I had no idea where the broken cable tie was so I quickly thrust my hands behind my back, hoping he wouldn't check too closely. I was absolutely terrified, thinking that this might be it. The end.

'Hello?' I said into the darkness, my voice cracking.

'We're going to call your fiancé,' said the kidnapper. 'You will speak to him and tell him to do exactly what I order, otherwise you're going to die.'

His voice was still disguised, but he sounded agitated, and I knew that things were coming to a head.

'Please,' I said, my own voice taut with tension. 'I don't want to die.' I knew I was literally talking for my life here and I channelled everything I had into it, appealing to the small chink of humanity I was praying my kidnapper possessed. 'My poor baby ...' Tears welled in my eyes, and I was so carried away I almost rubbed my tummy for effect, before remembering at the last second that my hands were meant to be tied.

'And you won't die if he does what he's told,' said the kidnapper.

'Okay,' I said, blinking away tears.

I heard his finger tapping on the phone screen, and then he leaned down close to me. So close I could have grabbed him. Poked him in the eyes or thrown a punch. Either of which would have been utterly fruitless.

'Remember what I told you,' he said, putting the phone to my ear.

It rang once and then I heard Matt's voice come on the line, sounding scared. 'Hello?'

'Matt,' I said, hugely relieved to hear him. 'It's me.'

'God, honey, I can't believe it's you. Are you all right? Are they treating you well?'

'I'm fine,' I said, not quite stifling a sob. 'I promise. And you? Are you okay?'

'I'm good, don't worry about me. Is the baby okay?'

God, I was going to have to tell him. But not now. He sounded so eager, so desperate. 'Yes, she's fine,' I said quickly, knowing that I had to give him a clue to my whereabouts just in case. 'But it's cold and burnt-out in here.' And then: 'I've been told that you've got to do what the man tells you, or he's going to kill me. But if you do it, he'll let me go.'

'I'll do it. Don't worry, Kate. I'll get you out of there. I'm going to—'

The phone was abruptly pulled away from my ear and Matt's voice cut out as the kidnapper ended the call. I heard him stand back up and put the phone away.

'What the hell did you say that for?' he demanded. 'That you were somewhere cold and burnt-out?'

'I don't know,' I sobbed. 'I didn't mean anything by it.'

He stood there in silence and I cowered, trying to look as subservient as possible.

'If you do exactly what you're told,' he said at last, 'you'll go free. But if you try to manipulate me, or do anything stupid, like try to escape, I'll kill you. Do you understand?'

I nodded, praying that he wouldn't check my bonds too closely. 'I won't, I promise. I just want me and my baby to be safe.'

There was another long silence, and I felt my heart beating in my chest.

Then the door opened and a wave of relief surged through me as he went out, double-locking it behind him.

I waited a full five minutes, just to make sure he'd really gone, before finally removing the blindfold and getting to work on the chain again. Five minutes later, I'd moved it to the end of the pipe, and it fell to the floor with a rattling clank. I was still attached to it, but for the first time I was able to move around freely.

I smiled. There might still have been a locked door between me and freedom, but for the first time I felt real hope.

50

Matt

'That was her,' I said to Geeta, the phone still clutched in my hand. 'Kate. She's alive.'

Geeta frowned. 'How did she sound?'

'Scared. She sounded scared, which isn't like her. She's a tough cookie. But she didn't sound like she'd been harmed, either.' Any suspicions that she might have been involved in setting this thing up had disappeared now. Her fear had been genuine, and I felt a desperate need to get her back.

'Did she give any clue as to what might be going on?' asked Geeta.

'She didn't get a chance to say much,' I said, but then something struck me. 'But she did say that it was cold and burnt-out where she was being held. And I've seen her twice on footage he's shared. Once she was on a stage that looked damaged by smoke. The other time she was chained up in a toilet, and again it looked like the place was damaged.'

'She's giving you a clue. There's no other reason she'd have said that. Tell me more about this stage. What did it look like exactly?'

I tried to picture the room in that initial footage, realising where she was going with this. 'I can't tell you much about it. It was just a stage, lit by two very bright lights, and Kate was standing on it with a noose around her neck and a rope going up towards the ceiling. I couldn't see the ceiling, so it must have been high. That's all I can really remember.'

'That might be enough. If there was a stage with a very high ceiling then she's not being held in any ordinary building.' Geeta's fingers drummed a steady tattoo on the dashboard and she was stroking her chin. You could almost see the cogs whirring behind her eyes. A lot of people over the years had inferred that she'd been promoted because of her colour and sex, but I knew better. The main reason was because she was damned good at what she did.

'What time did you get home last night?'

'About one. Something like that.'

'And what time did you last have contact with her?'

I took out my phone, checked the WhatsApp messages. 'I messaged her when I got to you. That was ten to eight. She messaged back at seven fifty-seven, said "See you later. Have a good evening." Three kisses.'

'Okay. She was taken at some point between eight and one, so that's a fair-sized window. He could have got her quite a distance in that time. Were there any signs of a struggle, or a break-in?'

I shook my head. 'There was nothing out of place. Except obviously a dead woman in our bed.'

'And would the doors to the house have been locked?'

'Not necessarily. The front door locks automatically but

the back door doesn't, and Kate may not have locked it until she went to bed. It's a quiet little village, and we're used to Sri Lanka, where home security really isn't an issue.'

'So he could have walked in and ambushed her. But he'd need to have parked out the front of your house to have got her out and the other body in.'

'It's not overlooked.'

'Even so, it's still a big risk. The point is, there must have been at least two of them involved.'

Before she had a chance to continue, the kidnapper's phone started ringing again.

I picked up immediately, noticing that Geeta had come in close so she could hear what was being said.

'I've done you a favour,' said the voice that had tormented me for close to twenty-four hours now, 'letting you speak to your fiancée like that. Now it's your turn. Do you still have the drive?'

'I do.'

'Describe it. Exactly.'

I looked down at it, sticking out of Geeta's laptop.

'It's black, made of metal, with a white lever that pushes out the plug, and the make's Cruzer.'

'Good. Where are you now?'

I wasn't sure what to say. I had no idea whether he knew about Geeta or not, but if he didn't, I didn't want to put her needlessly at risk. I had to think fast. 'I'm at a cheap hotel in Ealing,' I said, hoping I hadn't hesitated too long. 'Lying low.'

'Get in your car now – the rental one.'

'I think the police are looking for it.'

'They're not that quick off the mark. If you keep a low profile, no one will stop you. Drive north-west out of London on the M40. Come off at Junction 5 and put the postcode SL6 9GG into your navigation system. Pull over at the sign on the road welcoming you to the village of Hedsor. Be there by nine thirty p.m. I'll call you then. Don't be late. And . . .' he paused, 'whatever you do, come alone. If you bring anyone else – *anyone* – Kate dies. Do you understand?'

'I understand. But I want to see her before I hand anything over.'

But I was already talking to a dead phone. Once again the balance of power had shifted. I knew Kate was alive. I had hope. I just had to follow these last instructions. 'Did you hear all that?' I said to Geeta.

I think she must have seen the hope on my face, but her own expression didn't reflect it. 'I'm going to come with you,' she said.

'He said come alone. I've got to do what he says. I can't risk losing her now.'

'Matt, think. They want that drive. It probably contains your fiancée's confession to killing a young woman. That young woman has relatives who want to avenge her, who've already tried to kill Kate once. They're not going to release her. They'll want her dead.'

'What do you want me to do, Geeta?' I said, exasperated. 'Not go? Give up? I've got no choice. She's the mother of my child. I've got to try to get her back. And I've got to hurry. I need to be at this place – wherever the hell it is – in less than an hour, and my car's near your place.'

'Then we need to pick it up right now,' she said, chucking the laptop onto my legs and pulling out of the parking spot. 'You drive. I'll stay in the back. He won't know I'm there. And if you're going somewhere isolated, that's going to be putting you in danger too. You're a loose end, Matt. You know too much. They may want you out of the way. It's worth having some kind of backup.'

She was right. Geeta was about the only person I trusted in the world right now, and even she'd betrayed me once.

'Meanwhile, you can make yourself useful,' she said, nodding at the laptop. 'If the kidnapper wants to meet us in Hedsor, it means he's probably holding Kate not that far away. It'll be somewhere between there and where she was snatched. You need to look for any big building that might have a stage – theatres, hotels, maybe. Somewhere that's been damaged by fire in the last year. Because if we can find out where she's being held, we can turn the tables on this guy.'

I nodded, hoping she was right, because right now time was slipping away all too fast.

51

Kate

I'll be honest. I was petrified when I found out for sure they'd involved Matt in this. This whole thing was nothing to do with him, but at least he was okay. The problem was, I was scared to think what they might be getting him to do, and whether he had the strength to do it.

I loved Matt deeply, but I've never been a hundred per cent sure if he truly loved me, and I've never been able to put my finger on exactly why I doubted him. After all, he'd never shown me anything but kindness and affection. But it struck me when I was there in that cell that I didn't *know* him, and I think this was because he was a far better actor than his career would suggest. In fact, I had no idea where the actor stopped and the individual began. Or even if there was a real Matt underneath, because I'd seen the way he changed his whole persona depending on who he was talking to. He drew people in, made them feel special, and they fell for it. Always. In that respect, he was a perfect hotelier. At first, I was so infatuated with him myself that I didn't notice, but as the months passed and the infatuation turned to something far more dangerous – true love – I found myself feeling peculiarly vulnerable.

I'd never felt vulnerable around David. I was a different person then. Happier. More complete. And it had all been stolen from me.

I'd been riven with grief for David for a long time afterwards, and had never settled in a relationship until I'd met Matt. Even so, it hadn't been a bad life, and I'd built up a solid and successful business through my own hard work. Mum would have been proud of me, I know that.

And then a few weeks ago it had all gone wrong in a way I would never have imagined.

I'd kept in regular contact with Dad over the years – although it had taken me a long time before I'd started calling him that. Our relationship was best described as awkward, which wasn't surprising under the circumstances. But he'd invested in the hotel, made sure I was financially secure, and we both tried hard to make things work. So when he'd called and told me he had inoperable cancer, with only months left to live, I'd flown straight to London to visit him, telling Matt that I was going to the funeral of an old school friend. He'd wanted to come with me but I'd said I'd prefer him to stay and look after the hotel, which hadn't gone down well.

Dad knew about Matt – it was hard to keep anything from him even from five thousand miles away – but when he'd found out that we were engaged, he'd been less pleased than I'd hoped, which was why I hadn't told him about the baby. 'You be careful before you marry him,' he'd said. 'He may well be after you for your money.'

I'd laughed and told him that I didn't have that much money for him to be after.

But Dad hadn't laughed. 'You will have,' he said. 'You're going to inherit the vast bulk of my estate. That's a hell of a lot.'

I'd been shocked. You might think that's ridiculous given that I'd known for many years how rich he was, but I hadn't expected him to leave so much to me. Not after everything that had happened between us. In truth, I'd never given it much thought, because he was still relatively young. Don't get me wrong. The money would be hugely welcome. It meant never having to worry about anything again.

But as any rich person will tell you, money brings problems of its own, and one of my biggest was Dr Piers MacDonald.

I'd started seeing him after Alana's death. I'd been having terrible nightmares in which I'd relive the moment she'd fallen to her death again and again, and always I was unable to help. And with David in prison, and my other friends deserting me after what had happened, as if I was some leper whose very presence put them at risk, my life had begun to fall apart. In the end, things had got so bad that I finally decided to visit a psychiatrist for help.

I saw him for a total of about three months. During that time, I was the most vulnerable I've ever been in my life. I was young and naïve, and because of that I finally and reluctantly gave in to his repeated requests that I undergo hypnotherapy.

But the treatment seemed to work and the nightmares

did fade away, though I was left with a strange feeling that something hadn't been quite right with the sessions. There were parts of them that I couldn't remember, as if I'd been put completely under, and it made me wonder how much I'd revealed about myself. But as time passed and my life took new turns, I largely forgot about Dr Piers MacDonald. It was only after Dad told me about my inheritance that I suddenly thought about him again. Because he was the only person I'd ever completely opened up to, and I wanted to make sure he would keep his promise of client confidentiality.

A few days before I headed back to Sri Lanka, I googled him, which was when I got my first real shock. He'd been struck off, not only for molesting clients but in two cases for blackmailing them too. And he was still alive.

He knew that I was Sir Hugh Roper's illegitimate daughter, and if he found out that Dad was dying, and that we now had a proper relationship, I had little doubt he'd try to blackmail me.

So I made the decision to contact him first, and after some unseemly haggling, we met up in a café the day after Matt and I returned to England. I paid him ten thousand pounds in cash in exchange for all the paper files he had on me, plus the recordings I was certain he'd made of our sessions.

In hindsight it was a very foolish move. I should have left him well alone, and if he had crawled out of the woodwork at some later date, simply brazened it out. I suppose the reason I didn't was because I knew I'd said deeply unflattering things about Alana. After all, I'd hated her by then for the way she'd killed herself like that, right in front of me. How horrible she'd been beforehand. I had no doubt that a lot of vitriol had come out of my mouth, and I may even have suggested that I was glad she was dead, although I don't remember saying that. Such things could easily be subject to misinterpretation, and yes, I was worried that if Dad heard them he might reconsider his decision to leave me so much of his money.

So that was why I agreed to pay MacDonald. Not because I wanted to cover up a crime, but so that I could move on.

Of course, the problem hadn't gone away. I suspected the reason I was here now was due to MacDonald approaching either that vengeful bitch Diana or her feckless son to sell them the information. And I had to assume that if it was one of those two behind it, then they weren't going to let me go.

With the building now empty, I continued my ongoing attempt to escape. There was no way I could get rid of the chain, because it was still padlocked to my leg, but I was able to gather up a lot of the slack and push it into the pocket of the coat my kidnapper had given me. I'd make a noise when I moved, but at least I'd still be able to run.

The problem was the bathroom door. It was a sturdy wooden block that had survived the fire with only the loss of its paintwork. I tried kicking it with my bare feet. That didn't work. It just hurt, and on the fifth attempt – a flying kick from a distance, giving it everything I had – I ended up losing my footing and falling backwards onto the toilet seat, jarring my back.

That was when exhaustion finally set in, coupled with a sense of despondency. The door was far stronger than I'd been expecting, and my captor had clearly put new locks on it. After all I'd achieved, I was still trapped, and would be until he opened the door again.

He'd be coming to kill me then; I was sure of that. It was a terrifying prospect. But I'd faced it before. In fact, I'd almost certainly faced this man before. When he'd murdered the person I'd cared most for in the world.

He hadn't managed to kill me then.

And things were different this time round. I might be cold, hungry and exhausted, but this time I had surprise on my side.

52

Matt

'I've narrowed it down to three places,' said Geeta, who'd taken over the search for locations where Kate might be being held while I drove her in my rental car towards the rendezvous. 'A big country house in Buckinghamshire that was badly damaged by fire two years ago and looks like it still hasn't been demolished. It's fifteen miles by road from where we're meeting him. Then there's a warehouse on an industrial estate in High Wycombe that was gutted in an electrical fire last month. That's about ten miles away, and as far as I can gather, it's still standing. And finally there's a hotel near Windsor that was closed down a year ago and then set alight in an arson attack. That one's the nearest, just eight miles from where we're going.'

We were entering a rural area with woodland on one side and agricultural fields on the other. The traffic had thinned out to nothing, even though it was a Saturday night and still early in the evening. The road here wasn't especially good, and the rain was once again pouring relentlessly down, adding to the huge puddles of water that had formed in the dips.

From her position crouched in the back of the car, Geeta continued tapping away on her laptop. 'Apparently the hotel had what the old website claimed was a large conference facility. I'm looking at an image of it now. The ground floor's really badly damaged but the upstairs still looks relatively intact. And it's well off the beaten track. If I was to choose the most likely location for Kate on the information I've currently got, that's the one I'd go for.'

I looked at my watch: 9.22 p.m. According to the sat nav, my ETA at Hedsor was 9.27. We were going to be early, but not early enough that I could risk a detour to the place that Geeta was talking about. Right then, I was simultaneously exhausted and terrified. I was running on empty and wasn't at all sure that I had the strength or stomach to negotiate with the kidnapper. I just wanted Kate back.

The narrow glow of car headlights appeared in my rear-view mirror some distance behind and I was immediately conscious of the kidnapper's instruction to come alone. 'You need to get right down in the seat, Geeta. If you're seen, you'll blow this whole thing.'

Geeta slid down out of sight as the other car gained on me. My hands felt clammy on the wheel, and I could hear my heart thumping in my chest. It felt like I was having a panic attack. I tried to slow my breathing, remembered that I'd faced worse already today and had somehow come through it. I'd even been something of a hero, taking on a man with a gun. I'd never done anything like that before in my life. I'd fantasised about it plenty of times, taking on the bad guys and bringing them to justice. Especially after the mugging. It was my therapy, acting out scenes where I was mugged, threatened, attacked, time and time again, sometimes by the laughing boys who'd done it in real life, sometimes by others. But in my fantasies, I'd fought back. Beaten and disarmed them. Sometimes kicked and savaged them while they lay on the ground, all my rage coming to the fore. And afterwards, I'd stand there sweating from the intensity of it all, absorbing my small, important, but ultimately fictional victory.

The problem is, a fantasy is so very, very different from the reality. I was driving to an isolated place where I would face a man who'd already killed at least once before, and who would no doubt kill me if he thought it expedient. And that was why I was glad I had Geeta with me.

I told her as much, keeping my eyes fixed on the rear-view mirror. 'But I don't know how we're going to play it. I can't risk you being seen.'

'I know,' she said, shutting the laptop. 'I've been thinking about that. Let's wait to hear what his instructions are, but it should be a straight swap. The drive for her. And it'll be somewhere isolated where you're not going to be disturbed. The thing is, from how you've described this, there's more than one of them, so I can't shadow you. The best we can do is have a phone line open between us. If I hear you're in trouble in any way, I'll start the car, sound the horn and come riding to the rescue. Hopefully that'll scare them off.'

I sat up a little straighter so I could see her in the mirror, crouched down but looking back at me. 'You'd do that for me?'

'I want to know what's going on,' she said, her face hard. 'I've been used here too. And like you said earlier, one day it might make a good book.'

'I'm hoping none of this ever comes out,' I told her.

'Matt, be serious. When you've got Kate back, you're going to have to go to the police. If what you told me is true and MacDonald's death was an accident, then there'll be scope for leniency.'

I knew deep down that what she was telling me was right, but it was hard to take on board. 'Do you think I'll serve time?'

Geeta sighed. 'You can't rule it out. You got rid of a body as well. But I'll stand up for you, and if Kate's story supports yours, then that'll count in your favour.'

I had that niggling feeling again. That there were things happening that I had no idea about, and that nothing was quite as clear-cut as Geeta would have me believe. But I had to push such thoughts aside, because right now I had bigger fish to fry.

The car was coming up fast behind me, and I wondered if it was him – the kidnapper – and whether he meant to take the flash drive from me by force. My hands tightened on the steering wheel. It was woodland on both sides of us now, an easy spot for an ambush. I slowed down as I came to a sharp bend, conscious that the car was right up my tail. I glanced at the dashboard clock: 9.28 p.m. The sat nav was saying that our destination was one minute away, and as I rounded the bend, I saw the lights of houses up ahead.

A car was coming the other way, and I sped up a little,

seeing the sign for the village, with a lay-by just in front of it. This was where the kidnapper had told me to stop. I slowed again, indicating. The car behind didn't. 'We're here,' I said. 'Stay down.'

I pulled in and the car accelerated past, leaving the road empty. I kept the engine running, staring into space, as the clock clicked to 9.30.

And then, right on cue, the phone rang.

53

Matt

I debated putting the phone on loudspeaker, but decided against it in case it made the kidnapper suspicious.

'Are you there yet?' he asked as soon as I answered.

I sat back in the seat and ran my fingers through my hair, conscious of Geeta lying across the back seats, knowing she was perfectly visible to any passer-by if they came close enough. 'Yeah, I'm here,' I said. 'Facing the Welcome to Hedsor sign.'

'There's a turning just up on your left. Can you see it?'

I leaned forward and peered out of the window. There it was. A track running off with no signposts attached. 'I see it.'

'Follow it for approximately two hundred metres. You'll come to a dead end. There's a stream ahead of you partially hidden by trees, and a footbridge going across it. Park the car, then proceed to the middle of the footbridge and wait for my next call. And make sure you're alone.'

'I'm not going to do anything stupid. I just want Kate back. Is she with you?'

'She's not far away. Now go.' He abruptly ended the call.

I pulled out of the lay-by. 'Did you hear any of that?' I whispered to Geeta.

'Enough,' she whispered back. 'I'm going to call your phone now. Answer it, then put it back in your coat pocket. Also, there's a retractable baton under the driver's seat. Put that inside your jacket, just in case someone comes for you. And drop the car keys into the cup holder.'

'Okay,' I whispered. 'I'm not going to speak any more in case anyone's watching.'

The track was dark and narrow. I passed two houses on my left. Both had their lights on and cars outside. It felt strange to be so close to people living their normal lives while mine was being steadily ripped apart. The houses gave way to thick woods on either side. I drove slowly. The track was muddy, and under water in parts, and the car bumped and jarred across it. I could hear my phone vibrating in my jeans pocket and I pulled it out with one hand, pressing answer before dropping it in my coat pocket as per Geeta's instructions. I kept the other hand firmly on the wheel as I rounded a long, shallow bend and found myself in a small parking area surrounded by thick trees.

There were no other cars there and I turned mine round so I was facing back the way I'd come, reversing it onto a footpath running parallel to the unseen river so that it was out of view. I cut the engine and the lights, and sat there for a few moments in near darkness, watching the rain pound persistently on the windscreen, wondering if there was someone hidden in the trees watching me. It was a foul night and I imagined Kate out in it somewhere nearby, cold and wet, while she and the kidnapper waited for me.

'Don't forget the baton and to leave the keys,' whispered Geeta from the back.

I hadn't forgotten, but I was suddenly reluctant to leave the keys behind. Could I entirely trust Geeta? She might even be setting me up right now. My paranoia was suddenly running riot. But I had to trust someone and I'd spent four years of my life with her. I was certain she wouldn't be involved in kidnapping and murder.

Or was I?

I pulled the keys from the ignition, dropping them into the cup holder before leaning forward casually and reaching underneath my seat for the baton.

'Remember,' she hissed. 'Don't give it to them until you've seen her.'

I didn't dare say anything in response, and without even glancing at her, I slipped the baton into the inside pocket of my coat, checked that the flash drive was still there, and stepped out of the car and into the rain.

A strong wind was blowing, but it was surprisingly mild thanks to the thick cloud cover, which also made it very dark. The lights of the village and the houses we'd passed on the way up here were all now completely obscured by the trees.

I took a long look round. A new metal signpost a few feet away told me this place was called Trowbridge Woods, and showed a number of circular walks, but there was nothing and no one moving out here tonight. I should have been feeling hopeful. It was a relief to know that Kate was alive and that in my pocket I had the means of getting her back. But instead I felt a heavy sense of dread as I walked over to the footbridge, keeping my head down to stop the driving rain getting in my eyes.

The footbridge stretched for about twenty yards across a fast-flowing stream that the rain had turned into a raging torrent on the verge of bursting its banks. On the other side, a well-kept path cut through the thick wall of trees and undergrowth, with a picnic area a little further on to the right.

I mounted the bridge, almost losing my footing on the sodden wood, and started walking slowly towards the middle, using the strip of felt running down its centre to keep a steady grip. I looked round as I walked. There was no sign of anyone, and only the steady patter of the rain broke the silence. But I could sense that I was being watched, and I had to resist feeling for the baton.

I stopped in the middle, as instructed, and waited in the blackness, my hand gripping the kidnapper's phone, eyes scanning the dark under cover of my hood.

I waited. One minute passed. Then two. I shivered against the cold. The longer I stood there, the more nervous I became, and I was thankful I had Geeta listening in. I'd been thinking about her a lot these past few hours. She didn't have to do any of this. Not many people had gone out on a limb on my account over the years, and it made me wish then that I'd been a better boyfriend when we'd been together. Now, of course, it was way too late.

The phone vibrated in my hand. It was him.

'I'm here,' I said, wiping the rain from my eyes. 'Where you said.' I looked round but still couldn't see anyone.

'Keep walking,' said the voice. 'When you get to the far end of the bridge, place the drive on the handrail and then keep going. Do not look back.'

'Where is she?' I demanded, loudly enough for Geeta to hear on the open phone line, using all my old acting skills to make myself sound confident. 'I want to see her before I give you anything.'

'She's nearby. Probably only a couple of hundred metres from where you are now.'

'Then let me speak to her.'

'That's not possible, I'm afraid. I'm not with her, but I can tell you that she's bound to a tree with a gag preventing her from speaking and, I suspect, getting very cold and very wet while we're wasting time here. Now, can you see the picnic area ahead? Walk towards it; do not look back at any time or the deal's off. When you get to the first table, you wait. As soon as my associate has picked up the drive and authenticated it, I'll tell you where to find Kate.'

I wanted to argue with him, to hold my ground, but in the end, I'll be honest, I didn't have the balls. If she was hidden out there somewhere tied to a tree, there was no point in me wasting any more time. And if she wasn't . . . that meant Geeta was right and I wasn't going to get her back.

Either way, it was time for this thing to end.

'I'm coming,' I said, starting towards the far end of the bridge. The line immediately went dead again.

At the end of the bridge, I stopped, took a deep breath and removed the drive from my coat, placing it carefully on the handrail, acutely aware of how vulnerable I was out here. There could have been someone creeping up behind me right now. I listened hard but could hear nothing, and knew better than to turn round.

Instead, I kept walking in the direction of the picnic area thirty yards away, quickening my pace, desperate to get this over with. There were four tables, with logs fashioned as stools, set in a rough circle round a mature oak tree. There were also two children's swings in one corner. The place was probably very pretty in summer, but it looked lonely and sinister amongst the bare trees.

I waited by the first table, my back to the bridge, scouring the trees for any sign that Kate was in there somewhere. But still nothing moved. It felt like I was the last person left in the world. I stared at the kidnapper's phone, willing it to ring, but somehow deep down I knew that it wouldn't.

And it didn't.

I waited one minute. Then two. Then three, my frustration building, until finally I swung around and stared back at the bridge.

There was no one there.

I tried to think what to do. Then I heard it. The sound of a car starting and pulling away somewhere further off in the woods, in the opposite direction to where we'd parked. That was when I knew we'd been set up.

Cursing, I turned and ran back the way I'd come, my feet crunching loudly on the gravel track.

As I reached the bridge, I saw that the drive was gone. I kept running, careful to keep to the felt in the middle, shoving the kidnapper's phone back in my pocket and pulling out my own, shoving it to my ear. 'Geeta! Start the car!' I yelled. 'They've double-crossed me.'

But there was no answer, and it took me a couple of seconds to realise that I was shouting into a dead phone. That she was no longer on the other end of it.

I didn't have time to think what that might mean. I just kept running, going flat out now, pulling out the retractable baton as I rounded the line of trees running parallel to the stream and came back into the car park.

In the gloom, I could see that the rental car was still there. Intact and with no one visible inside. Panting from my exertions, I ran over and yanked open the driver's door, opening the baton with a twist of my wrist like Geeta had once shown me.

She wasn't in the back, but her laptop was still there, propped upright in the footwell where she'd been hiding earlier, and the keys were still in the cup holder where I'd dropped them. I immediately grabbed them and shoved them in my pocket.

As I pulled my head back out of the car, I caught movement out of the corner of my eye. I swung round fast, holding the baton, and saw a figure coming out of the trees towards me in the darkness.

It took me a second to realise who it was.

'Geeta? What are you doing? We need to go.'

She didn't say anything. She just kept coming towards me.

That was when I saw that she was staggering, her eyes fixed straight ahead, not focused on me.

And then she simply crumpled to the ground, falling gently onto her side on the asphalt, reaching one hand out in front of her as if to ward me off.

To the day I die I will always remember the way her fingers clenched and unclenched, and how her arm dropped to the ground, and I knew, even from ten feet away, that she was dead. Even so, I ran over and crouched down beside her, which was when I saw the gaping wound in her throat, still pumping out blood onto her top and the ground beside her. Desperately I felt for a pulse, but even though her skin was still warm to the touch, I found nothing.

Her eyes were closed. Her expression neutral. She was gone forever. Just like that. The woman I'd once loved, and who'd gone out of her way to help me, dead because of her kindness.

I fell backwards onto the asphalt and sat there frozen in the rain, so that I hardly heard the sound of a second car starting, just beyond the trees from which Geeta had emerged, accompanied by the faint glow of headlights.

I jumped to my feet, but already the car was pulling away, the headlights disappearing into the night.

I was too late. This whole thing had been a trap and I'd fallen for it. They – whoever they were – had never had any intention of returning Kate to me. They'd set me up. They'd set me up from the very beginning. I'd only ever been a pawn in someone else's game. And now here I was with the dead body of my murdered former lover, and no other suspects around.

The longer I stayed here, the more danger I was in. Not from whoever had killed Geeta, but from the law. I risked being framed for two murders. Possibly more. I had to get out.

I ran back to the car, jumped inside, flung the baton into the back seat and yanked open Geeta's laptop.

I had one lead. It was flimsy. It might well be nothing.

But right now, it was the best I had.

I started the engine and, forcing myself to look away from Geeta's crumpled corpse lying forlornly at the edge of the car park, pulled away in an angry screech of tyres, my hands shaking on the wheel.

54

Sir Hugh Roper

I didn't arrive home until shortly after 9.30 that night. My chauffeur, Jonathan, can testify to that. After asking him to drive me round my old London haunts while I tried to think, I'd got him to stop on the way home at a small family-run Italian place near Hampstead Heath where I'd once been a regular. They still respected me enough to get me a private table in the back, where I'd eaten a dish of tagliolini with Taleggio and black truffle, washed down with a glass of Amarone. It was the first food I'd had all day but it did nothing to ease the intense, stomach-clenching frustration I was feeling.

Nigel Burns was the man I needed to speak to most because he was the only person who might be able to come up with a solution. I'd tried his number three times in the previous hour and was still waiting for a response. He must have looked at his phone by now, which meant he was avoiding me.

A rat deserting a sinking ship. Just like Thomson, who also seemed to have fallen off the face of the earth, which was even more unnerving since he had a quarter of a million reasons to stay on my good side.

As soon as I was through the front door, I got Jonathan to light the fire in the main study, then told him to wait in the living room on the far side of the house in case I needed him again tonight. Although at that point, even I knew that was wishful thinking.

He was barely five minutes gone, and I'd just poured myself a large malt, when I finally heard back from the elusive Thomson.

'Where the fuck have you been?' I demanded, needing someone to take my anger out on. 'I've been trying to get hold of you for hours.'

'I've been arrested,' he said. He sounded more worried than I'd have liked.

'On what charge?'

'Suspicion of affray.'

God, this was all I needed. 'Affray? What the fuck do you mean? What have you been doing?'

'I confronted Walters at a house in Wembley,' he said, keeping his voice down. 'He was there with an associate. There was a fight and I was outnumbered. Someone called the police, and I was arrested nearby.' He paused, lowering his voice still more. 'You'll be pleased to know I got rid of the gun. They haven't found it.'

It immediately occurred to me that this could be a set-up. That this call might be monitored, possibly even by that arsehole Doyle, in exchange for some sort of immunity deal. Well I wasn't going to play along with that. 'I don't know about any gun,' I told him. 'I just want my daughter back. Have you got any further in finding out where she is?'

'No, but I think Walters might be telling the truth. I'm certain he doesn't know where she is. But if you can get me out of here, I'll keep looking. I won't say anything to the police, I promise. They haven't got much on me. But I do need a decent lawyer. They're holding me at Wembley.'

My feeling was that with Obote being either an informant or an undercover police officer, they had a lot more on Thomson than either he knew or was letting on. I also suspected his usefulness to me was now finished, but it was important I got one of my good lawyers down there to monitor what was being said, and if necessary give him an added incentive to keep his mouth shut. 'Leave it with me. I'll have my best person with you in an hour.'

I finished the call and phoned Stransky, my chief lawyer, appraising him of the situation. It might have been late on a Saturday night, but I pay him a very fat retainer, and thankfully he answered straight away and said he'd sort it. It was nice to have someone I could still rely on in these turbulent times.

Finally I sat back in my chair with a long sigh and took a generous gulp of the whisky, a rare fifty-year-old Macallan that would cost you ninety grand a bottle if you bought it today, but which I'd got for less than half that, trying to savour the taste. But it didn't work. It might as well have been some twenty-quid stuff you got in a backstreet pub for all the pleasure it gave me.

I put down the glass and leaned forward over the desk

with my head in my hands, a black gloom overwhelming me. I could have ended it all right then. I had a syringe full of pure morphine in the top right-hand drawer that I was keeping in case things became too much and I wanted to go out on my own terms. I was tempted. Very tempted. At one point I even had my hand on the drawer handle.

But then I heard the sound of tyres on gravel, and headlights lit up the room. Someone had arrived.

Intrigued, I got to my feet and went over to the window, pulling back the curtain.

And frowned when I realised who it was.

55

Kate

I was sitting there shivering under the blanket when I heard a car pulling up outside.

I took a deep breath. This was it. The moment of truth.

In the time he'd been gone, I'd been psyching myself up to fight, because that was going to be my only way out of here. But now that he was back, I felt a cold, wrenching fear.

The front door opened and I heard slow, heavy footsteps coming up the stairs. It was him. There was no doubt about it. I felt completely alone. Like I'd been alone for so much of my life. And that was all thanks to the Roper family. They'd ruined my childhood and destroyed the only chance of happiness I'd ever had when they'd murdered David and left me in a coma. And now their henchman was here to finish the job they'd started so long ago.

Unless I changed the script.

Slowly, quietly, I got to my feet. The chain, bunched up in the coat, made no sound. I gently lifted the lid from the toilet cistern, holding it in both hands like a shield. It was heavy, especially as I was low on energy, but manageable, and the fact that I was only going to have one chance at this focused my mind. I thought of Matt, pictured him smiling, and it gave me renewed strength.

The footsteps stopped outside the door. I hardly dared breathe. Waiting in the darkness, trying not to think about the possibility that in a minute's time I could be dead.

Think positive. Think positive.

I'm going to get this bastard.

The key turned in the lock and the door slowly opened.

I tensed my whole body, standing now only a few feet from the door, terrified at the thought of failure.

And then he was there in the doorway, a silhouetted figure holding a torch in his gloved hand.

Before he had a chance to react, I launched myself at him, raising the cistern lid above my head and slamming it into his face with a howl of exertion and a strength born not only of pure desperation but of anger too, for all the injustices that had ever been done to me, and by God, there'd been too fucking many.

The blow landed hard, sending him sprawling backwards, yelping in pain.

I threw the lid down on his foot, eliciting another yelp as it struck home, and he fell onto his behind, clearly dazed.

I rushed past him, giving him as wide a berth as possible. As I'd suspected, my prison had been an en suite bathroom, and now I was in the adjoining bedroom, which was empty bar a blackened mirror hanging from one wall. I made for the door but barely got two paces before I felt a hand grab my leg and yank me backwards, causing me to lose my footing and fall hard onto the stone floor, jarring my knee. As I looked back, I saw my kidnapper, still prone on the floor himself, reaching for something behind his back.

I didn't hesitate. Lashing out with my free foot, I kicked him in the face – once, twice, three times, bucking like a donkey. Blood was clearly visible behind the balaclava now. I was hurting him, and that gave me strength. His grip on my other foot loosened, and I lashed out with that one too, kicking him again and again until he was driven backwards across the floor and his grasp was weak enough that I was able to break free of it.

'You bitch,' he hissed, no longer making any attempt to disguise his voice. His hand came back into view, clicking open a flick knife with a wicked-looking five-inch blade, lunging at me with it.

Luckily he'd been more than a little dazed by my attack, and his reactions weren't as fast or as accurate as they might otherwise have been, giving me a precious second to roll out of range before scrambling to my feet.

But the chain had fallen out of the coat and now dragged on the floor behind me as I went for the door. Before I could make it out, I felt it tighten as he grabbed it and started pulling me backwards. He was already up on one knee, the knife firmly clutched in his gloved hand, the chain in the other, as he prepared to get to his feet and drag me back into his grip.

Five feet separated me from the tip of the blade and certain death. But I wasn't giving up now, and as he tugged me towards him, I darted to one side, taking the last of the chain's slack with me, and pulled the mirror from the wall, hurling it straight at him.

With the knife in one hand and the chain in the other, there was no way for him to deflect it, so he let go of the chain and used his arm to fend off the blow. I'd thrown it so hard that the glass shattered, sending shards in every direction.

I pulled the chain back towards me, throwing it over one shoulder, and charged through the open door so fast I banged my shoulder against the opposite wall in the process. Spotting a thin, blade-sized shard of glass on the floor that had somehow managed to fly out of the room, I quickly picked it up, knowing that I needed a weapon.

'Get back here or I'll kill you!' screamed the kidnapper as he clambered to his feet, real fury in his voice.

But I wasn't stopping for anything as I took off up the corridor, guided by a single dim ceiling light that bathed everything in an eerie unnatural glow. My feet clattered on the bare concrete of the floor, the chain rattling noisily and making it difficult to run properly.

The corridor was short – no more than ten yards long – with numbered rooms on the left and right, confirming that I was being held in an abandoned hotel. As I reached the end, I stole a glance over my shoulder and saw him come stumbling out of the bedroom door, one hand clutching at his face but the knife still clearly visible in the other.

Almost immediately, he started running after me, which was when I noticed for the first time how tall and broad he was. And even injured, he was faster than me.

I had a choice. Turn left or right. I slowed a moment, looking both ways, remembering that when he'd taken me for the lie detector test we'd gone right, and that, from my bathroom cell, it had sounded like the front door to the building was on the left. So I turned left and ran through the gloom. The corridor here wasn't lit and I was running straight into darkness, with no idea whether I was heading towards the exit or not. I let out a little slack from the chain as it was impeding my left side, but it was too much, and I stumbled, almost falling over it.

I knew then that I couldn't outrun him. He'd catch me. I had to hide. Quickly.

A door ahead on my right was slightly ajar, and I darted inside, closing it quietly behind me, hoping it would automatically lock. It didn't. I searched for a door chain in the darkness and couldn't find one. I tried to stop myself from panicking, unsure whether or not he'd seen me come in.

I could hear his footsteps, running then slowing. Then stopping. I heard the door of the room next to mine open.

Slowly, very slowly, knowing he'd be coming in here next, I slipped the chain back over my shoulder and crept into the bathroom, using touch as much as sight in the near-total darkness.

The door to the next room closed.

'I know you're in here somewhere,' he called from the corridor, almost directly on the other side of the wall. 'I'm not going to hurt you. I came here to let you go. If you come out, I'll take you to your fiancé. He's waiting for you.'

It was the first time I'd properly heard his voice. His

311

accent was reasonably educated, and he sounded older than I expected, possibly in his fifties. Ordinary, but with a degree of confidence that suggested he'd been successful in life. But there was also an edge to it, an anger that he was trying hard to suppress, and I knew that if I went out there, he'd kill me. There was no way he was letting me go. I might not have seen his face but I knew things about him. His height, his build. And, of course, his voice. To release me now would be suicide, and this man was too professional to take unnecessary risks.

The layout inside the bathroom was similar to the one I'd been kept in, with a bathtub and shower screen, which I knew would provide no cover. I closed the door as quietly as I could and stood there in the darkness.

Which was when I heard him stop in the corridor just outside the bedroom door and slowly open it.

He was coming in here, and I was trapped.

56

Matt

I had to make a decision, and my guess was that the most likely place Kate was being held was the burnt-out hotel near Windsor. I drove like a crazy man to get there, and as soon as I saw the place, I was certain it was the one. It was by far the closest to the rendezvous point and had the necessary privacy.

The building itself was set back behind a screen of trees at the end of a short access road, with grounds large enough that there were no neighbours within a hundred and fifty metres. There was a high padlocked gate at the entrance with a Keep Out sign on it, surrounded by tall temporary fencing to keep out trespassers.

I didn't hang about. One of the very few advantages of being a fugitive is that you get to break the law with impunity. With no one on the road behind me, I simply turned sharply and drove straight at the gates, the power of the impact smashing one of them from its hinges.

I drove rapidly down the access road, headlights on, making no effort to hide my approach, and a few seconds later the trees gave way to a car park in front of a large, bland modern building three storeys high, boarded up and partly damaged by fire. It was impossible to tell whether there was light inside because of the boards, but there was another car already in the car park – a Land Rover Discovery with dirty number plates – so someone else was obviously there. I pulled up beside it, turning the rental car around in case I had to make a quick getaway.

I was out of the car fast, baton in hand, going straight to the Land Rover and putting my hand on the bonnet. It was warm to the touch. This was the kidnapper's car. He'd driven out of here and murdered Geeta, and now he was back. That was my theory. I had no actual rescue plan, and I was about to enter an abandoned building, having announced my presence, to confront a murderer who had the element of surprise in his favour.

But I was less scared than I'd expected. Perhaps it was because I'd been through so much. Perhaps it was anger over Geeta, who'd died simply because she'd been brave and kind enough to help me. Or simply a father's desperation to do whatever it took to protect his unborn child.

Anyway, I didn't hesitate but went straight over to the glass doors that at one point would have led through to the hotel's reception. This part of the building was the least damaged, and I peered inside into a dark foyer, still covered in cheap carpet. From somewhere upstairs a dim light glowed.

I tried the door and it opened with a gentle whine. Knowing this could be a trap, I kicked it all the way open, waited a few seconds, then stepped inside, swinging the baton, finally ready to fight.

I stopped, took a deep breath, smelling the stale smoke, my eyes becoming accustomed to the gloom. I couldn't hear anything. Nothing at all.

There was a staircase leading up towards the dull light. If anyone was here, that was where they'd be. I still couldn't understand why I was being set up like this. And why they couldn't just let Kate go. Or indeed, even why they were still here. They'd got what they needed. Why not just disappear? This whole thing just didn't feel right. Why were audiotapes of sessions Kate had had with a psychiatrist eighteen years ago so important? And to whom? That was the thought that nagged me, because if what I'd heard was true, Kate – the woman I thought I knew – had the most obvious motive for keeping them secret. Which could only mean that she'd set this whole thing up herself.

All these thoughts flooded through my mind in a matter of seconds, and then, just as I put my foot on the first step, knowing that the answer to the puzzle lay somewhere upstairs, I heard it.

A woman's high-pitched scream.

57

Kate

The kidnapper's torch beam was visible through the glass panel at the top of the bathroom door. He was just feet away.

As quietly as possible, I climbed into the bathtub and crouched down behind the screen so I was at least partially obscured. My heart was thumping in my chest, the fear almost making me whimper, because I didn't think I'd have the strength to take him on again. And now he'd stopped right outside the bathroom door, and I was sure he had realised that the fact it was shut meant I had to be in there.

The door opened, inch by interminable inch, and I held my breath as his shadow appeared in the doorway, illuminated by the torchlight.

A vision hit me then. A memory from that horrendous afternoon sixteen years before, when I'd lost David. Running through the cottage, a figure in black chasing me, just like I'd been chased tonight. Getting closer all the time. And the terror. God, the pure terror I'd felt then, and was feeling again.

The torch beam shone through into the bathroom, easily

visible through the frosted Perspex of the screen, and I knew that he'd see me at any moment.

I wanted to believe his lies. I wanted to believe that he wouldn't kill me. But something deep inside told me with total certainty that this was the man who'd murdered David and put me into a coma from which sometimes – just sometimes – I wished I'd never emerged.

He was standing just outside the bathroom door. I couldn't hold my breath much longer. My grip on the piece of glass tightened, and with surprise I realised my hand was hurting. I looked down and saw blood pooling in the palm. I felt sick. Sick and exhausted and on the verge of a panic attack.

That was when he stepped inside. I could see his silhouette behind the torch beam. The knife in his hand. He turned the torch my way. I felt it illuminate me even though I was crouched down.

A drop of blood landed in the bath with a loud splat.

The beam lowered until it was shining right in my face.

'There you are,' he said gently, his knife glinting in the torchlight.

He took a step towards me and I tensed.

And then we both heard it. The sound of a car pulling up outside. He inclined his head a little.

Everything seemed to freeze in time. He didn't move. Neither did I. And then I heard the door being kicked open with a loud bang downstairs.

The kidnapper cursed under his breath, turning his body towards the sound, and I knew this was my only chance.

With a loud, blood-curdling scream, I lurched upwards and threw all my weight into the shower screen, sending it flying out of the tub and into the kidnapper.

As he stepped back and batted it away, I dived at him, driving the glass into the first part of flesh I could find, skewering him in the upper arm of his knife hand, my momentum making me bounce off him and away, thank God, from his blade.

I landed hard on my side against the bathroom door, with the chain hanging loose beside me. I looked up to see him standing above me, but he was unsteady on his feet, the glass embedded almost to the hilt in his arm, the knife hanging loosely in his hand. He was clutching at the wound with his other hand, growling with pain.

The advantage was with me and I made full use of it, driving my stronger right foot into his knee and sending him staggering backwards. The next second I was on my feet, but I didn't run. As he came forward again, swapping the knife into his other hand, I launched a kick that struck him straight between the legs.

This time he bent double and fell back onto the toilet seat, dropping the knife. I rushed forward and grabbed it but as I picked it up, he lunged at me, and that was when pure instinct kicked in. I drove the knife into his chest, pulling it out and stabbing him again and again, ignoring the strange gasping noise he made, and the slick, wet sound of the blade ripping through flesh, stopping only when he toppled sideways off the toilet seat and collapsed to the floor.

For a long second I simply stood there looking down

at him, getting my breath back. I let the knife drop to the floor with a loud clatter, knowing that this man was no longer a threat to me. He was dead. I'd killed him. It was a strange feeling. A part of me felt disgusted, but there was also a grim satisfaction at what I'd done. A man had held me against my will and had planned to kill me, and yet somehow I'd vanquished him.

Finally I moved, picking up the torch and shining it down on his face. I needed to know who he was and who he worked for.

Reaching down, I pulled the balaclava from his head and flung it to one side, revealing the bruised, partly bloodied profile of a craggy-faced man with a strong jaw, and thinning grey-flecked hair in a widow's peak. As I'd suspected, he was aged somewhere at the tail end of his fifties.

I experienced a hard mental jolt. Something about this man was definitely familiar. I'd seen him before. A long time ago. Another vision tore across my mind. Trying to get out of the upstairs cottage window on that sunny afternoon, desperate to escape, and then a struggle. The man chasing me, grabbing hold of my arm and yanking me round so that I was staring straight at him.

I closed my eyes, tried to picture him as he had been then, not sure how much was memory and how much the suggestive power of the mind. But as I opened my eyes again, I was sure that the man who'd come for us that day, who'd destroyed everything, was the same one I was looking at. And I felt a rage that had me shaking as I contemplated the terrible injustice of it all.

That was when I heard footsteps coming hard up the stairs. Was this the other kidnapper? I wasn't sure that I had it in me to fight again, but then I heard a voice call out my name from somewhere down the corridor, and I almost wept with relief.

It was Matt.

58

Matt

I sprinted up the stairs. I could hear a commotion further up, banging and crashing, but no more screams. As I reached the second floor, it suddenly stopped. Dead.

So did I. The noise had been coming from the floor I was on, and the corridor running off to my right was the only one lit by dim overhead lights.

I listened but couldn't hear anything. But that scream? I was sure it was Kate.

I made a decision. My grip tight on the baton, I called her name.

There was a long pause. If she was dead, I was just giving away my position. But if Kate was dead, then I no longer cared anyway.

But then I heard her call back from somewhere down the corridor, the fear still in her voice. 'Matt? Is that you?'

Relief flooded through me and I ran towards her voice. 'It's me, honey. I'm coming for you. Are you okay?'

And then a door opened just in front of me and I automatically jumped back.

It was hard to believe that the wild-eyed woman covered in blood and with a chain round her ankle was Kate, and for a moment we both just stared at each other. Blood was spattered all over her, but the only place she looked like she'd been cut was her hand. More blood dripped from an unseen wound onto the carpet, but she didn't seem to notice.

I dropped the baton and pulled her to me, holding her tightly, stroking her hair. 'It's all right. You're safe now.' I felt so blessed that I'd got her back, and my hand drifted down to her tummy, stroking it gently, hoping our child was safe.

She buried her head in my shoulder, taking a deep breath. 'Oh God, I'm so glad you're here. I thought he was going to kill me.'

'Where is he now?' I asked her.

'In there.' She motioned with her head towards the door from which she'd emerged. 'The bathroom. We had a fight.' She paused. 'He's dead.'

I was shocked but tried not to show it. 'Are you hurt?'

'Just my hand.' She showed me her open palm. There was a deep gash that was still leaking blood.

I didn't have anything to bandage it with, so I pulled off one of my socks and wrapped it round in a makeshift tourniquet.

'Thank you,' she whispered, smiling up at me, a look that always made me melt, even if it was diluted somewhat by all the blood on her face. 'How did you find me?'

'It's a long story,' I whispered, not wanting to talk about it yet, even though I would have to soon. 'We need to get you out of here. You're freezing.'

'Can you do something for me first?'

'Of course,' I said. 'What is it?'

'The kidnapper. I need to know who he is. He's probably got ID and a phone. It'll be the key to the whole thing. Will you come with me to search him?'

'Shouldn't we leave it to the police?' I said, not liking the sound of that at all.

'I know it sounds strange, but I need to know if my father or one of his family are behind this. There's a lot I haven't told you.'

'I know,' I said, nodding. 'And I wish you had. I've had to find out a lot for myself today.'

'I'm sorry. I'll make it up to you. But I need to know who this bastard was.'

I was desperate to get out of there, especially as I knew there was more than one person involved in this, but, like Kate, I also wanted to find out who had been tormenting me these past twenty-four hours. And I wanted to see if he was in possession of the flash drive I'd left at the bridge. 'Okay. Let's go,' I said.

She went back inside the room and I followed, switching on the torch app on my phone even though there was a beam of light coming from somewhere inside.

'He's in there,' said Kate, motioning towards the bathroom. 'If you don't mind, I'll wait here. Can you see if you can find the keys to this chain?' She rattled her ankle.

To be honest, the last thing on earth I wanted to do was rifle through the pockets of a still-warm corpse for the second time that day, like some kind of latter-day grave robber, but I didn't want to look cowardly in front of Kate either, so, taking a deep breath, I stepped inside.

He was in the bathroom just as she'd said, lying on his back, one arm half draped over the toilet seat, his head almost touching the back wall. I shone the light on him. He was a hard-looking middle-aged man, pale in death, with a cut on his forehead and bruising on his face. But even so, I recognised him as the man Laura had photographed earlier at the rendezvous, receiving the flash drive from Piers MacDonald. The same man who'd hired Geeta to set me up.

But why had this man wanted the master copy of the flash drive so badly? It still didn't make sense.

I shone the torch round the room, seeing evidence of a violent struggle. The shower screen had been ripped from its hinges and now covered much of the floor. It was splattered with blood, as were the wall tiles and the floor where the body lay. A torch and balaclava lay close to the corpse.

I turned off the torch app on the phone, not wanting to look at him, then crouched down and felt first inside his jacket pockets, finding nothing, then in his jeans, pulling out a mobile phone, a set of keys, and a money clip containing some notes. But no identifying documents.

And no flash drive.

I searched the body again. I even resorted to switching the phone torch back on and checking round him, just in case I'd missed something. Only when I was certain that I hadn't did I finally get back to my feet and leave the room, eager to escape the sickly smell of mildew and death.

Kate was standing where I'd left her. She looked calmer

now, although she was shivering. I asked her if she was okay and she told me that she was. 'Just hungry and thirsty and tired, that's all. Did you find out who he was?'

I shook my head. 'There's no ID on him. Just some cash, keys and a phone.' I handed her the keys, and she knelt down and tried each of them in the padlock holding the chain to her ankle until she found the right one. I thought again about the flash drive. 'Has this man been here with you the whole time?' I asked her.

She shook her head. 'No. He went out about an hour ago and he only just came back.'

'And you didn't search the body?'

Again she shook her head. 'I told you, no. This just happened. Why do you ask?'

'I was made to deliver a flash drive to him in return for your life. But it's not here.'

She looked at me. 'Really? What was on it?' It sounded like a genuine question, as though she had no idea of the contents.

I didn't want to get into the details of what I'd discovered about her today. At least not until we were out of here. So I told her I didn't know.

But the cloud of suspicion that had been lurking at the back of my mind was beginning to get stronger. Only one person in the world benefited from this flash drive being out of circulation, and that was Kate. But surely she wouldn't have searched the kidnapper for it, because how would she even have known of its existence, let alone the fact that he'd be carrying it?

I was becoming paranoid and I needed to calm down. I'd got Kate back. That was the most important thing.

'There's at least one other person involved,' she said, throwing off the chain. 'Two people snatched me and I heard him on the phone to someone while he was here. Maybe he'd already given it to them.' She didn't seem worried about either the drive or its contents, which made me question why she'd paid a blackmailer for all her psychiatric notes.

'Yeah, maybe that's what happened,' I said, although I wasn't convinced. I pulled out the phone I'd taken from the kidnapper's body and pressed the home button. The phone was an older Samsung and password-protected. 'It's locked, but I can see three missed calls here from the same number,' I told her.

She asked to look, and I handed her the phone, wondering whether it was worth trying to break into it like Geeta had with MacDonald's phone.

Kate was staring at the screen, an uncertain expression on her face.

'What is it?' I asked.

She took a deep breath. 'The number showing up on here. I recognise it. It belongs to my father.'

59

Sir Hugh Roper

'What a pleasant surprise,' I said through the intercom on my study desk. 'Twice in one day.'

Diana glared sourly up at the security camera above the front door. She was wrapped up in a different coat from the one she'd been wearing earlier, and it looked like her hair must have been glued in place because the wind was doing nothing to mess it up. 'Let me in,' she demanded.

'I'm in the study,' I said, knowing that whatever she wanted wasn't going to be good, but at least her presence provided a distraction from my gloom. I pressed the buzzer, then settled back in my seat and waited.

Five seconds later, she stormed into the room, threw her handbag down on a chair and faced me with her back to the fire.

'So,' she snapped, 'you went to see Tom, after all these years, and rather than seek a reconciliation with him in these your last weeks on earth, you effectively accused your own son of having something to do with that bitch's disappearance.' Her words had the hint of a slur in them, as if she'd fortified herself for this confrontation with a few stiff drinks, but she still stood ramrod straight, bristling with energy.

I looked at her and remembered the woman I'd fallen in love with; the intensity of our passion; the triumph of starting a young family together and giving them everything I'd never had. And I felt a terrible weariness as I finally realised the part I'd played in destroying it all.

'I'm sorry,' I said, words that had so rarely come out of my mouth over the years. 'To you and to him. I didn't want it to come to this.'

She looked surprised, but of course she'd never heard me apologise for anything before, and her expression softened a little. 'You need to apologise to Tom. Make amends with him.'

I took a sip of the whisky. 'I will, if either you or he tells me where Kate is.'

'We don't know, Hugh. Can't you get that into your thick head?'

We glared at each other and again I felt a huge weariness. What if Diana was telling the truth and it was nothing to do with them? But it had to be. There were no other suspects. It was time to take a different tack. 'I think it's too late for us to make amends, but I am prepared to leave him something in my will.'

'How much is something?' she asked, a glint of interest in her eyes.

'I'm prepared to leave him ten per cent of everything,' I said. Which was a lie. I wasn't going to leave him a damn grain, but if Diana and Tom – both people who were very interested in money – were keeping Kate somewhere, this might make them think twice about having her killed.

'Ten per cent?' Her lip curled as she spoke.

'It's a lot of money, Diana. More than he deserves.'

Her expression hardened again. 'What? And the bitch who killed our poor Alana *does* deserve it?'

'How many times do I have to tell you, Alana's death was an accident.'

'No, Hugh. It wasn't.'

There was a firmness to her tone I didn't like. 'How could you possibly know that?'

'Alana wouldn't have slipped and fallen. Even drunk. She never went close to the edge of that roof garden because she was scared of heights. But you wouldn't know that, would you? Because you never spent any time with her.'

'You never said that before.'

'Of course I did. More than once. But you weren't listening. You never did.'

'Is that why you tried to have Kate killed?'

'I told you. It wasn't me who tried to have her killed.'

'Well I know I didn't do it.'

'And I know *I* didn't do it,' she said.

We were at an impasse. I hadn't been responsible for the attack on Kate and Griffiths, so it had to be Diana. And yet once again she was refusing to admit it, making me realise this whole conversation was pointless.

I sighed and finished the last of the Macallan, while she sat down heavily in the chair opposite me, suddenly looking tired.

We were silent for a few moments, neither of us sure what to say.

'Do you mind if I have a drink?' she asked.

'Help yourself,' I said, concluding that the drunker she got, the more likely her tongue was to loosen, and while she went to pour herself one, I put in yet another call to Burns. If he didn't pick up, then this would be the last time I ever used his services, and I'd sue him for all the money I'd paid him for his fucking half-arsed consultancy.

But this time he did answer, and I was just in the midst of demanding where the hell he'd been when the voice at the other end spoke for the first time.

'Dad? Why are you calling this number?'

60

DCI Cameron Doyle

You see, the big problem I've got with this whole sorry mess is that nothing's cut and dried. Hard evidence is scarce. Yes, I've got suspects admitting to killings that we know happened, but it's either self-defence, in Kate's case, or an accident, in Matt Walters'. No one's confessing to being the bad guy, which I know is not uncommon in murder cases, but there are no independent witnesses to state otherwise. Geeta Anand is dead, as is Piers MacDonald. MacDonald's girlfriend, Laura Walton, the woman who reported his murder, has disappeared off the face of the earth.

Yes, we've got Clint Thomson in custody, although at this juncture I think it's worth pointing out that his real name is Brian. He changed it to Clint in honour of Mr Eastwood, which just goes to prove he's something of a lughead. However, Clint isn't actually telling us anything. He got himself heavily lawyered up, courtesy of his boss, and has been giving the classic 'no comment' response to every question he's been asked. In reality, we haven't got much on him. He wasn't carrying a gun when he was arrested, and we can't use Obote's testimony against him because it would be thrown out of court as soon as it became clear that an undercover police officer had stood by while a civilian was threatened with a firearm. So he's probably going to walk.

Which leaves me relying on the testimony of my three suspects to piece everything together, and as I've told you before, I think they're all lying to varying degrees, leaving me no further forward as to who was behind this thing.

But it seems Matt Walters has his own suspicions. He thinks there was something off about his fiancée when he came riding to her rescue, and it's time to exploit this. So I come right out and say it. 'Do you think Kate set up the kidnap herself, Matt? And used you as a pawn?'

'No way,' he says straight away, an expression of utter shock on his face, although something tells me he's trying just a little bit too hard. 'I don't believe that,' he continues. 'I told you, she was in a terrible state when I found her. There's no way that was an act, and I ought to know.'

From what I hear about Matt Walters' acting abilities, that may not be the best recommendation, but I let it go. It's interesting that, unlike most people in a loving relationship, he doesn't add that Kate would never use him like that.

It's DS Tania Wild who speaks next. 'Logistically it's possible though, isn't it, Matt, that the man Kate alleges was her kidnapper, Nigel Burns, could have been her accomplice. He could have tied her up and made it look as if she'd been held against her will. It wouldn't have been hard. Obviously, too, she'd have a motive to get rid of him, wouldn't she? To make sure no one found out about her plan. It would explain the missing flash drive you allegedly left at the bridge in Hedsor, and which still hasn't turned up.' Tania speaks softly, reasonably, as if what she's saying is the most obvious explanation.

Walters, though, looks at her aghast. 'No way. Why would she even do that? She didn't need to.'

'Well,' I say, joining the conversation, 'you said yourself that Kate had a motive for getting rid of all the copies of the drive. And she'd garner a huge amount of sympathy as a kidnap victim.' I'm not sure I believe any of this, but it's important that it's not discounted either. I need to make sure that Walters is telling us the whole truth.

'I don't buy it,' he says, firmly, but once again there's still a doubt in his voice that he can't quite hide. He might not accept this theory, but he's not wholeheartedly dismissing it either.

Tania picks up on this too. 'Don't try to protect Kate, Matt, because let me tell you, she's not protecting you.'

He knows this. You can see it in his face. His bottom lip actually quivers and I think he might cry. He takes a deep breath, composes himself and looks at us both in turn. 'She's the mother of my baby,' he says.

I let Tania give him the bad news, which she delivers without looking at me for permission, in a voice that's sympathetic but with just the barest hint of glee. 'She's not pregnant, Matt.'

His whole body jolts when he hears this, like the chair's just given him an electric shock. This is definitely news to him. Not even Ben Kingsley could pull that one off as an act, and Matt Walters is no Ben Kingsley. 'What? I . . .' He keeps looking at us both, his mouth opening and shutting like a fish, and then replies: 'I don't believe you.'

'I'm sorry, Matt, it's true,' I tell him, meeting his eye. 'We're not allowed to lie about something like this in an interview.' Which isn't entirely true, but he doesn't need to know that. He just needs to believe us.

Tania gives him a sympathetic smile. 'Kate has admitted that she was pregnant but that she lost the baby over a week ago, before you returned to England.'

We let the ramifications of this settle in. If Kate could lie to him about this, she could lie to him about anything.

He puts his head in his hands so that his face is covered, and I wonder if he's crying. When he takes them away again, I see there are tears in his eyes but that he's determined not to break down in front of us, and I admire him for that.

'So why don't you tell us what happened at Roper's house, Matt?' I say. 'The truth.'

61

Matt

I wanted to go straight to the police after I'd got Kate away from the abandoned hotel, but she insisted on going home first to shower and change, and stupidly, I didn't argue. In the end, I guess I wanted to put off handing myself in as well, since I knew the chances were I'd be held in custody, potentially indefinitely.

But once Kate was cleaned up and in fresh clothes, she said she still had things to do before we alerted the authorities. 'I have to see my father,' she told me. 'Right now.'

Her tone was terse, angry, and I remember thinking that this woman seemed very different to the one I'd left at home the night before.

'Are you sure that's a wise thing to do? If your father was in contact with the kidnapper then he may have been behind the whole thing.' Although this did beg the question of why he had sent that psychopath with a gun after me. But either way, I didn't think it was a good idea. Especially as I felt sure that Roper had been the one who'd hired Geeta to set me up, and the last thing I needed was that coming out.

But Kate wasn't having it. She was insistent. And worse, she wanted me to come with her. 'If he's behind it, he won't hurt me, not now. Not if I confront him. But I have to see him face to face and find out what he knows.'

'But what about the baby? You need to get checked over.'

'The baby's fine, Matt. And this isn't going to take long.'

I knew there was no point in arguing – Kate wasn't the type to back down when she'd made her mind up about something – so I agreed to drive her there, knowing she was too traumatised to go alone. I just hoped that the business with Geeta didn't come out.

The drive to Sir Hugh Roper's house took just over twenty minutes. On the way there, we finally talked. She asked what had happened to me in the previous twenty-four hours. In truth, with my bruised and bloodied face, it looked like I'd gone ten rounds in the ring, and I was surprised – and maybe a little disappointed too – that it had taken her this long to ask the question.

I gave her a blow-by-blow account of the worst day of my life, leaving out none of the details. Except Geeta. I made no mention of her. That would come out eventually, but I didn't want to get into a discussion about her now.

'Oh God, Matt, that's terrible,' Kate said when I'd finished. 'We'll get you a good lawyer, I promise. You'll beat any charges.'

'I hope so,' I said, although somehow I doubted it. 'And now it's your turn to talk. I think after everything that's happened, and the fact that I'm now wanted for murder through no fault of my own, I deserve to know about you. Your real story.'

So she told me. About her childhood, growing up poor in a single-parent family. Losing her mum at sixteen, finding out the real identity of her father, his rejection of her, and her attempt to connect with him through his other daughter. Alana's death when Kate had told her the two of them were sisters, and the guilt she'd felt as a result, leading her to make the fateful visit to Piers MacDonald for therapy. And then finally the murder of her boyfriend and the attempt on her own life.

I could tell it was hard for her to open up, and when she'd finished talking, I felt a great surge of emotion. I truly loved this woman and I remember feeling appalled that I could ever have suspected her of being involved.

As the car finally fell silent, a phone started ringing. We both looked round to see where it was coming from, then Kate pulled the kidnapper's phone from her jeans pocket. She looked at me. 'It's my father.'

'You'd better take it, I guess,' I said, although I wasn't sure it was a good idea to give him advance warning that we were on our way to his house.

Kate pressed the green button, and a burst of invective came down the line.

'Dad?' she said, putting the phone on loudspeaker. 'Why are you calling this number?'

'Kate, is that you?' He sounded genuinely shocked. 'Are you safe? Where are you?'

'We're about to pull into your driveway,' she answered,

her voice hardening. 'I need some answers. Like why are you calling the phone of the man who kidnapped me?'

'Nigel? He was behind this?' Again he sounded incredulous. 'It was nothing to do with me, Kate, I promise you. Nigel Burns was my head of security for thirty years. I was asking him to find you.'

Kate took a deep breath. 'We'll be with you in a few minutes,' she said, and ended the call.

'Do you think your father really is behind this?' I asked, as she directed me into a partially hidden driveway with a gatehouse and a grand stone arch enclosing two huge wrought-iron gates.

She screwed her face up in concentration. 'I don't think so. If it was him, I can't understand why he'd do it now. If he genuinely thought I had anything to do with Alana's death, why not do it before, or at the very least make sure I didn't inherit?'

And that was the issue. None of the scenarios made sense. 'Whoever's behind this wants proof that you killed Alana,' I said, 'but they don't want that proof being made public. Otherwise, why make me chase round after the flash drive that MacDonald gave to his girlfriend if they already had the information they needed? And more to the point, why have me kill him after he'd delivered the drive? If he really did have information that you'd killed Alana, then surely they'd want to keep him alive.'

'Jesus, Matt, I don't know,' she said, sighing. 'All I know is that I was kidnapped by the man who almost killed me sixteen years ago, and who was obsessed with finding out whether I killed Alana, to the point where he made me take a lie detector test. And do you know what? I didn't kill her, and nothing in those notes, or on that drive, is going to say otherwise. And before you ask, the reason I paid that bastard MacDonald for my notes, and the illegally made audiotapes of our sessions, was because I didn't want anyone else gaining access to them. They were private.'

'Look, I believe you, honey,' I said hurriedly. 'I really do.'

She seemed to calm down, sitting back in the seat and taking a couple of deep breaths as we drove up the long, straight driveway, through perfectly manicured lawns that led up to a vast country house straight out of *Downton Abbey*. There were plenty of lights on inside and three cars parked in the huge turning circle directly outside the imposing front door.

I turned the rental car round and parked a few yards away from them, facing the exit, before cutting the engine and looking at Kate. 'Are you sure about this?'

She nodded, and we looked at each other for several seconds. Then she leaned over and kissed me on the lips. It felt good. I wanted the kiss to last. I wanted to hold her properly again.

But she was already getting out of the car.

I opened my door and jumped out after her. By that point I'd faced so much danger that the thought of going inside filled me more with curiosity than fear. I needed to find out what was really going on, and figured that entering the lion's den was going to be the best way.

'Okay,' I said, catching her up. 'But I'm going to record

everything on my phone. I need all the evidence I can to get me out of this.'

'You haven't done anything wrong, Matt. We'll clear your name, don't worry.'

But there was something brusque in her tone that would have bothered me if I'd had more time to think about it. Instead, I followed her up the steps to the front door, standing behind her as she banged the old-fashioned brass knocker and turning on the record function on my phone.

Sir Hugh Roper's voice came over the intercom, telling her that he was in the study, and the front door buzzed and opened.

Kate led the way into a grand entrance hall with a massive chandelier dominating the ceiling. It was clear she knew the place well, because she went straight to a door on the right, gave a cursory knock and opened it. Sir Hugh Roper was standing there waiting for her. I recognised him instantly, although he looked older and frailer than he did in his pictures, and with a noticeable stoop. But there was no disguising the relief on his face at the sight of his daughter.

He immediately took her in his arms and buried his head in her shoulder. 'Are you okay, my darling?' he asked. 'I thought you were dead.'

Kate was holding him just as tightly, giving me an unwelcome pang of jealousy, although if I was going to be the beneficiary of all his money, perhaps I'd be making a supreme effort too.

Finally they broke off the hug, and with a hostile glance over his shoulder at me, which instantly confirmed that he'd been the one who'd hired Geeta, Roper moved out of the way.

The study was enormous, the size of my old London apartment. A fireplace with a blazing hearth took up half a wall, giving the place a warm, cosy feeling that was immediately undermined by the woman standing beside the mahogany desk glaring at us.

I guessed this was Roper's first wife, Diana, and she was an altogether more formidable prospect than him. A short, stern woman dressed younger than her years in jeans, leather jacket and heeled ankle boots, with subtle touches of plastic surgery about her face, she had that naturally hard look of someone you wouldn't want to cross. And from the expression on her face it was obvious, if I hadn't known it already, that Kate had crossed her very badly indeed.

'What the hell is *she* doing here?' she hissed furiously.

'She's my daughter, Diana,' Roper snapped back.

Kate glared back at the other woman with the same level of vitriol. 'And what's *she* doing here?'

'She came to talk to me,' said Roper. 'Can I get you a drink?' He didn't offer me one.

'A large brandy, please,' answered Kate.

I looked at her. 'What about the baby?'

'She'll survive one drink,' she said without turning my way.

'You're pregnant?' said Roper. 'From him?' He almost spat out the last two words.

She nodded. 'I was waiting to get to three months before I told you, just in case anything went wrong.'

I didn't say anything, not wanting to draw attention to myself. I knew I was on thin ice here.

Roper looked torn. Pleased on one hand that he was going to be a grandfather – even if he'd never live to see his grandchild – but clearly not happy that I was the father. 'Congratulations,' he said to her with a half-smile, before going over to a drinks cabinet filled with every kind of alcohol imaginable, all of it expensive-looking, and poured her drink.

All the while, Diana and Kate glared at each other from a distance of ten feet apart, like two fighters sizing each other up. Kate might have had thirty years and at least three inches in height on Diana but I wouldn't have bet my house on her winning any fight. And me? I'll be honest with you, it felt as if I wasn't there. No one was taking any notice of me at all, so I just stood in the background watching the whole thing unfold.

'So you're pregnant, are you?' said Diana, her voice utterly cold. 'How very convenient. Planning on carrying on the family name? But which family exactly?'

'Why don't you sit down, Diana,' said Roper. 'You've caused enough trouble as it is.'

'What? And have a nice civilised drink with the bitch who killed Alana? I don't think so, Hugh. You might have no spine, but I still retain one.'

Roper went to speak but suddenly doubled over with a coughing fit, only just managing to hang on to the brandy. He quickly recovered himself, holding a handkerchief to his lips and handing Kate her drink. 'We need to get you seen by a doctor,' he told her.

'I could say the same thing about you,' she answered. 'I'm okay, but I've spent a very unpleasant twenty-four hours locked up in an abandoned hotel and I want to know who was behind it.' She gave Diana a pointed look.

'It was nothing to do with me, sweetie,' said Diana, taking a gulp from an outsized tumbler. 'If I'd had anything to do with it, you wouldn't be here.'

Kate's expression darkened in a way I hadn't seen before. 'I almost wasn't.' She turned to Roper. 'I managed to escape and kill the kidnapper.'

'Something you've had practice at,' said Diana.

Kate ignored her and kept her gaze on her father. 'We know now he was someone connected with you.'

'The phone I called you on belongs to Nigel Burns. He was meant to be keeping an eye on you while you were back in the country. That's why I've been speaking with him today. I even saw him this morning.'

'Well, he abducted me from our cottage. And now he's dead.'

'Have you called the police?'

'Not yet,' said Kate. 'But I will do. I wanted to see you first. You didn't have anything to do with this, did you?'

Roper shook his head. 'God, no. I would never do that to you. You're all I've got left.'

'What about your son?' demanded Diana. 'What about him?'

'We've had this conversation already,' he said to her. 'He's dead to me. You know that. If Burns was behind this, then he was working for someone else.' He stared at Diana pointedly.

'He was definitely working for someone else,' said Kate. 'It wasn't this man Burns on his own. It was another attempt to make me admit that I was in some way responsible for Alana's death. He made me take a lie detector test. And I'm damn sure he was the same man who came to kill David and me all those years ago.'

'I don't know anything about that either, I promise,' said Roper.

Kate turned back to Diana. 'But she does, doesn't she?'

'I had nothing to do with any abduction,' snapped Diana. 'In fact, it wouldn't surprise me if you'd made the whole thing up just to get some attention and sympathy.'

'How dare you talk to me like that, you bitter old bitch.'

'I'll talk to you exactly how I want. You don't scare me. You're just a nasty little commoner with plenty of cunning but not an ounce of class.'

'Do not speak to her like that in my house, Diana!' shouted Roper, his voice booming round the room, the effort taking it out of him.

But his appeal had no effect. Diana was unleashing her wrath now, swinging her glass round as she spoke. 'You're pathetic, Hugh,' she snarled. 'You always were. What kind of man rewards his daughter's killer with an inheritance and leaves his son hanging out to dry?'

'I didn't kill her!' yelled Kate.

The atmosphere was toxic and I had a feeling that anything could happen. The two women were facing off like banshees, the fury evident in both their expressions, and Roper was in no shape to stop them. I wasn't sure anyone would have been able to. But Kate was the woman I loved, and the mother of my child, so I felt compelled to intervene even though everyone was ignoring me.

'Please, let's all calm down,' I said, stepping forward to get between the two women, and then Roper stopped me dead with his next comment.

'You don't have the right to speak,' he spat, looking at me with an expression of utter disgust on his face. 'I know all about you, Walters. Where you were last night, for instance? With your ex-girlfriend. Did you tell Kate about that? Because I've got the pictures to prove it in case you didn't.'

Kate looked at me. 'Is this true, Matt? You said you were out with friends.'

'It's not like it sounds,' I said, thinking I could still keep this from getting out of hand, because I hadn't actually done anything with Geeta.

But that was before Roper spoke again.

'You didn't meet Kate by chance either, did you? You were hired by my son Tom to go out to Sri Lanka.'

This time Kate's eyes widened as if she'd been slapped. She stared at me incredulously. 'Is this true? Tell me it isn't.'

'Of course, he's an actor,' crowed Diana. 'It was me who had the idea to hire him. I saw him on that awful TV show.'

'No one hired me, for Christ's sake!' I shouted, desperate to regain some control over the situation. And then, turning to Diana: 'And I've never clapped eyes on you in my life before.'

345

'That's right, you haven't,' she answered, wearing a triumphant smile. 'But you've met my son, Tom. He was the one who paid you to ingratiate yourself with this bitch. To get some answers from her about Alana. Something you singularly failed to do.'

'This is bullshit,' I said. I turned back to Kate, pleading with her to believe me. 'I don't know what the hell she's talking about, I promise. Don't believe her. She's just trying to poison you against me.'

'Tom told me the same thing,' said Roper. 'About hiring you.'

'Check his bank account if you don't believe me,' Diana said to Kate. 'He was paid five grand in August last year, plus we bought his flight for him. Sri Lanka via India so it looked like he'd been travelling. Less suspicious that way. I've still got the electronic receipt.'

Kate was staring at me aghast. Roper was still wearing the same expression of disgust. Diana just looked pleased with herself, as if her investment had just paid off. 'I think the receipt's somewhere on my phone,' she said, going to the desk and removing it from her handbag.

'Tell me they're lying,' said Kate.

I'm an actor. A much better one than I've ever been given credit for. But I was faltering. You see, I haven't been entirely truthful. Yes, I was hired to meet Kate and, if possible, become part of her life. I never knew the identity of the people hiring me. I never knew that Kate was related to Sir Hugh Roper. I wasn't told what information to glean from her. Just to get her to open up about her past, and to report back regularly. But I fell in love. And that's the truth. I realised then that there was no way I could betray her, and that was why I dropped all contact with the man who'd paid me. I wanted to put the whole sorry episode in the past, because I was ashamed of what I'd done. Instead, I wanted to look forward, to start a family, to lead a completely new life. With Kate.

And that's the truth.

But how was that ever going to happen now?

'It's not what you think, darling, I promise,' I said, taking the only approach I could, given that Diana was now checking her phone and would at any moment provide the proof that she had purchased my plane ticket. 'I'm in love with you. I always have been. You've got to believe that. We've had an amazing, incredible year together ...'

Kate put her drink down on a nearby table and took a deep breath. 'You filthy, rotten, lying bastard.' The words were delivered like slow, heavy punches to the gut, and I knew then that I'd lost her. Whatever happened, there was no way back from this.

But I had to try, because every bridge I had was already burned. 'Please. Don't do this. We've got something ... Our baby, our family.'

Her expression seemed to lose its anger and become almost vacant. 'Get out of my sight. I never, ever want to see you again. Go.'

I stood there in a state of complete shock as Kate – the love of my life – turned her back on me.

But Diana, it seemed, wasn't finished yet and she walked

over to Kate, holding out the phone. 'See,' she was saying, 'it's on here, the receipt—'

'Fuck off, you old bitch!' roared Kate, shoving Diana backwards with both hands, sending her tumbling onto her behind, the phone flying into a corner of the room.

Kate looked down at her with an expression that I can only describe as pure hatred, while Diana sat there regarding her with the same savage loathing. And then she said something that made even me flinch. 'No wonder your daughter committed suicide, having a mother like you. She always hated you, you know.'

Diana was on her feet with the speed of someone half her age. 'What do you mean, she committed suicide? You said she fell.'

'She jumped,' said Kate coldly. 'And she always told me how much she hated you.'

Everything happened very fast then.

'I'll kill you for that!' screamed Diana, and rushed at Kate, the brandy glass clutched in her hand like a weapon.

At the same time, Kate reached over and grabbed a poker from a stand by the fire and swung it one-handed like a baseball bat straight into the side of Diana's head, with such force that it knocked her sideways and into Roper, who was moving in to intervene. Both of them fell over in a heap.

Diana rolled off him and came to rest on her back near me. Her head was bleeding profusely from a deep wound and her eyes were closed. I didn't know if she was dead or not, but she wasn't moving at all, and if I'd had to take a guess (and remember, I'd seen no fewer than four corpses in the last twenty-four hours), I'd have bet a lot of money that she was number five.

I didn't even try to find a pulse. I was still rooted to the spot, finding it hard to believe what I was seeing. I looked at Kate. She was staring down at Diana, the rage gone from her face now, with shock taking its place, the poker hanging loosely from her hand.

I didn't know what to say. Or to think. It was as if this nightmare I was trapped in, which I couldn't imagine getting any worse, somehow always did.

'My God,' said Roper, sitting up straight like he'd had an electric shock. 'Is she . . .'

Kate nodded, her features crumpling. 'I'm sorry, Daddy. I didn't mean to do it. She . . . she . . .'

'It's all right,' he said, starting to get to his feet. 'We'll sort this somehow . . . we'll sort this.'

Feeling once again like a voyeur watching someone else's performance, I took a step towards Kate. 'Honey, put the poker down and let's all work together to—'

The glare she gave me stopped me dead, and her grip on the poker actually tightened. 'I thought I told you I never wanted to see you again. Now get the fuck out of here.'

I considered persisting. Usually I'm pretty good at the art of persuasion, but the key's to know when you're beaten, and right then I knew for certain that not only did I have no chance of persuading Kate to change her mind about me right now, but that staying put might even result in serious injury.

So with a last glance down at Diana, who still hadn't moved, and whose blood was now soaking into the carpet,

I turned and walked out of the study, moving quickly just in case Kate suddenly decided to lash out at me with the poker too.

There was no one out in the entrance hall, and I strode through it and out of the front door, eager to get some fresh air and try to make sense of what had just happened, and decide what the hell I was going to do now.

It had started to rain again, and I stood on the steps, my anxiety building, as I realised this was the end of the road. I had nowhere left to turn except the authorities. I tried to get my breathing under control, but I was terrified of what was coming next. My fiancée didn't want me, and everything I'd striven for had gone up in smoke.

I walked slowly over to the rental car, stopping beside the driver's door and reaching into my pocket for the keys. But before I got to them, I broke down in sobs, leaning against the car and allowing the tears to flow.

Which was unfortunate timing, because I never heard the footsteps until they were right behind me.

Feeling my heart leap with a mixture of fear and hope, I swung round just as the blow struck me on the temple. My head snapped back and I fell back against the car, and bounced off again, just in time for the second blow, which broke something in my face.

Before I could focus on my attacker, or even catch a glimpse of him, my vision darkened and I had a vague sensation of sliding gently down the door into unconsciousness.

After that, I really don't remember anything until you arrived.

62

DCI Cameron Doyle

'That's not how Kate tells it,' I say, when he's finished.

Walters looks genuinely affronted. 'What's she saying then?'

'What do you think?' asks Tania.

'I don't know,' he answers, exasperated. 'I've just told you what happened.'

'She says you killed Diana Roper-King.'

Walters snaps upright, shaking his head. 'That's bullshit. It's lies. I had no reason to kill her.'

'Well that's not quite true, is it?' I say. 'According to Kate's statement, Diana had just exposed you as an actor who'd been hired to get Kate to fall in love with you. She was about to show Kate – who was understandably very upset by this revelation – proof of your duplicity when you grabbed a poker and struck her once round the head with such force that she was immediately knocked unconscious. You then struck her twice more as she lay dying. Which is consistent with her injuries.'

'No! No! No!' he cries out, his voice rising several octaves as it carries round the enclosed room. 'That's not how it happened. Kate did it.'

'Apparently you tried to flee the premises but were overpowered by Sir Hugh Roper's chauffeur, Jonathan Wolfrey, and he and Kate tied your hands and placed you in a locked pantry, which was where you were when the first officers arrived on the scene, responding to Sir Hugh's emergency call.'

'Sir Hugh confirms Kate's version of events pretty much word for word,' says Tania.

'He's lying. They're both lying,' says Walters. His eyes dart from me to Tania and back to me again. 'They're covering up the fact that Kate killed her. Why don't you check the murder weapon for prints?'

'We did,' I tell him. 'Yours were the only fingerprints on the handle.'

'And Roper's chauffeur's statement also backs up their version of events.'

Walters shakes his head, running a hand through his hair. 'Does Kate say the kidnap was all bullshit too?'

I shake my head. 'No. She's told us about her abduction, and her story tallies with yours there, although she never saw the body of the woman you claimed to have found lying in your bed. We think Kate was kidnapped by Nigel Burns, who was a former employee of her father and whose body we've now recovered from the building where he was holding her. We also think that Burns was working for Diana Roper-King, who believed Kate was responsible for her daughter Alana's death.'

Walters looks sick. 'This is a set-up,' he says, downing the glass of water on the table in front of him. 'I'm telling you the truth.'

And the fact is, he may well be. The problem is, I don't know. Nor does Tania. We've got to go with the evidence, and the evidence says that the most likely culprit is Matt Walters. There may not be enough to convict him of Diana's murder, but that doesn't matter because he's almost certainly going to go down for the murder of Piers MacDonald anyway. That means Diana's case will be closed, with him being attributed as the killer whether he was or not.

I don't like it. Kate White has questions to answer. She had traces of Diana Roper-King's blood on her when she was arrested, but claimed she got splashed with it when Walters struck Diana the first time. She also had a strong motive for killing her, given that she blamed Diana for the murder of her former boyfriend, David Griffiths, and suspected that she was behind the kidnapping too.

But the fact is, we're never going to prove it, whereas with Walters we've got a chance of a conviction. And I'll be honest with you, we need some sort of a result here. We've got five dead bodies and a media who are going to be baying for villains to pin them on. Put bluntly, Walters fits the bill. And so it looks like Roper's going to go to his grave a free man.

That bugs me. But something else bugs me even more. As I've told you already, we've always suspected Roper of being behind the murder of David Griffiths and the attempted murder of Kate, and he knows full well about our suspicions. So it would have been easy for him to pin the blame on Diana by pretending that she confessed to Griffiths' murder during their conversation in his study. But he didn't. His statement says that she denied it, just as he himself has always done. Like a lot of things about this case, this doesn't make sense. Because who else could it have been?

I've been a copper thirty years – a detective for twenty-five of them – so I understand that not every loose end is going to be tied up and not every narrative makes perfect sense. But this seems especially wrong.

And I'm still thinking about this particular loose end when, two hours later and with a surprising sense of reluctance, I charge Matt Walters with the murders of Diana Roper-King and Piers MacDonald.

63

Matt

In the end, I knew they were coming. The murder charges.

After hearing the last of my testimony, the two detectives – a craggy guy in his fifties who looked like he'd seen it all before, and a younger woman who pretended to be sympathetic but clearly wasn't – had asked me several times if I just wanted to come clean and tell the truth, suggesting that my story was never going to cut it with a jury. I'd stuck to my guns and finally demanded access to a lawyer.

One had duly been appointed for me – a young guy, probably not even out of his twenties, the only legal aid solicitor available at such short notice – but it was clear from the look on his face when I told him my story that he didn't believe it either.

But I wasn't going to admit to anything I hadn't done, because the fact remained, I was telling the truth. So my lawyer, acting on my instruction, had told the police to either charge me or let me go.

Even knowing what was coming, it was still a shock to sit there and hear myself being charged with two murders

I hadn't committed by the lead detective, his monotonous, almost bored tone the very antithesis of the dramatic flourish in which the charges were read out to the bad guys on *Night Beat*.

And I'm innocent. I really am. Everything I've said in this room has been true. And yet no one is going to know the truth, or that I was set up and turned into a scapegoat by the woman I'd sacrificed everything to save.

The room fell silent and I leaned forward over the desk and put my head in my hands, as if by doing so I could somehow escape the disaster that was swamping me.

And my life as I knew it, with its many downs but some good ups, ended not with a bang but a whimper.

Six weeks later

64

Kate

So here I am, back in the world, and I can finally speak freely.

Question: do I feel bad for setting Matt up to take the rap for Diana's killing (which I wouldn't describe as murder, more justified homicide)?

Answer: a little, but not enough to cause me lack of sleep.

That's not because I'm a monster. Far from it. But Matt betrayed me. And it wasn't a small betrayal either. What he did – inveigling himself into my life purely for money, playing with my emotions, taking advantage for his own selfish ends – was, and is, unforgivable. I'd had my suspicions of him in the early days, the way he rocked up out of the blue at the hotel, a very handsome man travelling alone, and how he seemed to fall very quickly in love. I kept him at bay for a while because I thought he might be some sort of gold-digger – not that at the time I had a great deal of gold – and because he was the kind of pretty boy who'd be way too shallow for someone like me, and who'd almost certainly continue to have a roving eye.

But on the flip side, he seemed fun; he seemed kind; he seemed interested in me (in hindsight I now know why); and of course he was drop-dead gorgeous, which didn't hurt. And so slowly yet surely (and perhaps against my better judgement) I'd let him into my life.

And don't get me wrong. I'd loved him. Deeply. Painfully. If I'd kept the baby and never found out about his betrayal, then it's possible we could have had a life together back in Sri Lanka.

But then of course the abduction had happened, and everything had gone to shit, so I was in a distraught state anyway when I'd finally found out what the bastard had done. But the fury I'd felt then ... that had been something else. When Diana had gone for me, I hadn't even thought about what I was doing. I'd done it instinctively. And frankly, I've never regretted it for a moment, after all the terrible things she'd done to my family. The vicious old hag had got what she'd deserved.

I'd almost killed Matt too. I'd wanted to, but he didn't deserve that, and I'm not the kind of person who plans a killing. Diana attacked me, so I reacted. Matt didn't, so I didn't kill him.

However, he might not have deserved death but that didn't mean he didn't deserve to be punished, which was why I did what I did. It hadn't been hard. As soon as Matt had left the room, I'd told Dad that I couldn't go to prison for killing Diana, and he said that I wouldn't have to, but only if I was willing to sacrifice Matt.

And, of course, I was.

Dad's chauffeur, Jonathan, had overpowered Matt and knocked him out. I'd helped drag him inside, where we'd lain him down beside Diana's body. I struck her on the head twice more so that her blood splattered his upper body. Then we'd wiped my prints from the poker, placed it in Matt's hand so that his were on it and, as he started to come round, we tied him up and locked him in the pantry. Dad called the police and we worked out our story. Ruthless, yes, but if a job's worth doing, it's worth doing properly. And it had worked. Dad and I had walked free and Jonathan is now a quarter of a million pounds richer thanks to a payment into a Panamanian bank account.

And now it was time for me to begin my new life. Matt was the past. After being charged with the murders of Diana and that blackmailing rodent Piers MacDonald, he'd been remanded in custody. He'd asked me to visit several times through his lawyer, but I'd refused. There was nothing to say.

The last few weeks haven't been easy. There'd been a shit storm of publicity surrounding Diana's murder and my abduction. It had all the ingredients for a perfect story. Money; the mysterious death of a young woman witnessed only by her illegitimate half-sister; the bloody revenge of the mother. The murder of the mother by the half-sister's fiancé, whom the mother had hired in the first place for a honey trap. Jesus, who wouldn't want to read about all that?

I'd had hundreds of requests for interviews but had refused them all. I just wanted to draw a line under the whole thing, and I was thankful that nothing had come out about the fact that MacDonald had possessed the means to blackmail me.

But I still had one big problem. Who was the person behind it all? The one who'd ordered my kidnap and arranged for Matt to kill MacDonald? Because whatever you might be thinking, it wasn't a set-up I'd arranged myself. And it wasn't Burns either. He was just a dupe, working for someone else. And I wasn't sure that the someone else was Diana. She'd denied it vociferously when we'd all been in the study just before she died, and I have to say I believed her. That only left two people I could think of. One was Tom, the half-brother I'd never met, although from what I could gather, he was something of a waster who didn't have any kind of relationship with Burns, so it was highly unlikely to be him.

And so once again we get back to Dad himself. Because, ultimately, who else is there? Perhaps he really did just need to know for sure that I hadn't pushed Alana to her death that night, and having me abducted was a foolproof means of confirming it one way or another. It would explain the use of Burns, a man he trusted, and the lie detector. It would also explain the killing of MacDonald, using Matt – a man he *didn't* trust – to do it; and perhaps, most damning of all, the fact that no audiotape copies of my sessions with MacDonald have come to light. Anyone wanting to destroy my chance of an inheritance and take revenge on me would have made them public by now. But Dad wouldn't want a scandal. If he'd thought I was responsible for Alana's death, he would have just quietly disinherited me.

And he hadn't done that either.

Poor Dad.

He'd gone downhill rapidly after the events of that night. I think the drama of it took most of the fight that was left in him, and he'd been bedridden at home for the past fortnight as he finally approached the end. I'd been spending several hours every day with him and had seen the pace at which he was deteriorating. It therefore hadn't been a surprise when his doctor had told me on the phone this morning that he only had hours to live.

I parked the car on the driveway outside his house and climbed out.

It was a beautiful sunny day with a near-cloudless blue sky, but there was a biting December chill in the air that I still couldn't get used to. My plan wasn't to stay in England. It no longer felt like my home, if it ever truly had. It wasn't to go back to Sri Lanka either. Now that I had money coming – real money – I wanted to travel. To see the world in style and start my new life of wealth wherever I felt comfortable. I had no interest in the business, even though with thirty-five per cent of the shares (less any tax I had to pay, which wasn't going to be much the way Dad's accountants had organised things), I was the company's single biggest shareholder and had an automatic seat on the board. In the last few weeks Dad had tried to get me enthused about the world of luxury housing developments and I'd tried very hard to sound like I was. But put bluntly, once he was gone, so was I.

As I walked towards the entrance, I saw a tall blond

man I recognised instantly from photos as Tom Roper, my half-brother, being led out of the building by Dad's security man, Thomson. Tom had attempted to visit Dad a number of times these past few weeks, and Dad had always refused to see him. Their estrangement, it seemed, was complete, and I didn't want to get involved, even though I was sure Tom blamed me for it, as if it had nothing to do with his own behaviour over the last twenty-five years.

I stepped behind a tree, not wanting to be seen, and waited while Tom stalked off to his car and drove back up the driveway far too fast. Even from some distance away I could see his face was like thunder. Alana had always said her brother was an arsehole, and she was right. He'd tried to sell his story to the newspapers after the abduction, but I'd got Dad's lawyers to send a letter telling him I'd sue for libel if he said a single critical word about me, and coward that he is, he immediately beat a hasty retreat.

Dad's bedroom was on the second floor, and Thomson had returned to stand guard outside by the time I got there, his hands behind his back.

'Good morning, ma'am,' he said with a smile. He always looked pleased to see me, but then I'd already employed him to be my bodyguard after Dad had gone, so it was worth his while. 'Your father's got a visitor at the moment. Shall I tell him you're here?'

'Who is it?' I asked. Dad didn't get many visitors and I couldn't think of anyone he'd be wasting his last hours with, because when it came down to it, I was the only person he had left in the world.

'It's his stepson, Edward. He's been in there a while.'

I'd never met the stepson. Dad didn't talk about him much, and it was clear they didn't have a close relationship, although I knew Edward was heavily involved in the business.

'Can you let Dad know I'm here?' I said.

Thomson nodded and knocked on the door, opening it to announce my presence before closing it again without speaking. 'You can go in, ma'am, but he's asleep.'

I thanked him and went inside.

Dad was propped up on the pillows of his outsized bed, looking frail and wan. The sight reminded me of when I'd watched Mum die all those years ago. How awful it was to see someone you cared about degenerate from a healthy, vibrant individual to a bag of skin and bone. It reminded me all too much of my own mortality.

Edward was sitting in a chair by the side of the bed and stood up as I entered. He was, I have to say, a distinctly underwhelming-looking young man – slight of build, with a baby face topped with hair that was already retreating fast. I'd been told he was around my own age, but he had all the gravitas of a twelve-year-old.

'Hello,' he whispered, coming around the bed and putting out a hand. 'I'm Edward, Sir Hugh's stepson. You must be Kate. I was sorry to hear of your ordeal.'

'Thank you,' I said. 'It's all in the past now.'

He waited for me to say something else, but I let the silence hang there. I didn't want to continue the conversation in case it turned to business or the inheritance. I don't want to sound mercenary, but Edward was of no interest to me, and I had no doubt he would be a pain in the arse when he found out that he wasn't getting anything in the will. Easier to put the wall up between us now.

'Well, I was just leaving,' he said after an awkward few seconds. 'Good to meet you.'

'And you,' I said with a polite smile, stepping past him.

I waited until he'd left the room, then sat down on the other side of the bed so I could see out of the window. Dad looked the most peaceful I'd ever seen him, lying there with his eyes closed, breathing softly. I stared at him for a few moments, wondering how different it all could have been if he'd acknowledged my presence all those years ago. I'd only been seven when he'd divorced Diana, so we could have had a proper relationship and done the daddy-and-daughter things I'd so wanted to do when I was growing up. My life could have been fun. There would never have been the tragedies, the long, lonely exile halfway round the world. I'd fantasised about it so many times, but sitting here watching him take the final breaths of his life, I knew it was time to let go, to forget the injustices that had been visited on me, to forget the ghosts of the past like Alana and David, and to look forward for once. But there were still questions that needed answering before I moved on.

One of Dad's eyes popped open, jolting me from my thoughts, and he smiled at me with surprising vigour. 'Has he gone yet? He was boring me to death. Quite literally.'

I smiled back. 'Yes, you're safe now.'

'Thank God for that.' He tried to sit up, but the effort was too much for him.

'Stay there, it's all right,' I said, touching his arm gently. 'I can get you anything you need.'

'I'm good,' he said. 'They've been filling me with morphine. I can't feel a damn thing any more.' He turned his head slowly and looked up at me, and there was real love in his eyes. 'I'm glad you came.'

'I was always going to come. We've wasted too much time already. There's no point wasting whatever we've got left.'

He sighed. 'I know.'

We were both silent for a long time, and I suppose that was our problem. We really had nothing in common. Our relationship had been cobbled together when I was already an adult, and in the intervening years we'd seen each other rarely. Did I love him? I wasn't sure. Was I sad that he was dying? Yes, but nothing like as sad as I would have been if he'd at least tried to be a father to me back when I was young. And right now, I didn't know what to say to him. Well, I did, but it wasn't something he was going to want to hear.

'Are you all right, Kate?' he asked, clearly seeing something in my expression.

I took a deep breath. 'Can I ask you something?'

'What is it?' There was a disapproving look in his pale eyes, and I could tell that he was wary.

I was going to ask if it was him behind my abduction, but somehow I simply couldn't come out with the words, because even if it had been, I knew he'd never admit it. Not now. And maybe it was just best to let bygones be bygones.

He saw my hesitation. 'I wasn't responsible for Griffiths' murder, or your attempted murder, if that was what you were going to ask,' he said. 'I may not have been a good father to you growing up, but I would never have done anything to hurt you, whatever anyone else might say.' He tried to squeeze my hand, but there was only the lightest pressure. 'I'm hurt that you could think I'd ever do something like that to you.'

I squeezed his hand back. 'I didn't think that. I just needed to know for sure.'

'You thought I might make a deathbed confession then?'

I smiled wanly. 'I'm glad you didn't.'

But of course there was no way he'd be making a deathbed confession to that particular crime. I knew he wasn't responsible for David's murder. And nor was Diana.

Because it was me.

There you go. It's out there. I killed David.

It had all happened very suddenly. I'd come home from work early, because I'd been feeling under the weather, and had discovered David up in our bedroom with some photos of Alana I'd never seen before strewn across our bed. He'd clearly been sitting there staring at them – although he did make an effort to hide them when he heard me come in – and I could tell he'd been crying.

And then he dropped the bombshell. He wanted to split up. He still missed Alana terribly and didn't feel right continuing with our relationship.

I was devastated. I couldn't believe it. I'd been so happy and now he was ending everything, just like that. I cried and begged him to stay, but he said he was leaving. That was when I got angry. I yelled at him, told him he couldn't go, my fury boiling over, but he pushed past me, saying he'd come back to collect his things.

And that was when I grabbed the knife I kept under the bed – because I always thought the Ropers might one day send someone to harm us – and went for him.

I don't remember what happened after that. The next thing I knew, I was waking up in a hospital bed looking up at my father but I guess I must have cleared up and removed any incriminating evidence, and then, in a fit of despair over what I'd done, and perhaps as an ironic nod to Alana, I'd thrown myself out of the window.

It had taken me years to get over what I'd done, and years before I allowed myself to fall in love again. And look how that had turned out. So from now on, I was going to stay single. It was a lot easier that way.

Dad and I sat in silence for a few moments, both lost in our own thoughts.

'So, in the spirit of confessions, can I ask *you* something?' he said eventually.

I knew what was coming.

'I know you've told me many times that Alana's death was an accident, and then you said that night in the study that she actually jumped, but I want you to know that if there's anything you want to add . . . if there was more to it, then now's the time to tell me. It's the past. I wouldn't love you any less.'

I looked him right in the eye. 'I've never lied about it, Dad. You have to know that. I would never have hurt her.' I pictured her then, the spiky-haired wild elfin girl with the sly grin that always spelt trouble. We'd had good times. Some of the best I've ever had. 'I loved her.'

'So did I,' he said. 'I love you too.'

And then he closed his eyes, his breathing slowing as he slipped into sleep.

I sat with him a while. I didn't know how long he'd last like this; it could be hours or even days. Eventually, though, I became restless and decided to take a stroll round the grounds.

As I walked back through the house, I felt liberated. I'd suffered ordeal after ordeal in my life, and perhaps nothing was worse than the twenty-four hours I'd been held in a filthy cell by Burns. But now it was over. I'd survived everything thrown at me.

And do you know what? I'll let you into a secret, if you hadn't guessed it already.

I did push her.

She'd turned on me, furious that I'd dared tell her the truth about our relationship, talking to me like I was nothing, destroying everything we'd had with her venomous words . . . and I'd gone for her. Charged into her, sending her backwards towards the ledge. I remember her eyes widening with fear and her mouth opening to cry out . . .

And then I gave her that final shove and she was gone, hurtling through the darkness below.

Almost immediately, I'd felt terrible about what I'd done, but that was quickly replaced by a need for self-preservation. I decided on my story, accident rather than suicide, and rushed back in to tell David that she'd slipped and fallen.

The rest you know. I did feel guilt. Huge guilt. Hence my ill-fated visits to Piers MacDonald. But yes, I got over what I'd done. It was a moment of madness provoked by Alana herself, and admitting it wouldn't have brought her back.

The problem was, I had admitted it to someone. MacDonald. It had been in one of our last sessions, when he'd put me under. The thing about hypnotherapy is that even though your eyes are closed and you're in a trance, you're still awake and aware of what you're doing or saying. At least I was. On some level I needed to admit it, to tell someone, anyone. I knew I couldn't tell David. He was convinced I'd had nothing to do with it, and would have been horrified if he'd known the truth.

I knew my sessions with MacDonald were confidential. So I just let myself go, and when he put me in a trance and took me back to that night, I told him everything word for word. It felt both cathartic and terrifying, I remember that.

Afterwards, when I was back in the room, I felt terribly vulnerable and I remember telling him that I hadn't meant to push Alana over the edge, that it had all been an accident.

He'd told me it was okay, that I was safe confiding in him, and I'd genuinely believed him. But although we'd continued the sessions for another couple of weeks, things between us had changed. He tried to get me to talk more about my feelings of guilt, but I clammed up and soon stopped going.

All the memories had come flooding back after I'd paid him for my files and had listened to those sessions. It made grim listening. Even if you took out my single admission that I'd killed Alana, there were so many things I said that pointed to my guilt. Anyone listening would know what I'd done. None of it would be admissible in court, of course, but given that I was standing to inherit a huge amount of money, the recordings were dynamite.

And someone, somewhere still had a copy. Yet whoever it was had yet to make their move, which meant either that it had indeed been Diana, or that perhaps whoever it was would be willing to let it lie.

But life never works like that.

I was barely out of the front door when who should appear from behind the very same tree that I'd sheltered behind earlier but Edward. He walked purposefully towards me, an irritatingly knowing smile on his face.

'We didn't really get a chance to talk earlier,' he said, drawing alongside me.

'There's nothing for us to talk about,' I told him without slowing down, heading for the side of the house and the back garden.

'I think there is,' he said, pulling something from his trouser pocket and opening the palm of his hand so I could see it.

In spite of myself, I looked down. It was a flash drive.

'Recognise this?' he said. 'You probably don't. But I'm sure you know what it contains. I do.'

The look in his eyes said it all, and I wondered if he'd shared its contents with Dad, then dismissed the thought just as fast. Dad would never have told me he loved me if he knew about this.

I stopped. Edward stopped too. He was still grinning. I felt like wiping it right off his face. 'What do you want?'

'Nothing that you can't manage,' he said in his irritatingly high-pitched voice. 'You'll be the largest shareholder in Peregrine Homes, so for starters you're going to make sure that I become the next CEO. Then you're going to gift me a manageable percentage of the shares, no more than ten per cent, in lieu of the inheritance I never had. After that, you're going to vote for any changes I want to make.'

I looked down at the drive in his hand then back at him. 'Make whatever's on there public, I don't care. I'm inheriting anyway.' If I had to, I'd rush back upstairs and smother Dad just to make sure he didn't make a last-minute change to the will, but I knew it wasn't going to come to that. This little prick could do nothing. He was just a chancer.

But he was still smiling, and I didn't like that.

'Yes, you might be able to weather the reputational storm if it came out about you killing Alana, and I very much doubt that it would lead to a conviction in court, although it would be a lot worse than you think. But I also have something else.' He reached into the pocket of his suit trousers with something close to an amateur magician's flourish and pulled out a phone. He pressed a couple of buttons,

then handed it to me. 'Have a look at this. It makes gripping viewing.'

The screen showed a still from a video taken inside Dad's
study, the angle suggesting the camera was high up on the
main bookshelf facing the door. There were four people in
shot, standing round in a rough circle. It was clear there
was a discussion going on between them, but there was
no sound. I recognised them all instantly: me, Matt, Dad
and Diana. And the footage was from the night of Diana's
murder.

I pressed the play button, and Diana, who had her back
to the camera, immediately rushed towards me. As she did
so, you could quite clearly see me grab the poker from
by the fire and strike her with enough force to send her
hurtling sideways.

I turned away from the screen and shoved the phone back
into his hand. I felt sick. There was no way of sugar-coating
that. The evidence was all there.

'How?' was all I managed to say.

'I've had the camera in Father's study for months,' he
said matter-of-factly. 'I needed to know what he was up to
vis-à-vis the business. It was just blind luck that it caught
your little escapade.'

He'd trapped me. My mind worked furiously to think of
a way out. There was only one solution. Edward had to die.

But it seemed he'd already planned for that. 'Please don't
think, Kate, that just because you have the killer instinct
– and I know that you do have it – you can get rid of me
somehow. It doesn't work like that. I'm very well prepared.

If anything happens to me, all of this will automatically be made public via three different lawyers in three different countries. You will not only face ruin, but life imprisonment too. However . . .' he paused, his smile growing even wider, like that of a little boy pulling the wings off a fly, 'if you do what I ask – and I think you'll find it's very reasonable under the circumstances – none of this will ever see the light of day. Nor will there ever be anything linking you to Alana's death. I have control of all the copies made by Piers MacDonald. And since he's dead, and so is the poor detective who followed you to your meeting with him, no one can put any of it together. I've thought of everything. My only concern about the whole thing was Nigel Burns. I had to pay him a lot of money to kidnap you and I thought he might prove to be the kind of loose end it's hard to get rid of. But you managed that for me, so thank you.' He gave a little bow.

I didn't know what to say.

'I can see you're shaken up by all this,' he continued, 'and I can understand that, but you'll be doing the right thing. I'm more than ready to head up Peregrine Homes. My stepfather might not have believed it, but as you can see, I too have the necessary killer instinct. In fact, I think we'd make a great team.' He leaned forward and patted me on the arm, his hand lingering, his face close enough to mine that I could see the fluffy hairs above his upper lip and smell his fish-paste breath. 'You're a very attractive woman,' he whispered into my ear, 'and one who needs to make sure I stay alive, healthy and, of course, happy. And what would make me happiest right now is if you'd agree to join me for dinner this evening. I have a reservation at eight p.m. at the Waterside Inn in Bray. Usually you have to wait a year to get a table, but I pulled some strings. What do you say?'

He stared at me with far more confidence than was warranted for a man like him, his teeth bared in a predatory leer.

I had no choice, and we both knew it.

'Of course,' I said, trying and failing to smile back, wishing I could smash his face into a bloody unrecognisable pulp with the same poker I'd used on Diana.

'Good,' he said, giving my arm a squeeze. 'And make sure you wear stockings and a nice pair of heels. I'll pick you up at seven thirty.'

He turned on his heel and walked away with a jaunty little wave, leaving me standing there rigid with shock and disgust as all my chickens came flocking back home to roost.

And somewhere in the back of my mind, I could hear Alana's bawdy laughter echoing down the years in mockery as she finally had her revenge.